The Becket Factor

The
Becket Factor

Michael David Anthony

All characters in this book are completely fictitious. In particular, Bishops Maurice Campion and William Harvey-Watson or other members of the clergy bear no relation to any figures, present or past, in either the Anglican or Orthodox Churches. Visitors to Canterbury will be reminded of some of the places mentioned, but would be ill-advised to use it as a guide or attempt to book rooms in either the Bugle-Horn or the Old Swan.

THE BECKET FACTOR

A Felony & Mayhem mystery

PRINTING HISTORY
First UK edition (William Collins Sons & Co.): 1990
First U.S. edition (St. Martin's Press): 1991
Felony & Mayhem edition: 2008

ISBN-13 978-1-933397-95-5

Manufactured in the United States of America

Dedicated in loving memory to my father, Daniel Ernest John Anthony, sometime honorary Canon of Bristol Cathedral and Rural Dean of Malmesbury, and to my mother, Marion Gwyneth Anthony.

For their encouragement, suggestions and help, I am especially indebted to my friends Robin Buss, Peter Clarke, Tim Dowley and Katherine Frank.

The icon above says you're holding a book in the Felony & Mayhem "British" category. These books are set in or around the UK, and feature the highly literate, often witty prose that fans of British mystery demand. Other "British" titles from F&M include:

ROBERT BARNARD
Death on the High C's
Out of the Blackout
Death and the Chaste Apprentice
Skeleton in the Grass

LIZA CODY
Dupe

PETER DICKINSON
King and Joker
The Old English Peep Show

CAROLINE GRAHAM
The Killings at Badger's Drift
Death of a Hollow Man
Death in Disguise
Written in Blood
Murder at Madingley Grange

REGINALD HILL
A Clubbable Woman
Death of a Dormouse

ELIZABETH IRONSIDE
Death in the Garden
The Accomplice
A Very Private Enterprise

JOHN MALCOLM
A Back Room in Somers Town

JANET NEEL
Death's Bright Angel

SHEILA RADLEY
Death in the Morning
The Chief Inspector's Daughter

For more information, please visit us online at
www.FelonyAndMayhem.com

Or write to us at:
Felony and Mayhem Press
156 Waverly Place
New York, NY 10014

AUTHOR'S NOTE

The exact number of Archbishops of Canterbury is controversial. Some authorities omit Reginald FitzJocelyn (1191) and John Ufford (1349) who both died before consecration. Some count Thomas Arundel (1397) twice over since he was deprived by Richard II and then restored by Henry IV. However, using each of these names once, I calculate there have been 103 archbishops between St Augustine (597) and the present Primate, Dr Robert Alexander Kennedy Runcie.

May, 1990

The Becket Factor

Human souls...bear the weight and see through the dusk of a gross atmosphere, gathered from wrong judgments daily passed, false opinions daily learned, and early habits of an older date than either judgement or opinion. Through such a medium the sharpest eye cannot see clearly. And if by some extraordinary effort the mind should surmount this dusky region, and snatch a glimpse of pure light, she is soon drawn backwards, and depressed by the heaviness of the animal nature to which she is chained. And if again she chanceth, amidst the agitation of wild fancies and strong affections, to spring upwards, a second relapse speedily succeeds into this region of darkness and dreams.

—*Siris*
George Berkeley (1685-1753)
Bishop of Cloyne

(HAPTER 1

A boy began singing.

Faint, ghostly-beautiful, the sound echoed down the darkening nave. Figures bowed reverently over the whispering audio-guides, lowered their earphones and turned to listen, then gradually, from all over the cathedral, came a growing clatter of feet as the late afternoon visitors hurried towards the brightly-lit choir.

On the topmost tier of the steeply rising pews the grey-haired man appeared to be sleeping. He was slumped forward, his body wedged awkwardly in a half-kneeling position, his eyes closed, his face furrowed.

Harrison's mind was on God—or rather, on that image of a god he had been given as a child, an image that had stayed young as he had grown old. A print of Holman Hunt's *The Light of the World* had hung in the nursery; the same pale, bearded face that had gazed through the cot-bars later faced him morning and evening in the school chapel. Now more than half a century later, he knelt, concentrating on holding that face before him, finding it comforting that it should be so vividly there, unchanged after so many had faded or utterly disappointed.

The anthem ended. As a young priest rose to intone the prayers, Harrison opened his eyes. Although the majority of the congregation were visitors, he recognized the middle-aged woman across the aisle—shabby, solitary, one of many such who came seeking solace daily in the peaceful world behind the Christ Church gatehouse. Others he knew: retired clergymen, muffled in coats, a King's School master, white-haired, with the face of a boy. He glanced at the cluster of figures in the entrance opposite. One stood slightly back from the others. The lean face was too alert for a casual visitor, the dark overcoat too formal, too well-cut. Memory stirred—this was a public face, a face he should know.

As if sensing the close observation, the man looked up. For a second their eyes met, then whoever he was had gone, stepping back out of sight behind the railed corner of the Chichele tomb.

'Endue thy ministers with righteousness.'
'And make thy chosen people joyful.'

Harrison repeated the response automatically, staring down to where the man had stood. Then the priest's voice intruded; immediately, all thoughts of the stranger were gone.

'...that his soul, together with the souls of all the faithful departed, rest in peace.'

Cratchley dead! Harrison felt a jolt of loss. It wasn't as if he'd known the old Canon well, but over the years he'd grown used to the sight of him hurrying by in black cassock: always that quick flap of the hand in greeting, the oddly conspiratorial grin. Now he too was gone—another landmark torn away, the wilderness left that bit more barren.

People were moving: Evensong was over. Harrison rose and followed out into the nave. All over the vast building came the murmur of voices, for the rain had brought larger than usual numbers out of the winter streets. As he descended the steps of the north-west transept, he found his way blocked by a group of tourists clustered round the portly Head Verger.

'It was the fourth knight, Richard Brito, finished him.' The speaker's face and bald scalp gleamed; there was a relish to his voice. 'He drove down through Becket's head so hard that the sword-tip broke off against them stones.' With a sweep of his gowned arm, the Verger gestured towards the roped-off section of worn pavings below the stairs.

Despite the speaker's enthusiasm, there was disappointment in the faces of his party. Harrison understood: an obscure little spot below a back staircase was hardly a stage for martyrdom. But that's the way of it, he thought; what was Golgotha itself but a mound among rubbish pits? Suddenly he was back in the yard behind the Famagusta cinema, seeing the face staring up out of the dustbin at him, milky-eyed. Other bodies came: a headless corpse in a sewer: those bullet-riddled obscenities floating, bloated and fly-blown, in the irrigation ditch outside Nicosia.

'Welcome back to Canterbury, sir.'

The Verger grinned, puffing slightly as he led his flock past up the stairs.

'Thank you, Mr Simcocks.' Harrison forced a smile. 'It's good to be home.'

The crowd pushed against him as they passed. 'I always thought they killed Becket in front of the altar,' said a woman, complaint in her voice. 'I'm sure that's how it was in the film.'

Harrison hardly heard her: her voice was lost behind the hum of the flies about the blood beside the Larnaca road.

The footsteps died. Pushing the nightmares back, he continued down. Opening the huge, iron-studded calefactorium door, he stepped out into Great Cloister.

Thin rain was drifting between the columns. With relief, he felt it cool on his face. He stood, savouring the cold dampness for a moment, then eager to be home, he walked on. He had taken only a few steps, however, when a voice called his name.

❁ ❁ ❁

'Colonel! Colonel Harrison!'

Canon Rope came hurrying up, one hand clutching the collar of his raincoat closed beneath his chin. Momentarily Harrison's mind leapt back to the man in Evensong: the elegant black coat had been buttoned right to the throat. 'I noticed you back in your usual seat. A good break?' The elderly cleric smiled up into his face as they shook hands.

'Thank you, yes.'

'And Mrs Harrison?' Rope peered closer.

'A little tired after the journey.'

As if by unspoken command, they began walking on, their footsteps echoing under the low vaulted roof.

'You've heard about Cratchley?'

'Just now.'

'Happened only yesterday morning. Went off in his sleep, apparently. He'd only called on me the night before.' There was a resentful note to the old man's voice; he could have been speaking of an unwarranted slight, some trivial betrayal.

Harrison nodded, remembering the two old men had been friends.

'The Dean, of course, was upset,' continued Rope. 'He was fond of Cratchley.' He suddenly laughed. 'Remember Jezebel?'

'Ingrams's dog?'

'The creature started having fits. Cratchley would have it the thing was possessed—absolutely insisted on exorcising the wretched beast.'

'Did it work?'

'Apparently—at least the fits stopped. The animal lived a perfectly normal life for another two years.'

Laughing, they walked on.

'How is Ingrams?' asked Harrison; he'd noticed the Dean hadn't been in Evensong.

'Much encumbered, I fear.' Rope sighed. 'And our Archbishop's sudden wish to step down will add to his burden—and talking of such, I notice the men are still not finished in the crypt.'

'Not finished yet!' Harrison felt a wave of annoyance: he'd expected the re-laying of the floor to have been completed before his return. Damn Keates! he thought, a momentary vision of the cathedral Clerk-of-Works rising before him. Would the confounded fellow never get a move on?

'Well, Colonel, who are you betting on?'

'Betting on?'

'The next occupant of the Augustine throne, our next Archbishop—who will it be?' Rope chuckled. 'Safe old Haverwell of York or someone rather more exciting perhaps?' Halting under the Selling gatehouse, he grinned round, rubbing his hands.

Ahead was the wide quadrangle of Green Court. Fine rain shone like dust-motes in the lamplight; across the lawn, flitting shapes emerged at intervals from the foyer-entrance of the King's School prep rooms to vanish almost at once in the drizzling darkness.

'Cratchley was the same dear fellow to the end.' Rope's voice was again wistful as they stepped together from under the archway. 'He'd been conducting one of his spectaculars—you remember he enjoyed taking groups to see the crypt by floodlight. *Pilgrimage Today*, I think this one was called. Anyway, over cocoa afterwards, he complained of being stung.'

'Stung?'

'It was at the moment of his grand finale. He would always get his group to stand under the Bell Harry Tower, then turn off all the lights. After that, level by level, he'd illuminate the interior of the tower right to the roof. Extraordinary sight!

Like looking deep into a lily-pond—delicate tracery, layer upon layer, stretching right up to...' Rope's voice died; there was a pause, then he chuckled. 'Think of it, at that very moment—staring up into that sublime beauty, poor old Cratchley gets himself stung!'

They had entered Bread Yard. Lights glistened on the cobbles. At his garden gate, where the shrivelled rose-heads blew in the wind, Harrison hesitated. 'I would ask you in, Canon, but my wife...'

'My dear fellow, I wouldn't dream of it.' Rope touched his arm. 'Good night,' he said, walking on.

Harrison pushed through the gate. At the door he fumbled for his key.

'Colonel Harrison!'

Rope had paused under an overhead light. 'Think of it, Colonel—a bee in December, and right on the BTM!' His dentures gleamed. With a wave, he vanished laughing into the shadows.

'Richard!'

He turned from closing the door to find his wife behind him; her knuckles were white on the wheels as she thrust her chair forward. 'That man is here!' she hissed.

Harrison's mind leapt back to the face looking up from the presbytery floor. He shook his head in disbelief. 'Good God, Winnie, who the hell is he? What does he want?'

For a second there was blank incredulity on her face, then the fury rushed back. 'Who?' She spat the word out. 'Your beloved Greville—who else!'

'The Brigadier?' Harrison stared. 'Impossible!'

Wrenching the wheelchair round, she pointed down the hall. 'He's in there,' she whispered fiercely, 'in our sitting-room, drinking tea!' Her dark eyes were suddenly bright with tears. 'Get rid of him, Richard! Make him go!' Her fury had crumbled, and only fear and pain remained.

He glanced at the hand gripping claw-like at his wrist.

'Right!'

He threw his coat over a peg, noting as he did so the two strange coats, one formal black, the other brown tweed, then pushed past towards the sitting-room. As he entered, a tall, hollow-cheeked man clambered up from the settee. Brigadier Greville himself was leaning against the bureau, gazing absently down into his cup. For an instant Harrison saw him in repose: the large head slumped forward, the heavily lidded eyes, the grey, wrinkled folds of the jowls hanging slack and loose. An old man! He felt a painful jar. Then Greville was looking up, his features leaping to life—and then the remembered dazzling smile. In a moment, he was across the room and Harrison was receiving a warm half-hug.

'My dear Dickie!'

'Brigadier!' muttered Harrison awkwardly.

'Not so formal, old chap.' Greville grinned ruefully. 'We're both in the bowler-hat brigade now.' He tapped his chest. 'A Whitehall wallah, would you believe it!' For a few seconds longer Greville stood smiling, then turned towards the man standing in front of the settee. 'Let me introduce you to Gillie here, my successor-to-be.'

Gillie was very tall, well over six foot. There was not the hint of a smile on his thin lips as he shook hands.

Civilian, thought Harrison. Ex-police.

'The Colonel and I served together in Cyprus.'

'Aye.' The highland accent was as soft as the eyes were hard.

'My wife's given you tea, I see.'

'Brave woman, Winnie.' Greville picked up the wedding photograph from the bureau. He glanced at it absently, then smiled round. 'This work for the Church, Dickie. Secretary to the Diocesan Dilapidations Board—what does that entail?'

Harrison flushed. 'Estate management basically.'

Glancing around him, the Brigadier nodded approvingly. 'Very nice: quiet life, house with the job, even roses round the cottage door, I noticed.' The grin faded; the heavy face became a grey, melancholy mask. 'Well, I'll be out to grass soon myself—won't be sorry.' He was old again. 'Worn down, Dickie!' Shaking his head, he turned to stare out through the window. 'It's a different bloody world.'

Gillie sat looking down at his scrubbed fingernails. For a moment the only sound was the tick of the hall clock.

'Why are you here?'

Greville turned and smiled. 'Just for old time's sake; we had to be in Canterbury to go over the ground.'

'For the enthronement? But that's months away!'

'Did you know Canon Cratchley, Colonel?'

Gillie's sudden question caught him off-balance. 'Cratchley?' He looked round at the questioner. 'Yes, slightly. Why do you ask?'

'He was found dead the day before yesterday.'

'So what?' he snapped, nettled by the cold stare.

'Of course, he was getting on a bit, wasn't he, Dickie?' Greville's voice glided between them like oil.

'Early seventies, that's all.'

'Dicey heart, though?'

'So I believe.'

'And the head? Gaga would you say?'

Harrison shook his head. 'He was a bit eccentric, nothing more.' He paused. 'Look, what's this all about?'

Gillie's voice was slow and precise. 'He phoned Brigadier Greville last week.'

'Cratchley phoned you!' Harrison stared incredulously.

The Brigadier laughed. 'Queer old bird! Met him in

Alexandria during the war. He was some sort of naval padre, I remember.'

'But this phone call—what did he want?'

Greville smiled. 'Lot of silly nonsense.'

'Yet you're here!'

'The man's dead, Colonel.' Gillie stared coldly.

Greville broke the silence. 'We just wondered if there had been any gossip round the cloisters.'

'About Cratchley? I've been away.'

'You've heard nothing since you've been back—no tittle-tattle? Nothing unusual?'

From the courtyard came the sound of voices. Turning, Harrison looked out into the darkness, remembering Rope's laugh in the gloom. He thought of Winnie; she'd be in the kitchen, longing for them to go, longing for the safe life to resume.

'Well, Dickie?'

'A bee in December,' he murmured. Raindrops ran like tears down the pane. 'It was nothing!' He swung round. 'A joke, damn it! Nothing at all!'

The faces, both intent, watched him steadily. He sighed. 'Apparently, Cratchley was stung by something when he was taking a party round the cathedral the night he died.'

When he spoke, Greville's voice was quiet, consoling; he could have been a doctor hearing the symptoms of a cancer. 'This sting, Dickie. Where on the body—any idea?'

'Buttocks.' Harrison looked away. 'I'm sure it's nothing.'

'Of course.' The Brigadier sighed. 'All the same, I suppose we'll have to take a look.' He turned. 'Autopsy? Can something be arranged?'

His companion nodded.

'Right, then,' said Greville, 'we'll leave you to the quiet life.' He picked up Harrison's copy of *The Times* and smiled. 'I notice you got most of the clues in the crossword today.'

Harrison flushed. 'My quiet life,' he said, turning to the door.

As Gillie stepped outside, Greville grasped his hand. 'Sorry about this. All nonsense, of course.' He smiled affectionately. 'Don't worry, you'll be left alone.' He went to leave, then hesitated. 'Oh, just one little thing: Becket Factor—does the phrase mean anything at all?'

'Nothing.'

Greville nodded. 'As I say, just a lot of crazy nonsense.'

'They've gone.'

There was no reply; his wife sat at the kitchen table, staring down at the oilcloth. 'Tea?' he asked, endeavouring to sound casual. Again there was no response. He went over and switched on the kettle. 'Look,' he began, 'honestly I didn't—'

'Don't! I don't want to hear!'

Helplessly, he gazed at her, waiting for her to face him. When she did, he was shocked to see her crying.

'Richard, you promised!'

'They just came. Believe me, it was none of my doing.'

Lowering her face, she remained staring down at the table.

He gazed at her numbly: she looked smaller, more wasted than ever. 'They won't be back, Winnie, I swear.'

'The kettle's boiling,' she said shortly.

Filling the teapot, Harrison could feel loneliness like a stone weighing on him—worse was his almost tangible awareness of hers.

'So why did he come after all this time?' She was looking round, her face blank and cold. 'But I suppose it's useless to ask.' Bitterness made her voice ugly.

'Just a lot of crazy nonsense,' he answered, unconsciously echoing Greville's words. 'With the IRA and the rest of it, I suppose they're concerned about the security aspects of the Archbishop's enthronement.'

Her expression showed utter disbelief. 'Are you still in touch with him?'

'The Brigadier? Of course not.'

'Yet he knew you were here.'

He shrugged, then held up the teapot. 'Sure you wouldn't like a cup?'

'All right.' It was some sort of truce. With relief, he began to pour. Doing so, he sensed a change. He looked round: she was looking at him, eyes bleak with unhappiness. He went and put an arm round her shoulders, but she stiffened, leaning away.

Out in the hall, the clock began striking the hour.

As Winnie's friends made abundantly clear at the time, theirs had been an unlikely relationship from the start. She had been at art college when they met, youngest of the large and somewhat chaotic family of a failed North Country architect. Vivacious and headstrong, a talented rebel, she was the very antithesis of him—the stiff, shy son and grandson of military engineers, almost perversely about to join his first regiment in Germany when thousands of his fellow countrymen were thankfully exchanging their uniforms for a demob suit and trilby.

That he'd ever attended that party in Chelsea had been extraordinary. Too polite to refuse a brother officer's invitation, he'd gone dreading the evening—and yet, at the same time, curious about that mysterious bohemian world he visualized existing somewhere between the borders of Pimlico and the sleazy western extremities of the King's Road. To his surprise, he enjoyed it—drinking cheap wine from tin mugs and dancing to jazz: it had been another country, a land temporarily outside duty and class, where he'd relaxed as never since childhood. Then Winnie had arrived—one of a group coming late from another party. Their eyes had met as she'd entered; he'd seen her hesitant smile, then amazed himself, pushing through the crush, in love before he even reached her.

Engaged before the end of the week, they married on his first leave, both of them blissfully happy in a grim, grey post-war world of shortages, ration books and the ever-widening political chasm across Europe. As the cold war deepened, his duties changed: seconded to counter-insurgency, he went to Austria. Within a few months, he was permanently transferred to Intelligence. A year later he was brought back to a desk in Whitehall, and for the first time he and Winnie set up home together, renting a small house overlooking Battersea Reach.

It was their best of times: she as happy as she'd hoped, he happier than he'd ever expected. Between them, there was completion—he giving her the security and dependability she'd hungered for, she bringing a warmth, a gaiety, a world of speculation and imagination that his narrow upbringing and cold, undemonstrative parents had never given. Content, they'd waited for the children to come. Instead came the polio.

The hall chimes ceased. From the distance, like a vast echo, came the continuing boom of the cathedral clock.

'Go on—you go through to the sitting-room,' said Harrison. 'I'll bring the tea in.'

He watched her go, manoeuvring herself out into the hall. There would be no more pain for her, he determined—whatever the truth of this curious business about Cratchley, the past would somehow continue to be kept at bay.

Winnie lay awake, unable either to sleep or read. After helping her to bed, Harrison had returned to the sitting-room next door; she visualized him that moment, there at the bureau, re-reading his report ready for his meeting in the morning with the Archdeacon.

Pulling herself up on the pillows, she thought again of

the man who had stepped so suddenly and mysteriously out of the winter afternoon. Two months after the polio had struck, Richard had first brought him home; it had been Major Greville then—charming, witty, urbane, a wartime hero, decorated for his service with the Italian and Yugoslavian partisans. Richard had been in awe; she more reserved in her judgement. However, he'd won her round, dropping in when Richard was overseas to inquire after her welfare and pass on whatever bits of news he had—always reassuring, always so tactfully sympathetic—and when the section had moved to Cyprus, it had been he who'd arranged for her to go out and join Richard there.

She'd hated Cyprus from the start: even as she'd been wheeled from the aircraft, she'd felt the spirit of the island, like some hideous incubus, begin to suck at her soul. The killing had already started; from the mountains, Grivas and his EOKA gunmen had begun their attacks; fear and distrust increased between British, Greek and Turk. Confined to an airless married quarter, she'd sat the barren days through, watching the trucks and armoured cars rumbling through the barbed-wire gates, brooding as never before on her physical helplessness, her childlessness and her ever increasing alienation from Richard.

The war changed him: preoccupied with his work, he grew increasingly withdrawn and moody. Although she had only the vaguest notion of his actual duties, there was an odour of guile about him; almost tangibly it hung in the air, estranging them, driving them ever apart. And there was always Greville. He haunted their life. Whenever Richard was home, he'd appear; through the window, she'd see them in the scrubby back garden, walking in circles, heads bent, whispering secrets like schoolboys, the older man's mouth moving, Richard's head bent to listen—a Faustus with his Mephistopheles.

The violence grew: trucks were ambushed, villages attacked,

and ever more frequently came the crack and rolling echoes of the saluting volleys from the military cemetery beside the camp—and then, at that dark hour, came Seferiades.

There had been something of the quality of dream about that first meeting: the grey Humber creeping at night along the dusty, rutted roads to the small mountain town; the moment of absolute silence as the engine was switched off; the Mediterranean night pitch black, the air oven-like—then, like phantoms, men emerging to carry her up the outside staircase of a white-painted house to where, on the oil-lit balcony, the tall, bearded figure stood waiting, dressed in black cassock and high stovepipe hat.

The sight of an Orthodox priest—a bishop—had been a shock, but sitting at the scrubbed table listening to the two men arguing politics, one insisting that the time for union with Greece—for *Enosis*—had come and adamant there must be a British withdrawal, the other, equally implacable, fearing the bloodbath of civil war, obstinate in his belief in the absolute rightness and necessity of British rule, she'd had the instinctive certainty that just when they'd needed it, she and Richard had found a friend.

She had never been religious. For Richard's sake she had agreed to a church wedding, later even accompanied him to Sunday services, but never once had experienced the slightest stir of that faith so rooted in him; yet there with the insects swirling in the lamplight and the incessant chirp of the grass-hoppers about them, she'd sensed the faith of the dark-bearded man opposite her reaching out, suggesting a greater dimension to reality than she'd ever imagined—an enfolding whole, to which all—her own crippled body and hopes, the decay of empire and the bigotries of nationalism and church—were nothing but distorted shadows of an eternal sublime, flickering momentarily on an imprisoning wall.

After that first time she and Richard had returned many an evening, stealing to that upper room at night to sit and talk, eating and sharing wine. And all the time Seferiades, the uncompromising, outspoken opponent of British rule, embracing them, drawing them back together, enfolding them in the benevolent, rock-like faith. And then had come the morning when the phone had rung during breakfast.

Lying back on the pillows, hearing the rain, she could see the moment in every detail: the pattern of sunlight on the wall, Richard in the doorway, his eyes not quite meeting hers.

'That was Greville—Seferiades is dead.'

She'd known it as if he had shouted it—known that in some way they'd murdered him, he and Greville together, just as surely as if they had taken the Sten guns themselves. From the window she'd watched the jeep disappear, numbly certain that, whatever else, it was love that had been defeated, and it was their marriage that also lay bleeding in the dust beside the Larnaca Road.

And now Greville is back, she thought, turning towards the window against which the rain was beating suddenly hard. Across the precincts, the cathedral clock began booming dully through the curtains of rain.

Hearing the clock, Harrison looked up from the report, and then remembering what Canon Rope had said about the workmen still in the crypt, he reached for his diary. The Archdeacon's appointment was at ten; he would have to deal with Keates first thing.

He scribbled a note, then, yawning, pulled himself to his feet. As he went to leave, he noticed *The Times* lying on the arm of the settee where Greville had left it. Picking it up, he turned immediately to the crossword on the back page. Just as he'd expected, the blanks that he'd failed to complete over breakfast in Salisbury were now filled in. He gazed at the thick pencil strokes contrasting so clearly with his own thin, careful script, imagining the triumphant grin on the Brigadier's face.

'Damn him!' he muttered. Going to the waste-paper basket, slowly and deliberately he began screwing up the paper. All at once he stopped. Quickly he smoothed out the sheets: there, a few inches above the crossword, was the face that had looked up at him from the presbytery floor that afternoon.

He stood gazing down at the photograph. The patrician stare was just as it had been, only the dress was different: then it was black, high-buttoned coat; now it was mitre and full canonicals, and the hand, with its episcopal ring, was gripped round the haft of a crozier. Beneath, read the caption, *'Derby's turbulent priest—Bishop Campion arriving to address striking Rolls-Royce workers.'*

Maurice Campion, of course! He should have recognized him at once—how many times had he seen that face on newsreel or in television debates. He frowned. But why had the Bishop been in Canterbury on a winter afternoon? Above all, why incognito?

He remained staring down at the photograph for a few seconds longer, then suddenly impatient, he crumpled the paper and threw it into the basket.

CHAPTER TWO

T he muffled clink of pick and hammer rose from the crypt; irritation rising, Harrison hurried down the steps and, between the pillars, glimpsed Keates glancing round. The sight of the familiar moon-round face inflamed him further; he strode forward, eager for battle.

The Clerk-of-Works muttered something to the pair of elderly men bent over their tools, then came forward. ' 'Morning, Colonel.'

Ignoring the greeting, Harrison burst out, 'I had hoped you would have finished down here by now, Mr Keates—I know the Dean expected it!'

Keates scratched an ear. Conscious of Dill and Pennyfeather enjoying the confrontation, Harrison lowered his voice. 'There will be an enthronement in the coming year! Damn it, man, it'll mean the eyes of the world upon us!'

Keates stared back woodenly while, behind him, the two men reluctantly recommenced hacking at the concrete in-fills between the massive pavings. Glowering, Harrison shook his head. 'Good God,' he muttered, 'at this rate, you won't have started on the gatehouse before Christmas!'

'That's all very well, Colonel,' answered Keates, 'but look at the thickness of them slabs!' He pointed at the pile of already-raised pavings. 'And it isn't just the lifting—we're having to dig down to lay a good level of hardcore. If we don't, they'll rise again.'

Harrison didn't reply: the fellow had a point. He considered suggesting the job be left, but aware of the slabs and gravel already heaped under the vaulting, he dismissed the idea. Giving up, he walked away, conscious as he did so of the smirks at his back.

Crossing the nave, he heard his name called. He turned to see the chubby figure of the Dean hurrying towards him, face wreathed in smiles.

'I heard you were back, Richard. How's Winifred?'

'Thank you, fine.'

'You've heard about poor Cratchley, I suppose?' The Dean stared up at the soaring splendour of the nave. 'How he loved this place!' Turning, he smiled ruefully at Harrison. 'But then, of course, he didn't have to keep it all together!' He glanced at his watch. 'Interminable meetings! I'll have to go.'

'And I've got the Archdeacon coming in to discuss the rationalization scheme,' said Harrison.

'Oh, poor you!' Ingrams laughed. 'Come on,' he said, taking his arm, 'I'll walk with you as far as your door.'

Harrison was fond of Ingrams. He found him by far the most compatible of the cathedral clergy. For his sake, over the years, he increasingly intervened in the practical affairs of the cathedral. In turn, the diffident and genial Dean had come to rely on him, confiding in him many of the anxieties of his often irksome and difficult office. Now, however, it was Harrison who found himself longing to tell the other something of the disquiet he'd felt since returning home to find his two visitors the previous day.

Greville's reappearance had had the effect of a boulder tumbled into a deep, stagnant pool: the waters had been stirred, and the sleeping creatures within now swam again. Of course, he would say nothing: natural reserve and long training held him fast. Nevertheless, the sudden doubt over Cratchley's death and the curious phrase he'd used to the Brigadier intrigued and disturbed him.

'When is the funeral to be?'

'Funeral?' The Dean glanced round. 'Ah, you mean Cratchley's—it's on Tuesday next at the crematorium.'

'Cremation?'

'At his own request, of course. Why do you ask?'

'I thought I might go.'

'Good!' Ingrams shook his head. 'There's only Sarah left of the family now.'

'Sarah?'

'His niece.' Beaming, Ingrams raised a hand in greeting as Lloyd-Thomas, the cathedral organist, hurried past, face sour as ever. 'The ashes are to be buried in Basset Underhill.'

'Titmouse's parish?'

Ingrams smiled. 'I was forgetting—your little *bête noire*! Yes, Cratchley was Rector there for twenty-five years. In fact, his wife's buried there.'

'I had no idea.'

Descending from the north-east transept and passing the Howley-Harrison Library, they walked together up the narrow passageway of Dark Entry to his office door.

'What killed Cratchley?'

'Killed him?' The Dean looked curiously at his companion.

'What did he die of, I mean?'

'Heart attack, I believe. He'd had two before.'

'Of course.' Harrison stared a moment at the black, dusty door, then sighed. 'Well, I'd better go in and prepare for the Archdeacon, I suppose.'

At exactly ten the intercom-buzzer sounded on Harrison's desk. Moments later he was confronting the angular features and steel-rimmed spectacles of Dr Crocker.

When he'd first handed the Archdeacon the report, Harrison had been optimistic about its reception. Now, however, as they began going through the proposals in detail, Crocker's pale face grew more marble-like by the minute. Heart sinking, Harrison pressed on. 'Regarding the matter of St Mary the Virgin at Sheepcote, you will notice that with the scheme already agreed in principle with the local Nonconformists, our costs could be halved.'

'Time-share—isn't that the modern phrase?' Crocker's venom was hardly disguised.

Harrison sighed inwardly. 'I had hoped you'd be more pleased. It has involved a great deal of work for the Board.'

'Undoubtedly.' Dr Crocker smiled thinly. 'Incidentally, Colonel, I notice you wish to close St Stephen the Martyr's.'

'I did attach the incumbent's report.'

'Ah yes, Gleeson, isn't it? Wasn't he among those of the diocese who signed that letter to *The Times* in support of women's ordination?' Crocker paused. 'Ah well, I have the cutting at home. I must check.'

Harrison swallowed. 'You will see from this report that he holds Communion at the church once a month. According to him, as often as not, he has no congregation at all.'

Crocker's face was steel. 'Then perhaps Mr Gleeson should consider holding services more often! The Church lives on tradition, Colonel—not on absenteeism and neglect!'

'The man has six parishes, Archdeacon!'

Crocker stared stonily back. Harrison struggled to keep his temper. 'I don't see how we could be justified in keeping St Stephen's open. After all, the original village was abandoned during the Black Death—for the last five hundred years, the church has stood among fields!'

'St Stephen's is one of the most historic of our Kent churches.' Turning to the window, Crocker looked up to where the veiled disc of the sun seemed to be rushing away beyond the cathedral towers. His voice became wistful. 'St Stephen's was a pilgrims' church before Chaucer. Once it held some of the most precious relics in England.'

'The Board does not suggest—'

'Pulling it down—of course not! You would merely have it turned into a folk museum!' He paused, his gaze fixed on Harrison. 'Stalls for trinkets, Colonel! Trippers' coaches! You consider that suitable on land consecrated since Augustine's mission to Ethelbert?'

'You did ask the Board to rationalize.'

'Rationalize, yes—not devastate! Not desecrate!'

There was a knock at the door. Harrison's secretary entered.

'Excuse me, Colonel, there's a message.'

'Not now, Mary.'

'It's from the Dean, sir. He wants you to meet him in the crypt—he says it's urgent.'

'In the crypt?'

'That's what he said.'

'I see. Thank you, Mary.' As the door closed, Harrison turned to his visitor. 'I'm sorry about this,' he murmured, getting up. 'Perhaps we can arrange another meeting.'

A ghostly smile glided over Crocker's face. 'It appears our Dean is an instrument of a blessed Providence—if nothing else, he's at least postponed the destruction of Holy Kent!'

❀ ❀ ❀

Ingrams was waiting at the foot of the crypt steps. As Harrison descended, he stepped forward. 'Ah good, Richard! Thank you for being so prompt. I'm afraid I must have annoyed the Archdeacon, breaking up your meeting like that. I wouldn't have done it if the matter wasn't so urgent.'

'Urgent?' Harrison glanced into the interior of the crypt. Keates and the men stood in a huddle together, their attention fixed on something at their feet.

'What's happened?'

'More delay, I'm afraid. Our friends appear to have turned up something.'

'Found something?' said Harrison, surprised. 'What?'

'Come and see for yourself.'

Keates looked up as they approached. 'Well, Colonel,' he murmured with gloomy satisfaction, 'this is a proper turn-up for the books right enough.'

Harrison glanced down: in the shallow pit from where the latest flagstone had been removed, there intruded what appeared to be the surface of yet another large slab. 'What is it?' he asked, glancing up at Keates.

Before the Clerk-of-Works could answer, the single word 'coffin' was muttered by Alfred Dill.

'Coffin?' Frowning, Harrison peered down again at the slab of weathered stone barely protruding from the surrounding earth and rubble. In the couple of places where the men had attempted to get their picks under to lever it up, six inches or so of vertical grey stone was exposed to view.

'Mr Dill's obviously right,' intervened Ingrams. 'Without doubt, it's a coffin. Medieval, I'd say.'

Harrison surveyed the object with increased interest, then, remembering all the work to be done, turned back to Keates. 'Well, it will just have to be moved.'

Keates shook his head. 'Can't do that,' he said with exasperating finality, 'not without permission—not corpses!' Dill and Pennyfeather nodded in support.

Harrison felt his temper rise: determined not to prolong the matter a moment longer, he made his decision. 'Right,' he commanded, 'leave it where it is. Simply shovel some hardcore over it and relay the slab.'

The three stared at him doubtfully. He was about to repeat his order more forcefully when he felt a touch on his arm. The Dean was shaking his head. 'It may be a little more difficult than that, Richard.'

'I don't understand.'

Without answering, Ingrams knelt at the edge of the slight pit and rubbed his fingers over the exposed lid. As he did so, for the first time Harrison noticed the crude design carved into the stone. As the remaining topsoil was brushed away, the design became clear. It was crudely simple: one long stroke curving into a half-circle at one end.

Ingrams rose and half-whispered, 'Right, let's have a quiet talk.' Harrison followed him out of earshot. 'Well, Richard,' he said, 'what do you make of it?'

'The design?' Harrison shook his head. 'It reminds me of nothing so much as a question-mark.'

The Dean smiled. 'Hardly.'

'Then what?'

'A crook,' murmured Ingrams softly. 'The shepherd's crook.'

'I don't see.'

'A crozier—the pastoral staff of a bishop!' The Dean's usually mild eyes were troubled. He leant closer. 'This could be very awkward. You realize what it means? I'm afraid we now have the Becket factor to contend with!'

'Becket factor?' Harrison gasped. For an instant he saw Greville's face again in the hall light, Gillie's behind, a blur in the darkness. 'I don't understand,' he said recovering, 'This Becket factor—what does it mean?'

His companion glanced past him. 'I'll tell you later,' he whispered. He returned to the huddle of men. 'Mr Keates, I would like it covered for now.'

'The coffin, sir? Right.'

Ingrams thought for a moment. 'I think we'd better arrange with Mr Simcocks to have the crypt closed for the moment.'

As Keates lumbered away in search of the Head Verger, the find was covered with a tarpaulin. When done, Ingrams touched Harrison's arm. 'Right, time for a quiet cup of coffee.' He smiled. 'I'm afraid I have a short history lesson for you.'

❀ ❀ ❀

'You will remember that in the time of Henry the Eighth and the dissolution of the monasteries, Thomas Cromwell and his men began destroying all the so-called papist relics.' Ingrams paused. 'How's the coffee?'

'Fine,' answered Harrison. 'Go on.'

'It was soon Canterbury's turn: before the high altar stood Thomas Becket's shrine—the most sacred in England.' Ingrams sipped his coffee. 'The monks weren't fools: they knew what was planned. The shrine would be stripped of its treasures and the saint's remains destroyed.'

'But were powerless to prevent it, I suppose?'

'Not quite.'

There came a squeal of laughter from the garden outside. Getting up, Ingrams went to the window and waved to his twin teenage daughters who, in spite of the cold, were playing a game of improvised badminton on the deanery lawn. Harrison felt a twinge of envy; whether it was for Ingrams with his children or for the carefree joy of the youngsters themselves, he couldn't tell.

'No, not quite powerless,' repeated the Dean, returning to his desk. 'Before the King's commissioners could arrive, the monks had time to remove the bones and re-bury them secretly within the cathedral. Whoever organized the removal chose his helpers well: no trace of the remains has ever been found, though there was a brief flurry of excitement at one time when a stone coffin was dug up during reconstruction work.'

'Like the one today?'

'Exactly.' Ingrams nodded gloomily.

Harrison frowned. 'But what's the problem? If these really are Becket's remains in the crypt, isn't that good?'

'Good? My dear Richard—it would be an absolute disaster! Don't you see, it's a political matter.'

'Political?' repeated Harrison, stunned.

'Oh yes,' continued the Dean, 'of course it's political—think of it, the bones of the most famous English Catholic saint in the very mother-church of Protestant Anglicanism!'

'I can see that might prove a little embarrassing.'

Ingrams looked pained. 'My dear fellow, you still don't understand. We're talking of the very survival of the Church of England!'

'Surely not,' gasped Harrison.

The Dean smiled sadly. 'Ah, how innocent you of the laity are!' Getting up again, he returned to the window and stared out. 'The Anglican Church is in danger as never before. It's threatened with schism. There are many for whom the very idea of women's ordination is anathema—sincere men like our Archdeacon, who dream of one day reuniting with Rome—who would, as they see it, keep us part of the apostolic tradition and thus fight every innovation and change.'

Remembering Crocker's cold face across his desk an hour before, Harrison nodded. 'Yes, but I still don't see what exactly is so dangerous if these are Becket's bones?'

'Why do you think Henry's commissioners were so keen on destroying them originally?'

Harrison shrugged. 'They could have represented a sort of talisman, I suppose—something around which Catholic resistance might have grouped.'

'Exactly—and that is what would happen now!' Ingrams's face was suddenly anguished. 'Think how it would strengthen the hands of the Anglo-Catholics.' He shook his head. 'I tell you, Richard, that thing we've dug up is like an unexploded bomb—one that could easily bring the whole Church down!' Sighing, he extracted a pipe from his cassock pocket and stared a moment gloomily into its bowl. 'But it's not the politics that frighten me most—it's the passions that underlie them!'

Harrison waited as the pipe was lit.

'When I was called away to the crypt, the vestments committee were discussing the choristers' new surplices. Discussing!' Ingrams grimaced. 'If a few bits of linen and lace can arouse such emotion, I shudder to think what the bones of Thomas Becket might do!'

'Can't we hush it up?'

'Impossible—the news will be all round the city already.' The Dean sighed heavily. 'No, all I can do is play it down for all I'm worth and just pray the experts can prove the coffin has nothing to do with Becket.'

Harrison took a breath. 'Cratchley? Was he Anglo-Catholic?'

Ingrams looked surprised, then suddenly he was laughing. 'Anglo-Catholic? Cratchley? Good Lord, no! He was very middle of the road, low if anything. Why do you ask?'

'I just wondered if he might have feared such a discovery?'

Again Ingrams laughed. 'No, he'd have loved it—for him, it would have been one of the cathedral legends coming to life.'

'But the political dimension?'

'Cratchley was a political innocent, Richard—for all his extraordinary qualities, there was a naïve simplicity to the man.' Ingrams sucked his pipe, then shook his head. 'You know, talking of Thomas Becket, I think there was more than a touch of the saint about dear, simple, old Cratchley himself.'

As he left the deanery, Harrison paused to look back. What in that quiet, safe world could have so alarmed a political inno-cent that he'd got in touch with the Brigadier? With a shake of his head, he turned away, leaving behind him the half-cleared cabbage patch, the compost heap and the Dean's three earthen-ware rhubarb funnels, over which trails of snail-slime wove in intricate patterns of silver.

'You haven't forgotten the accountant's visit this afternoon, Colonel?' The inter-connecting door between the offices was open and his secretary was looking in.

'Thank you for reminding me, Mary.' Harrison smiled. 'You'd better get off for your lunch.' As she left, he turned back to the latest letter from the Reverend Titmouse, vainly trying to concentrate his thoughts on the tangled matter of the Basset Underhill glebe. Suddenly he threw the letter down. 'Damn it, it just doesn't make sense!' he burst out. 'No damn sense at all!'

Since leaving the deanery, Harrison's thoughts had been dominated by thoughts of Cratchley: how could he have known about the coffin? Even if he had, what was the reason for calling in Greville? Could the old Canon really have thought that a potential furore in the Church would be of interest to whatever section of Intelligence the Brigadier now ran? If he had, he must indeed have been going senile as Greville had suggested.

Impatient suddenly at the absurdity of the whole thing, he got up to leave. Once outside, however, he stopped to look up at the cathedral's massive central tower—the great Bell Harry, under which, according to Canon Rope, Cratchley had experienced that bee-like sting the night he died. It was all quite absurd, of course; all the same, it was an extraordinary coincidence—the same phrase cropping up again like that.

Thoughtfully, he walked on towards Bread Yard. As he let himself into the house, he heard voices from the kitchen. 'Fatty Simcocks says they chopped off the top of his head, so they'll be bound to know if the skeleton really is—' The speaker broke off with a look of near-horror as Harrison entered; dropping the sausage-roll in his hand, he clambered to his feet.

'Richard, this is Simon Barnes.'

Harrison stared uncomprehendingly down at the small red-haired boy, now hurriedly wiping crumbs from his mouth. He was about nine years old and was dressed in the uniform of a choral probationer.

'Simon kindly helped me get lunch. We thought you'd be delayed by this find in the crypt.'

'We?'

'Simon and I.'

Harrison glared at the tiny intruder.

'Well, you'd better hurry back to school, Simon,' said Winnie, smiling, 'but you will call again, won't you?'

Barnes glanced at Harrison, then answered eagerly, 'Oh, yes, Mrs Harrison—thank you.'

'Now,' said Winnie as the boy left, 'is it really Becket's coffin? Margaret Ingrams phoned. Everyone's terribly excited. Come on, tell me—I'm dying to know.'

Despite his irritation at finding the boy, Harrison was amazed and pleased at the change in Winnie: her eyes shone and there was an enthusiasm in her voice he'd not heard in years. 'I don't understand, Winnie—why the excitement?'

'Oh, come on, Richard! Thomas Becket reappearing after all these hundreds of years! It's wonderful! Pure romance!' She broke off, laughing and blushing. Momentarily, he saw beyond her wasted body to the bright-eyed, long-ago schoolgirl in panama hat and pinafore. The change was miraculous. Ingrams was right, he thought—whatever it was that Keates and his crew had unearthed, it was much more than just some old stone that had risen from the rubble and dust.

Returning to his office, Harrison noticed a camera crew filming in the precincts. News of the find was clearly spreading fast. His secretary had heard all about it over lunch. She was still talking animatedly of skeletons and ghosts when the diocesan auditor arrived. Harrison was soon immersed in the accounts of a dozen small Victorian charities. It was dark before the final ledger was closed and the auditor had left. He was locking the safe before going home when the telephone rang.

'Ah, Richard, I'm so glad to catch you.' Ingrams's voice sounded weary. 'It's about this wretched find. I've been in touch with the British Museum. Apparently, we'll be lucky if they can send anyone before Christmas—for some reason, their medievalists are all away at some conference—Dallas of all places!' He laughed briefly. 'Anyway, in the meantime, I'm arranging a little meeting in the crypt tomorrow morning to arrange a few practical matters. Could you possibly attend?'

'Of course.'

'That's very kind.' The Dean chuckled. 'I gather the twins have just seen me on the news. They're full of it at the moment. Dad on the box! You can just imagine!'

'You gave an interview?'

'Lesser of evils. If I'd refused, they'd have only gone to someone else.' A heavy sigh came down the line. 'As it was, they also interviewed our Verger.'

'Simcocks? Good Lord!'

'Exactly! So much for my wish to play the thing down! I'm furious with him. After his public enthusiasm, I fear we'll be packed out with sightseers for weeks!'

Harrison returned home to find Winnie reading in the sitting-room. She smiled up as he entered.

'You've just missed Matthew on the news.'

'And Simcocks as well, I hear.'

Winnie laughed. 'Oh, Richard, you should have heard him!'

'I can imagine.' Harrison smiled and touched her shoulder. 'What are you reading?'

'Just something from the library. Margaret took me.'

'Let's see.' He took the thick volume from her. It was a history of the reign of Henry II. On the cover was a detail from a medieval painting, depicting the King confronting a bearded Becket. 'It looks interesting,' he murmured, flicking through a few pages. 'If you don't mind, I'd like to glance at it myself.'

After their meal, Harrison slumped in a chair with the book. It had been a long day and he felt drowsy. As he began reading of the loss of the White Ship, his eyes began to close; a few lines into the dynastic problems of the Capetian kings and he was sound asleep.

He woke to a faint gabble of voices. Blinking, he opened his eyes. The television was on. He gazed at it blearily: next moment he sat up. On the screen was the same face that had looked up at him during Evensong.

Elegant as ever, stiffly upright, Bishop Campion faced the camera across a polished expanse of mahogany.

'Turn up the sound a bit, would you?'

Winnie glanced round quizzically, but, saying nothing, squeezed the button on the remote control. Immediately the interviewer's voice boomed into the room. 'Surely, Bishop, according to the polls, the British public want to retain an independent British deterrent.'

The lean, patrician face raised a fraction; the slightly hooded eyes surveyed the questioner. 'The public's ancestors wanted the stake and the branding-iron; once the average Englishman would have regarded the rack and the ritual disembowelling and dismembering of traitors as an absolute necessity for national survival. Because a majority believes or wishes a thing, it does not make that thing either necessarily true or morally right.'

'That doesn't sound exactly democratic.'

Campion smiled. 'Perhaps not.'

The interviewer glanced at his notes. 'You have publicly demanded the cancellation of the Trident Submarine project and openly attacked the Government's economic policy. Aren't they, the nuclear deterrent and the success of private enterprise capitalism, the very two things that have between them not only kept the peace, but won it?'

'What we have seen in East Germany, Poland, Czechoslovakia and Romania did not spring from *laissez-faire* capitalism; it arose from the cathedrals of Cracow and Warsaw, from the tradition of Wenceslas and the spirit kept alive in the churches of ancient Christendom.' Campion's face was more hawk-like than ever. 'The great changes in Europe—what is happening and will continue to happen—are not because of our weapons, but despite them!'

'As a bishop, you have influence—you more than most,' resumed the interviewer, 'and if this influence led to a policy that left us defenceless, what then? I realize that in the age of Glasnost and Perestroika that doesn't sound very likely; nevertheless, nuclear weapons still exist—how can you then preach views which might, however improbably, threaten our national survival?'

'Nuclear weapons are wrong—wrong because they threaten God's creation—wrong because they absorb those resources needed to alleviate poverty here in Britain and the starvation of millions throughout the world.'

'But surely, even—'

'In the end there is no political system, state or institution, nothing—not even the Church itself—that should, or indeed can be, defended or preserved by wickedness.'

The scene shifted to a brightly-lit studio where a group of discussion participants sat in a semi-circle. 'A typically tough and uncompromising message from the Bishop of Derby,' began the chairman. 'Perhaps, David, you as a Government minister...'

'Turn it off, Winnie,' said Harrison.

'What did you think?' she asked as the screen went blank.

'Of Campion? Yes, he's impressive all right.' He laughed. 'Almost frighteningly so.'

'Do you think he'll make a good Primate?'

'Archbishop of Canterbury! Campion? You're joking!'

'A lot of people think he will be.'

'Nonsense! Who for instance?'

'Canon Cratchley for one.' Winnie laughed. 'You needn't stare like that. I'm not a leper. I do have visitors, you know.'

'No, it wasn't that. You say Cratchley thought Campion would be Archbishop? Winnie, are you sure?'

She smiled. 'He used the same word you used—impressive.'

'Good Lord!' Harrison murmured flatly. 'And he wouldn't have minded? A chap with those sort of ideas!'

There was a sudden tenderness in Winnie's smile. 'My dear,' she said, 'you are so out of date! Remember the fuss after the Falklands War. Your beloved Church of England has changed—it isn't the squire's preserve any more and it's certainly not the Conservative Party at prayer.'

'All the same...' His voice trailed off, then for no reason he could understand, Winnie wheeled over to him and, bending, kissed his cheek.

Harrison again sat up late that night, the questions turning in his mind: presumably the crypt-pavings had not been raised since the sixteenth century, then how could Cratchley have known the coffin would be there? And even if he had, why try to get Greville involved? Suddenly he laughed aloud: at least, one little mystery was cleared up. If it was true that Maurice Campion was really a serious candidate for the Primacy, then the explanation of why he'd been in Canterbury incognito was obvious—to use the Brigadier's phrase, the fellow had been merely going over the ground.

Getting up, he poured himself a whisky and went to the window. The cathedral loomed above, a black ship upon a black ocean. He thought of Winnie—the look in her eyes and her kiss. Gazing out, he felt an enormous peace and joy spread through him, almost as if some beneficent presence had indeed risen and was already reaching out from the deepest recesses of the vast building before him.

CHAPTER THREE

'It's not like the Dean to keep us waiting.' Simcocks was clearly finding the standing difficult. He breathed heavily as he leant against one of the pillars, and despite the chill his face and scalp were perspiring freely. He dabbed at them with a large handkerchief while Keates and the two workmen nudged each other and grinned.

Harrison glanced at his watch. It was already twenty-five past the hour. Simcocks was right; it wasn't like Ingrams to be late. Turning, he looked back into the shadowy recesses of the crypt.

Crocker hadn't moved. He was still standing beside where the coffin lay hidden under the tarpaulin. His hands were clasped in front of him, his head bowed: he could have been asleep, at prayer or merely lost in thought. Whichever, the Archdeacon was clearly a long way from them all.

From above came the sound of hurrying feet. A moment later the Dean appeared, looking flushed and ruffled. 'I do apologize, gentlemen. Something cropped up rather unexpectedly, I'm afraid.' Spotting Crocker, he hurried forward. 'My dear Archdeacon, I didn't see you back there. I'm so sorry for this delay.'

Crocker flinched slightly as Ingrams touched his arm. 'Pray don't mention it, Dean. I could not have awaited your arrival in a better place.'

Whether the Archdeacon was being ironic or not was impossible to tell. Ingrams hesitated uncertainly for a moment before turning back to the group by the crypt steps. 'To business then, gentlemen. As you all know, there will be a delay before the experts arrive. In the meantime, I'm determined that the crypt chapels should remain open for private prayer and contemplation—that must be our priority.'

Simcocks nodded enthusiastically. 'Prayer and contemplation—yes, sir, quite right!'

'One moment!'

Crocker had stepped out of the shadows; he stood before them, tall, gaunt, his face a bony mask in the dimness. 'Is there not a more urgent priority?' He pointed back to where the coffin lay covered. 'Surely the safety of that sacred casket over there must be our first concern.'

Ingrams frowned. 'Archdeacon, we are not yet at all sure what the coffin contains, and, as I've made clear, I consider it dangerous to speculate, but of course in principle I agree—our little find must be protected from the hands of the curious.'

Crocker's expression hadn't changed. 'It is not curiosity that frightens me, Dean.'

'I don't understand. What frightens you, Archdeacon?'

'Desecration!'

The word echoed through the low-roofed dimness. Harrison glanced round. Ingrams looked both bemused and embarrassed; Keates was gaping open-mouthed, while behind him Dill and Pennyfeather stood transfixed, gazing at the Archdeacon. The Verger, however, was peering around into the shadows, consternation in his sweating face.

'Surely not, Archdeacon.' The Dean looked pained and troubled. 'Who would do such a thing?'

The answer was immediate. 'Those at war with the Universal and Apostolic Church.' Crocker's voice trembled. 'By a miracle, the bones of St Thomas of Canterbury were protected from Thomas Cromwell's commissioners in 1536. If now, by another miracle, the saint has returned to us, we must guard against the latterday bigot, the unhappy or simply insane—any, for whatever reason, who would come here to smash and destroy.'

There was no doubting Crocker's sincerity—and such was the intensity of the emotion behind his words that no one spoke for seconds after he'd finished.

'Yes, of course,' said Ingrams at last, 'the coffin must be vigilantly guarded. Mr Simcocks can arrange for a couple of the younger ushers to be down here whenever the crypt gates are unlocked. And you, Mr Keates,' he continued, 'perhaps you could screen off the find from public view.'

The Clerk-of-Works appeared to wake from a trance. 'Screen off?' He gaped. 'How do you suggest, sir?'

Harrison took a hand. 'Come on, man, that shouldn't be difficult. Make up some wooden frames and tack hessian over them.'

'There's the work on the gatehouse to begin, Colonel.'

It was the Dean's turn to intervene. 'No, Mr Keates, the crypt must be our first concern now.'

Keates stared wordlessly at Harrison a moment, then lumbered away up the steps with Pennyfeather and Dill, mumbling an inaudible something under his breath as he went. Simcocks bustled out, followed by the Archdeacon. Harrison, too, went to leave, but as he did so Ingrams caught his elbow.

'Richard, a word if I may. This news I've just had—it's come as rather a shock.' He looked round. 'But perhaps we should find somewhere a little more private to talk.'

Crossing to a door, he ushered Harrison inside, and following, closed the door behind them.

They were in what had been designed as the chantry of the Black Prince and Joan of Kent, but which since the seventeenth century had been used by the descendants of Huguenot refugees. Despite the high Perpendicular windows, the light was dim, and the austere walls and dark-wood pulpit gave the little chapel, beautiful though it was, a sombre and melancholy feel.

Ingrams went and stood before the small altar. 'I had a call from Sarah Cratchley this morning. Apparently she's been contacted by Drood the undertaker. He says the funeral will have to be postponed.' He shook his head miserably. 'I've never known such a thing.'

Harrison's stomach had knotted. Hardly for a moment had he considered the possibility of the autopsy turning up anything—the implications were too incredible, too grotesque, to be true. Yet something had obviously been found—what other explanation could there be? Unbelievable as it was, he had to accept it—Cratchley had been murdered, done to death there in the darkness as he'd gazed up into the illuminated splendour above.

Ingrams sighed. 'All the arrangements! And there's Sarah—always such a highly-strung girl!'

Harrison made himself speak. 'What reason did they give?'

'They? Ah, you mean Drood's people?' Ingrams shrugged. 'Paperwork apparently.' There was silence, then the Dean laughed unexpectedly. 'Funny thing, Richard, but I was always telling dear Cratchley he'd be late for his own funeral.' He smiled sadly. 'Who would have ever guessed I'd be right!'

'Glad you could make it, Dickie.'

Leaning on a walking-stick, the Brigadier stood bareheaded under the gatehouse arch, the collar of his heavy overcoat turned up, a smile on his heavily jowled face. Behind him, despite the bitter cold of the late afternoon, the small square of the Buttermarket was abustle with shoppers and sightseers. 'Come on,' he said, glancing back, 'let's take a stroll round the precincts—it will be quieter.'

'Is that safe?'

Greville grinned. 'Two elderly gents seeking peace—nothing more natural, I'd have thought.'

With the clock striking four, Harrison and the Brigadier headed towards the west front. The already darkening grounds were almost deserted, and apart from the cry of wheeling rooks the only sound was the tread of their feet.

'You found something, then?'

Halting, Greville nodded. 'Ricin,' he said. Seeing the other's blank look, he laughed. 'You're a bit out of touch, old lad. Ricin's a fast-acting toxin. It's what they used in the Bulgarian umbrella job. You remember—the writer fellow they poked on Waterloo Bridge?'

Harrison was hardly able to believe what the other had so casually said. 'You surely don't mean...'

The Brigadier nodded. 'Afraid so—it seems we've got the Opposition involved.'

'What? The Eastern bloc?' Harrison shook his head in disbelief. 'Moscow killed Cratchley! Is that what you're saying? It can't be—it's absolutely absurd!' He paused, his mind reeling, then burst out again, 'But I thought the world was meant to be changed—Glasnost, Perestroika and all the rest of it!'

With a shrug, Greville bent and began tracing a circle on the path with the tip of his stick.

'But Cratchley of all people!' Harrison lowered his voice. 'A retired clergyman! For God's sake, why?'

Greville remained apparently concentrating on the movement of the stick. Moments passed, then he straightened and, with a smile, tapped Harrison lightly on the chest with the handle. 'Yes, Dickie, quite a teaser, I agree.'

Turning away from the west front, he walked on, following

the line of the nave. Harrison automatically fell in at his side. Ahead, a woman sat huddled on a bench. As they passed, Harrison recognized her as the woman who'd sat opposite him in Evensong. Here in the open, she looked thin and cold, pathetic as any winter sparrow. For a moment he thought of Winnie back in the house. He suddenly swung round. 'Damn it, it's got to be a mistake!'

The other shook his head. 'Hardly—there was enough toxin in the body to kill the proverbial horse. As you can imagine, I had it double-checked.'

'Then it must have been a mix-up—it has to be! Pitch black in the nave; the only lights up above in the tower; someone stabs at someone, and by mischance Cratchley gets in the way—it's the only logical explanation!' Harrison thought for a moment. 'This party he was taking round—any idea who they were?'

'A religious tour-group organized by the Lutheran Church, most of them West Germans and Scandinavians.'

Harrison felt a huge relief. 'That's it, then! It must have been one of those they were after! As I say, poor old Cratchley just got in the way.'

'Come on, Dickie!' There was something like anger in the Brigadier's eyes. 'The phone call, man! Cratchley wanted to see me, remember? Something had definitely alarmed him.' Greville glanced across the darkening lawns. 'Yes, and some bastard here knew it—of that I'm bloody well sure!'

Beyond the curved eastern end of the cathedral stood the ruins of what had been the monks' infirmary. Leading the way, the Brigadier walked across the grass and stood, his back to the dark flintstone, looking up. The sinking sun had deepened into a red ball of fire. Still bathed in its light, the soaring stonework above glowed honey-brown, while among the roofless ruins below the shadows gathered fast.

Harrison made himself speak. 'What are you going to do?'

Greville turned. 'Come on, man, you know why I'm here.' He smiled slightly. 'Are you going to make me beg?'

Harrison shook his head vigorously. 'No, I'm sorry, I can't help you. I swore to Winnie I've done with the work.'

The Brigadier sighed. 'Old friend,' he said quietly, 'don't you remember—there's still a debt to be paid.'

'Debt?' Harrison glared. 'What debt do I owe you?'

The other laughed. 'Not me—Him!' At the final word the stick was swung upwards so that it pointed at the flaming sky. For a moment its ferrule gleamed against the sun. 'Well, Dickie,' said Greville slowly, 'isn't that right? Don't we owe God a priest, you and me both?'

As if mesmerized, Harrison stared back through the gloom at the eyes fixed on his, then, with an effort, turned away. A hand touched his arm. 'It's a quiet pond, this place, Dickie. I need someone able to swim in it without causing the slightest ripple—and that, I'm afraid, is you.'

There was a giggle behind them. Turning, the two found themselves facing a small group of boys on the path. Through the dusk, Harrison glimpsed Simon Barnes's face. He went to speak, but Greville checked him, while the boys, lowering their heads, walked on quickly, giggling among themselves. With a last stifled burst of laughter, the small figures disappeared.

'Well, Dickie, will you do it? Will you find what this so-called Becket factor is and why they sent that butchering bastard in after a harmless old fellow like Cratchley?'

As Harrison stared into the gloom, the Brigadier stepped in front of him. From his wallet he extracted a card. 'You can get me on this number, night or day.' As Harrison reached to take it, Greville seized at the lapel of his coat; there was a fierce intensity to his eyes. 'Help me find them, Dickie!' His grasp tightened; his breath came in gasps. 'Smell them out for me! Do it, man! For Seferiades, for poor old Cratchley, smell me those murderous buggers out!'

❋ ❋ ❋

'The cathedral is now closing.'

Hardly aware of either the cry or the faint clatter of feet overhead, Harrison gripped the nearest timber support and shook it. It didn't budge. He tried the next. Taking a step back, he surveyed the entire length of the structure.

Yes, he had to admit it. Keates had done a good job. The hessian-covered frames, reaching from ceiling to floor, stretched in a dead straight line from the foot of the steps to the further wall, neatly and effectively dividing the crypt in two.

He walked over to stand where the Archdeacon had stood that morning. An extension light now hung from a hook over the tarpaulin covering. He ran his eye along the cable back to the junction-box, noting as he did so that it was securely tacked to the low ceiling at regular intervals. There was something humbling about the simple efficiency with which the tasks had been carried out: he made a mental note to praise the men for their efforts when he saw them next.

After parting from the Brigadier, he had gone straight to the cathedral. Evensong was almost over, and instead of taking his usual seat at the service, he'd let himself into the crypt, telling himself he ought to look at the finished partitioning: next day was Saturday, and with all the publicity, there were bound to be sightseers.

'The cathedral is now closing.'

The call was closer now. A door slammed. The crypt darkened suddenly as the main lights were turned off above. Harrison hardly noticed: he was gazing at the tarpaulin at his feet. Irrational though it was, he'd connected the seemingly miraculous change in his relationship with his wife to the emergence of the coffin; from the moment Ingrams had traced with his finger the strangely ambiguous motif on the lid, a healing magic had begun, nothing less perhaps than the resurrection of love. As he now stared down at the faded canvas, he felt his anger rise. Why had the past returned to trap him at this moment? What cursed fate, or weakness perhaps in him, was dragging him back into the intoxicating dark worlds of deceit? Anger and self-loathing rose up, blending and overwhelming him.

I'm back, he thought, grimacing, back like a dog to his vomit!

Stooping, he seized the near edge of the tarpaulin and savagely yanked it clear. Under the glare of the bulb hanging a few feet above it, the coffin-lid was brightly illuminated. Rough, pitted and grey, the slab of worn stone lay brutally exposed. On it, the deep-carved shape that had first appeared as a mysterious enticing question-mark now resembled nothing more than the slash of a hooligan's knife. All they had found was an ancient container of dry bones and dust—fit emblem, he thought, of all earthly hope, mocking with its pathetic crudity, the transitory and illusory dreams of humankind.

'Christ, God!'

His cry echoed hollowly through the emptiness. Then—as if in answer—there came a loud, jarring clatter from above.

He froze. The sound died. In the silence he felt his heart beating. Then came the noise again, even louder than before: someone was violently shaking at the wrought-iron gate that he'd padlocked behind him before descending the steps.

Recovering his senses, he dashed through the hinged screen to the foot of the steps. For the third time there came the frenzied clatter. Looking up, all he could make out was a pair of white knuckles frantically wrenching at the gate.

'I say!'

The shaking stopped dead. For a half-second a pale face stared down—then it was gone, and there was only darkness between the bars. He bounded up the steps in time to see a vague shape flit away into the blackness.

'Stop!'

His voice echoed feebly through the empty vastness. He fumbled frantically for his keys; unlocking the gate, he went to follow. As he did so, a torch-beam blazed into his eyes.

He froze, blinking into the glare. From behind the light a sharp voice spoke.

'Colonel, would you kindly explain exactly what you are doing here!'

❀ ❀ ❀

'Stop shining that confounded light in my face!'

The torch switched off. As Harrison's eyes adjusted to the darkness, the Archdeacon's angular features materialized before him with Simcocks's face peering over his shoulder, a round, sweating Iago playing to a spectral Othello.

'Well, Colonel, can you explain?' Crocker's voice was icy. 'What was all that noise?'

'The gate, damn it! Someone was shaking it.' Away at the western end of the nave, a door slammed. Hearing it, he burst out angrily, 'Standing here talking, we've lost the blighter!'

'A nutter!' breathed Simcocks. He glanced fearfully about, then squeezed past Crocker to face Harrison. 'The coffin, sir? Is it safe?'

'Quite safe.'

'I think we'll take a look all the same,' said Crocker, pushing by. The Archdeacon's torch flicked to and fro as he descended the steps. Harrison and Simcocks, following closely, heard him gasp as he reached the gap in the screening.

'No!'

Before Harrison could explain, Crocker dashed towards the coffin; reaching it, he moved in a low crouch back and forwards, leaning low over the lid, then glared up. 'Why is this uncovered?'

'I wanted to see what we'd found precisely,' answered Harrison, his face reddening.

'Indeed!' Crocker slowly rose to his full height. A nerve twitched in his face. Swinging round, he stalked back to the gap in the screening, then turned. 'I shall be taking this matter up with the Dean.' Allowing Harrison no time to reply, he pointed at the heap of tarpaulin lying beside the shallow pit. 'Please have everything tidied before you leave, Mr Simcocks.' He glanced significantly at Harrison. 'And make sure everything is well secured.' Then he was gone, his footsteps ringing away.

Simcocks began tugging at the tarpaulin. Harrison, still trembling with rage, knelt to help.

'You mustn't mind him, sir,' said Simcocks, inclining his head towards the gap in the screening where the Archdeacon had delivered his parting shot. 'He's a bit edgy at the moment—there's this.' He nodded down at the spread tarpaulin, then whispered confidingly, 'And there's his sister, of course.'

'What do you mean?'

Simcocks leaned closer. 'The big C!' he hissed, then grimaced horribly. 'It's terrible what they've cut out of her—doesn't bear thinking of!'

In silence, he followed Simcocks out. As the Verger first locked the lower door, then began winding the padlock-chain round the gate, he thought of Miss Crocker—a grey-haired woman, tall and gaunt like her brother, who shared with him the house in Green Close. He'd heard she'd been ill, but operations for cancer, he'd had no idea.

'There's plenty of nutters around all right!' Simcocks's voice interrupted his thoughts. He looked round to see him examining the padlock earnestly with the aid of a tiny pocket torch. There was just light enough to see the satisfaction on the Verger's bulging features. 'But I reckon that should hold them back awhile.'

'I'll walk round with you when you finish locking up,' said Harrison.

Apart from the tread of their feet and the slight jangling of the keys, they moved in silence through the darkened building, locking and barring doors. Once done, they mounted the steps to where the lights still shone beyond the great carved choir-screen. As Simcocks went to the discreetly hidden switchboard, Harrison looked up into the great hollow cave of darkness above where the interior of the Bell Harry Tower rose invisible over his head. It must have been about here, he thought, that Cratchley was standing when he was stabbed.

With a series of little clicks, the choir lights went off. Now, apart from the beam of the Verger's torch and the distant lights in the north-west transept, the cathedral lay in complete blackness.

'Tell me, Simcocks, what did you think of Canon Cratchley?'

The thin beam of light wavered uncertainly. 'He'll be very much missed, sir.' Simcocks sounded like an elderly butler.

'Not one of your nutters, then?'

There was an intake of breath in the blackness. 'I was referring to the laity, sir.'

Harrison pressed on. 'All the same, Cratchley was an odd sort, eccentric, wouldn't you say?'

'The Canon was a very nice clerical gentleman—no harm to anyone.'

Clearly aggrieved, Simcocks ponderously led the way towards the Martyrdom Transept. As they descended the steps, Harrison tried once more. 'But what did he do, Cratchley, I mean?'

'Do?' The Verger gaped round. 'Do?' he repeated with growing perplexity: to him the clergy were part of the cathedral much as the pillars and altars; with his gold-tipped staff, he led them in procession, bowed them to seats and pulpits. He might as well be asked what the cathedral did. 'Well, he was mostly retired, wasn't he?' he muttered resentfully.

'Yet he always seemed to be rushing around.'

Suddenly Simcocks understood. 'Ah, that would be his books, sir—he was always at that.'

'Books? Writing them, you mean?' Harrison paused. 'Not political books, were they?'

'Oh, I wouldn't know about any of that,' answered the Verger, continuing down the steps. Harrison followed him to the calefactorium door. The Verger held it open for him to pass, but as he went to do so, Simcocks touched his arm. 'Of course, the old gentleman had his troubles.'

'Indeed?'

'What you said, sir—political!' Simcocks whispered the final word. 'That niece of his—near broke his heart, they say.'

'Sarah?'

Simcocks gripped his arm. 'Went the same way as my first dean.'

Baffled, Harrison shook his head.

'Hewlett Johnson, Colonel,' whispered Simcocks.

'You mean..."

'That's right, sir!' Simcocks interrupted, gripping tighter in a spasm of excitement. 'Commies—the pair of them! Both as red as the blood in your arm!'

Harrison left the cathedral walking briskly. Only as he emerged from Dark Entry did he slow his pace. Across the expanse of Green Court, boys were assembling outside the entrance to the King's School prep rooms. The bitter north wind, whipping at his face and making his eyes run, carried their shrill voices over the frozen grass. He paused, remembering Simon Barnes and his group of giggling friends.

Frowning at the memory, he glanced towards the archdeaconry where a solitary light shone from one of the upstairs
rooms.

A master's voice rang out in the distance. He had a blurred
vision of a short crocodile forming in front of the dimly lit
entrance. Then it moved away, a straggling, disjointed column
of small shapes flickering silently between dark shadows and
the pools of light to disappear into the arched gloom of the
Palace Street gateway. Standing there, Harrison thought of
another boy of that school—the young Christopher Marlowe,
son of a poor Canterbury shoemaker. For a moment, he visualized him: a wild, brilliant youth in doublet and hose, a bush
of brown hair swept back under a velvet cap—ahead Corpus
Christi at Cambridge, the London playhouses, *Tamburlaine*,
Faustus—and already, perhaps, within him the same ambition
that was to draw him also into the dark webs of espionage and
conspiracy.

An unearthly shriek jerked Harrison from his reverie. A cat
raced out of the shrubbery towards the deanery drive. He shuddered. The wind was biting cold. Quickly he walked on towards
Bread Yard, but as he entered the courtyard, he halted momentarily, dread suddenly in the pit of his stomach: of all the cottages,
his alone was unlit.

'Winnie?' he called in the hall. 'Winnie, are you there?'

Faintly he heard her voice from the bedroom. As he entered,
she turned on the bedside light. Her face was drawn and pale.

'What is it, my dear?' he said, going over to the bed. 'One
of your bad days?'

She nodded. 'It's got so suddenly cold.'

Harrison said nothing. He knew something of her pain:
occasionally, usually at some sudden change in the weather, the
knee, hip and foot joints with their shrunken, wasted tendons
and muscle, would ache continuously. At such times the slightest
movement was excruciating.

She pulled herself up a little on the pillow, wincing as she did so. 'Is it late? I must have fallen asleep.'

'Quite late, yes. I stayed behind to help Simcocks lock up. He tells me that Dorothy Crocker is ill—he says cancer.'

'You didn't know?'

He shook his head. 'Is she home?'

'Richard, she's been back nearly a month now. There's nothing more they can do.'

'I had no idea,' he murmured, seeing again Crocker's thin face glaring at him across the coffin. 'Well,' he said, getting up, 'I'd better go and make us supper.'

'I hear you've had a visitor.'

He stopped, his hand on the door-handle; for a second or so he remained staring at a hardened lump of paint on the panel in front of him like a frozen tear, then turned to face her. 'That brat Barnes told you, I suppose?'

'He and his friends saw you by the ruins—you and a flabby old man, they said.'

Damn them to hell, he thought. A sharp gust of wind rattled the window; a dustbin lid fell and clattered away on the cobbles. He went to speak, but the words didn't come. 'I'll go and see to that meal,' he said flatly, turning to the door.

He hadn't reached the kitchen when he heard the crash and cry from the bedroom. Next moment he was dashing down the hall.

Winnie was lying on the floor, the china table-lamp in pieces beside her. As he rushed forward, he saw her face contort as she raised herself slightly, arching to pull the hem of her nightgown over her knees.

Gently, he lifted her back on to the bed. Fingers clenched, head turned away, eyes closed with the tears squeezing from the corners, she lay in agony while he stood hesitating. Finally, as she cried out, he rushed to the bathroom for the pain-killers.

'How did it happen?' he asked, holding the glass as she gulped down the mixture.

'I was trying to get out of bed,' she gasped, her breath coming in shallow fast pants.

'For God's sake, Winnie, why?'

'For us!' She grimaced. 'I'm a fool!' A spasm of pain contorted her face. Rolling over, she bit on the pillow. 'I'll phone the doctor.' He started to get up, but her hand seized his wrist.

'No, it will pass.'

Helpless, he sat praying for the pain-killer to start working. Through the changing pressure of her fingers about his wrist, he measured each of the spasms rising to a crescendo, then felt its retreat, the breathing slowing, and then once more the tiny handcuff contracting until her half-stifled cry. Under the torture, he broke—and the words were suddenly spilling out. 'Winnie, listen. Greville came about Cratchley.' He talked fast, telling her of the walk with Rope, the account of the so-called bee-sting, the ricin in the body—everything, anything to take her mind from the racking pain. Whether it was what he said, or merely the drug working, as he finished he noticed she was breathing normally and that the pressure round his wrist had relaxed. As he lapsed into silence, she looked up at him steadily, her eyes cold. 'Why?' she asked.

'Why what?'

'Did you say you'd help him?'

'The Brigadier?' He looked away, thinking back to the moments outside the infirmary ruins: the fading light on the tower above, the giggling boys on the path, their faces pale in the dusk. 'I don't know.' He shrugged. 'Pride perhaps, frightened of being nothing more than an irascible old buffer—another dried-up relic round the place, just like that wretched thing in the crypt.'

'Just for vanity, then?'

Her scorn stung. 'Not quite,' he said, looking away.

'What, then?'

He swallowed. 'The Brigadier said something about owing God a priest.' He looked back at her. 'I think you know what he meant.'

She nodded, biting her lip. 'Seferiades,' she whispered. 'You killed him?'

'No! His own people did that. All Greville and I did was help discredit him—our meetings with him, yours and mine, our talks, it was to compromise him. Imagine the gossip: friend-ship with any British officer was bad enough—with someone in Intelligence, it was fatal.' He paused. 'God, he must have been blind not to see it!'

'He loved you—he loved us both.'

'I had a duty, woman! We were fighting a war. Christ, Winnie, what were we expected to do? Seferiades was openly preaching all that Enosis stuff. It couldn't go on. We had to undermine his authority somehow, surely you see that!'

She didn't answer.

'Honestly, I didn't think they'd kill him—not a priest!'

She turned slowly to look at him. 'This thing now with Greville, it's going to be your atonement, is it?' The scorn was back in her voice. 'Your debt repaid?'

'Something like that,' he said quietly, looking down.

From the hall came the beat of the clock; beyond the window, the rose-bushes rustled; Winnie lay regarding him as the moments passed, then pulled herself up on the pillows. 'Well?' she said, 'where will you start?'

He shrugged. 'I don't know. There are those books Cratchley was writing and there's the niece. Simcocks says she's a Communist, that she broke the old fellow's heart.'

Winnie snorted. 'Simcocks is a fool.'

'It's the only possible political connection I can see.'

Again there was just the beat of the clock from the passage.

'I'd better get the meal on,' he said, getting up wearily.

'You need to talk to Matthew.' Winnie was looking up. 'He's the best one to tell you about the books.' She paused, then smiled. 'If you like, we could both call in at the deanery tomorrow morning. I want you to take me into town anyway to choose a new lamp.'

'I don't understand. You're offering to help me?'

She reached out her hand. 'Bob Cratchley was a friend. If someone has killed him, I also want to know why.'

Making supper, Harrison felt a joy he would have hardly believed possible an hour before: after all these years, he'd managed to speak of Seferiades and admit his role in the killing; somehow, amazingly, a bond had survived both that and the new connection with Greville. Whether love had died and been reborn, or whether it had merely gone underground to have now re-emerged, he didn't know. Either way, he and she were together. Going to the window, he looked out.

The wind still blew hard. Above the wall of the yard, the cathedral was now a black galleon anchored in a racing, moonlit sea. Staring up at the streaming clouds, his mind returned to the crypt, to the frenzied rattle of the gates, the white knuckles round the iron, the pale face behind. Obviously something else beside love had emerged; another emotion, obscure and irrational, equally strong perhaps, had risen coincidentally from out of the rubble and dust.

CHAPTER FOUR

'I'm not quite sure what you've done to our Archdeacon, Richard.' The Dean chuckled as he dipped a biscuit into his coffee. 'He was here breathing fire and the sword before I'd even finished breakfast this morning.'

'I trust you don't think I was out to desecrate the coffin?'

Ingrams grinned mischievously. 'Oh, I don't know—according to him, you virtually wish to close down the diocese!'

'Matthew, you shouldn't joke,' said Margaret Ingrams. 'It's a difficult time for Stephen. There's his sister, remember: they've always been close.'

Frowning, the Dean stared into his cup, as if, beneath the liquid's impenetrable blackness within, lay hidden the key to the mysterious workings of an inscrutable omniscience. For a few moments the deanery drawing-room was silent apart from the asthmatical purr of the elderly Siamese on his lap.

'How is Dorothy?' asked Winnie.

Margaret shook her head. 'Very poorly, I'm afraid.'

'You heard about that lunatic rattling the crypt gates last night, I presume?' said Harrison, turning to the Dean.

'At some length.' Ingrams gave a tired smile.

'Who could it have been, Matthew?' asked Winnie.

'Some tortured soul.' The Dean gazed a moment out at the cathedral towers. 'The wounded come seeking balm and, not finding it, they rage against us and God.' He shook his head mournfully. 'It's extraordinary what terrible responses even a clerical collar can provoke. Just think of poor Cratchley getting stabbed.'

Harrison caught his breath. Did the Dean know?

'You hadn't heard? Of course, it was a while ago now.'

'What happened, Matthew?'

Before Winnie had her answer, there was a loud slam of a door from the back of the house. A girl shouted angrily, 'You can bloody well pull your own boots off!'

'But I can't,' came the answering wail.

'Oh dear!' Margaret rose quickly, smiling apologetically. 'I'm afraid Charlie does cause his problems, sweet as he is.'

'A boy?' inquired Winnie.

'No, thank goodness. Just a horse!'

Ingrams chuckled as the door closed. 'A favourite pony, I believe; the twins have riding lessons on Saturday mornings.'

Winnie smiled. 'You were telling us about this attack.'

'On Cratchley?' Ingrams began lighting his pipe. 'Yes, an extraordinary business—quite bizarre. It was the occasion of Pope John Paul's visit. He and the Archbishop prayed together at the martyrdom stones, you remember. Anyway, that evening, Cratchley was walking home through Dark Entry when someone came from behind and slashed him with a knife.'

'How awful!' exclaimed Winnie. 'Did he see who it was?'

Ingrams shook his head. 'It was pitch black in the passage, and his attacker fled before he could properly turn—though dear old Cratchley, of course, always swore it was Nell herself!'

'A woman!'

Ingrams laughed. 'Not a living one anyway! Nell Cook is supposed to have been walled up somewhere in Dark Entry in Tudor Times for poisoning one of the cathedral clergy; legend has it, she haunts the passage.'

'But this was no ghost, I take it?' said Harrison.

'Far from it—Cratchley had to have stitches.'

'What made him think of Nell Cook?'

'You know what Cratchley was like—his love of the cathedral stories.' He paused. 'But there was something else, I can't remember exactly—something about a dress.' Ingrams smiled. 'Anyway, it all goes to show that the cloth is not quite so safe a calling as is often supposed.'

Harrison glanced at Winnie, then cleared his throat. 'I hear he wrote books.'

'Cratchley? Oh yes, he was very prolific. I have tried to read them, but—' Ingrams flushed slightly—'not quite my sort of thing.'

'Political, you mean?'

Ingrams stared incredulously, but before he could speak, the door opened and his wife ushered in the twins.

'Whatever was the matter?' Ingrams smiled at his daughters who stood awkwardly together, faces flushed and averted.

'Sorry,' both girls mumbled at the carpet, then glanced sideways towards Harrison and Winnie, their look half an appeal, half an apology.

'I don't understand—so much emotion over a pony.'

'Oh, Daddy, it wasn't over a silly old horse!' burst out Judith. 'It was Jane. She shouldn't have been so rude.'

'I wasn't!' protested the other. 'I just said—'

'That's enough!' Their mother turned to Winnie. 'Apparently some women started shouting at them in the street.'

'How very embarrassing.' Winnie smiled sympathetically.

'Still,' said the Dean sternly, 'you shouldn't have been rude, Jane.'

'But, Daddy, it was horrible! Right in the middle of the Marlowe Arcade—a lot of nonsense about papist relics and heretics!'

'This confounded find!' sighed the Dean. 'It's stirring

people up. First the Archdeacon, then that poor soul last night, now this!' He looked despondently at his guests. 'I had Simcocks on the phone just before you arrived. Apparently, tourists are flocking to the crypt. I've had to agree to having the hinged screen opened.' He shook his head. 'One wonders where it will end!'

As Margaret and the twins wheeled Winnie into the hall, Harrison hung back. 'About these books of Cratchley's, Dean?'

Ingrams chuckled. 'Ah yes, what did you say—political? Extraordinary idea! My dear fellow, as I told you, Cratchley was one of Nature's innocents.'

'Then what was his subject?'

'Theology—what else?' The Dean smiled. 'Well, perhaps that slightly overstates it. He wrote for the SPCK—a series entitled *Our Bishops*. Very detailed, very exact, but rather, shall we say, a little too dry for my palate.'

'There,' said Winnie, looking round in her chair with a smile, 'your Becket factor for you!'

Harrison glowered. Since leaving the deanery, his depression had grown; now, confronted by the crowds flocking the wide path between the gatehouse and west front, his spirits plunged even deeper. 'Damn fools!' he muttered. 'What do they expect to see?' Almost angrily, he thrust the chair on against the flow of visitors, trundling it over the cobbles under the archway, out into the comparative quietness of the Buttermarket.

A group of Japanese tourists were clustered at the entrance of Mercery Lane. Most had cameras trained on the grimy splendour of the decayed gatehouse with its ornate statuary and double row of painted shields, the lower gaudy with coats-of-arms, the upper plain and simple with the stark emblems of the Passion. Wheeling Winnie past, Harrison wondered what these prosperous-looking orientals made of the nails, the spear and the crown of thorns. His spirits plunged deeper: his civilization was dust; Canterbury a museum, and the crowds come to gape at that worn slab in the crypt a parody of a past devotion, an empty imitation of a heritage dead as that of pharaonic Egypt.

The narrow, pedestrianized streets ahead were crowded with Saturday morning shoppers. By the time the lamp was chosen and Harrison and Winnie were again outside, the numbers had grown. Ahead came the strains of a violin, but with the density of the crowds, they couldn't see who was playing until they'd almost reached the source of the sound.

She was a young woman, thin and tall, whose short-cut black hair contrasted strikingly with the almost bloodless pallor of her face. Dressed in a khaki greatcoat, she played, her back against a wall, her eyes closed, while the laden shoppers edged past, leaving a semi-circular swathe around her.

'Let's listen,' said Winnie, 'just for a moment.'

Harrison nodded. There was an intensity and poignancy to the music. As he listened, his gaze fixed on the gaunt, almost mask-like face of the player, he thought of the shape leaping out behind Cratchley with the knife and what he'd seen looking up the crypt steps the evening before: the clenched fists around the iron, the pale blur of that face through the bars. Again he heard the wild, jarring rattle of the gate. The music soared like a firebrand. He felt a tingle in his spine: Ingrams was right—some force, terrible and macabre, had been stirred and was, invisible as yet, growing and forming itself in dimensions beyond his reach.

He felt a tug at his wrist. Winnie was looking up.

'Over there!' she whispered. 'Have you seen?'

He glanced round to see that a new figure had joined the

half-circle of listeners. It was Canon Rope. The elderly cleric apparently hadn't seen them. He stood a few feet away, nodding in time to the tune.

'Ask about Sarah,' breathed his wife.

'Right.'

Before he could move, however, Rope stepped forward and, dropping a coin into the open case, turned away.

'Come on,' said Winnie quickly, 'let's catch him up.'

'Ah, Colonel and Mrs Harrison! What a pleasant surprise!'

Even with having to manœuvre the chair through the crowd, Harrison had had no trouble catching up Rope. They came across him only a few yards down the street, apparently absorbed by the columns of property details in an estate agent's window.

'You're not thinking of moving out of Bread Yard, I hope, Canon,' said Winnie as he leant forward to shake her hand.

'Move out?' Rope grinned uncertainly, his slightly protruding dentures, over-large in his mouth, giving the impression of a small gnawing animal—something, Harrison thought, between a rabbit and a rat.

'I thought,' said Winnie, smiling up, 'that perhaps with these hordes in the precincts today, you might have been yearning for quieter pastures.'

'Ah, the find!' Rope rubbed his hands. 'Crocker's ridiculous box!' Grinning, he shook his head. 'A ten-days' wonder, Mrs Harrison, I assure you.' He turned and pointed across the street. 'No, there's the real news—there's the future, perhaps!'

Propped against a newsagent's shop was a billboard, reading: NATION DIVIDED! UPROAR AT BISHOP'S CLAIM.

Puzzled, Harrison and Winnie looked back at Rope, who

immediately burst out laughing. 'Neither of you has read our front runner's speech, I see.'

'Campion? Front runner for the Primacy, you mean?' burst out Harrison in disbelief. 'Surely not!'

Rope put a finger to his lips and, bending forward, eyes sparkling, whispered, 'I told you, my dear fellow—smoke-filled rooms!'

'Surely the Primacy lies in the gift of the Prime Minister.' Harrison nodded towards the billboard. 'From that, it looks as if he's dished whatever hopes he may have had.'

Rope's dentures gleamed. 'Campion will have his chance.' His bright eyes darting from one to the other, he leant closer. 'Even innocent old Cratchley could have told you that.'

Harrison glanced at Winnie; she gave the tiniest of nods.

'How about coming back for a glass of sherry, Canon?'

'And why not stay for lunch?' added Winnie. 'We've got rather a nice casserole of lamb in the oven.'

'An extraordinary man!' muttered Rope, peering at the piece of lamb skewered on his fork. 'A veritable lion!'

Harrison's irritation verged dangerously on anger: he wanted to talk about Cratchley and his niece, but his guest seemed interested in talking of nothing but the Bishop of Derby. Winnie, however, smiled across the table. 'Quite a ravaging beast, he seems, this lion of yours, Canon!'

'Ah, you mean his speech in the Upper House!' Putting down the fork, Rope leaned back to reach for Harrison's copy of *The Times*. Turning over a page, he began reading aloud.

"A people serving Mammon by the daily sacrifice of the sick and unable; a government bloated with arrogance, pitiless in its blind adherence to the materialistic idol it has both erected and serves." Yes,' said Rope grinning broadly, 'I think we may safely describe that

as a fair bit of ravaging.' Popping the pronged gobbet of lamb in his mouth, he began to chew, his mouth and jaw working rapidly in a short screwing motion. Harrison watched in fascinated distaste.

Finishing his mouthful, Rope caught his host's eye. 'Well, what if this ravaging beast does indeed seat himself on the Augustine throne—what then?' He leaned forward. 'But you, Colonel, I imagine, consider the Primacy is of little importance—the Church just a museum piece, is that right? A harmless relic, like that ridiculous box that's so exciting our poor Archdeacon?'

Harrison coloured: it was uncanny how exactly Rope's words echoed his own thoughts of that morning.

'Of course, in a way you are right, this is a secular age: houses, cars, foreign holidays, financial security—they are our values, yet even you, Colonel, must be discomfited by the moral poverty of our time. Hospitals—great charitable foundations of our Christian past—turned into moneymaking conveniences for the rich; our classical and humanistic heritage dumped in the name of utilitarianism—you see it and are offended, of course you are!' The speaker smiled sympathetically while Harrison stared glassily back. 'People look for an alternative, but from where? There is no effective opposition: the Labour Party is weak and demoralized—no longer trusted. As for the rest...' Rope gave a derisive laugh. 'But if there came another voice, a voice speaking with authority, what then?'

'You mean Campion?' Harrison felt lost. 'We need him, is that what you're saying?'

'Ah, that would depend!'

'On what?'

'On the nature of the beast.' With an infuriating grin, Rope bent again to his meal.

Exasperated, Harrison frowned at Winnie, then, taking a breath, reluctantly turned again to his guest.

'Odd business, Canon, this delay in the funeral.'

Glancing up, Rope grinned. 'With Cratchley playing the central role, did you really expect the curtain to rise on time?'

The joke jarred: not for the first time, Harrison found himself wondering at the nature of the relationship between the two old men.

'His death seemed very sudden,' said Winnie intervening. 'How had he been of late?'

Laying down his cutlery, Rope frowned. 'Physically fine, Mrs Harrison, but I must say, in those last weeks he seemed rather on edge, I thought.'

'Did you ask what the matter was?'

Rope shook his head and looked down at his plate.

'Do you think it was anything to do with his niece?' said Harrison.

'Sarah?' The Canon looked up, surprised, then shook his head. 'I hardly think so. They hadn't been close for years.'

Harrison frowned: the reply was a blow. 'Even so,' he persisted, 'perhaps she was mixed up in something political? She's quite a radical, I hear.'

Rope shrugged. 'Nothing very important: CND—that sort of thing. No, whatever was on Cratchley's mind, it was nothing to do with her. As I say, they weren't close.'

'His work, then?' said Winnie. 'Wasn't he writing a new book? Were his worries anything to do with that?'

'Possibly.'

'What was it on?'

'His book? Yet another eminent churchman—Bishop Harvey-Watson.' Rope smiled. 'I see the name means nothing to either of you. Harvey-Watson was Bishop of Manchester back in the 'fifties: an interesting man, quite an influence in his day—and that reminds me!' Rope began tapping hurriedly round his pockets. 'Ah, here they are!' Drawing out a bunch of keys, he dangled them over the table. 'Cratchley's cottage—I had to collect the Harvey-Watson papers for our librarian.' The dentures gleamed. 'I mustn't forget to return the keys to the Archdeacon this weekend or I shall really be in trouble.'

'Don't worry, Canon, I am sure Richard will take them back.' Winnie smiled at Harrison. 'You have to see Dr Crocker this afternoon, don't you, darling?'

'See Crocker?' Flabbergasted, Harrison stared at his wife's face, then understood. 'Yes, Canon, of course,' he said, swinging round to his guest. 'I should be delighted to pass them on.'

He reached out for the keys, but as he took them, Rope seemed to hesitate; holding tight to the ring, he looked directly into the other's eyes. 'You, Colonel, must think Cratchley's life a failure: an obscure priest, harmless eccentric writing books read by a few old fossils like me.'

Harrison flushed. Before he could answer, Rope was leaning further forward, intense earnestness on his face. 'Always remember, Colonel, we all have to fight towards truth.' The clutch on the key-ring grew stronger. 'Through painstaking research, Cratchley fought his battle; his life, like your own, was a long, hard battle through darkness towards the light.'

Winnie intervened, 'Now, Canon, I hope you're fond of chocolate mousse.'

Rope released his grip on the keys. 'Chocolate mousse?' He rubbed his hands eagerly. 'Wonderful! Absolutely delicious!'

The solitary figure paused and looked up at the huge window above him. Faint from within came a deep baying growl. With a furtive glance back, Harrison walked on, turning to follow the path across the lawn.

As the sound of the organ faded, he felt for the keys. Finding them, he clenched them hard. He was tense: the flat grass gave no cover, and moving out from the shelter of the cathedral, he felt increasingly exposed.

The very idea of searching Cratchley's cottage was extremely distasteful; that he, a respected member of the cathedral community, should be skulking through the grounds on a Sunday morning during Matins to make an illegal entry into a dead man's house was degrading. All the same, he needed something to report to the Brigadier. However, as he headed towards the south boundary wall, he wished he'd gone straight to the cottage as soon as Rope had left the afternoon before. It had been Winnie who'd dissuaded him. 'Go tomorrow during the morning service,' she'd said, 'no one will be around then.'

So far she'd been right—apart from himself, nothing moved except for the assortment of birds grazing on the heavily dewed grass. For all that, his unease increased at every step. Reaching the boundary path, he again looked back: still nobody, yet the serpent in his belly gripped tight. Then something made him look upwards. As he did so, his heart leapt.

A figure stood motionless on the Bell Harry Tower—a black smudge, insect-small against a leaden expanse of sky. Whoever it was appeared to be gazing directly at him over the balustrade. He stared upwards—and then the figure waved.

So unexpected was the action, so incongruous the sight—an arm, thin as a feeler, gesticulating wildly against the dark of the clouds—that he was utterly taken aback. Before he could recover, whoever it was had gone.

For a moment, all he wanted to do was to drop the cottage keys in the archdeaconry letter-box and get back to Bread Yard. Indignation, however, sprang to his aid: furious that Simcocks should have allowed anyone up the tower during a service, he strode on towards the sequestered garden in the south-eastern corner of the precincts known as the Oaks. Following the path round the wide oval of grass marking the site of the monastery fishpond, he reached the gate to what had been Cratchley's garden. He was about to push through when a touch of something white caught his eye.

Next to the gate was one of a number of small alcoves set in the surrounding walls that, in the time of the monks, had been beehives. From the deep-lipped shelf at the base protruded a tiny triangle of paper. Going over, he carefully peeled it from the damp stonework.

It was a torn sheet of unlined paper. On it, fuzzy and run, was scribbled: *Two extra pints today please.* Beneath appeared the initials: R.W.C.

Harrison stared down at the soggy, pathetic relic. For the first time, he felt a hatred for the old man's killer. Glancing again at the message, he frowned: two extra pints seemed a large amount for a reclusive widower alone. Taking out his wallet, he placed the paper between two banknotes, then, entering the gate, walked up the path towards the front door.

The key turned as smoothly as oil; glancing back, he stepped inside. Immediately he did so, he knew that the dead man was still in his cottage.

Cratchley was in the cottage all right—tainted and stale with years of tobacco smoke and unopened windows, the very air breathed him. His personality was everywhere: in the mackintosh and black beret behind the door, in the amateurish watercolours on the drab walls, in the piles of books and newspapers obstructing not only half the floor, but even the sides of the narrow stairs.

Harrison ducked through the low doorway into the front room, automatically glancing to the windows, half-expecting to see the familiar cassocked figure sitting at work at the table there. There was, of course, nobody: the wooden swivel chair was empty, and the room had itself the stillness and silence of a corpse. He looked about, remembering the ex-rectory furniture, overlarge in the tiny room. As he did so, he met the gaze of the face looking directly at him from the mantelpiece.

He walked over and peered at the photograph. There was amusement in the dark intelligent eyes; the wide mouth almost grinned. The young face was so alive, so vibrant with life, that it was hard to believe that Ruth Cratchley had been in her grave twenty years.

As the cathedral clock struck the half-hour he began work. Removing the bundle of correspondence stuffed behind a candlestick, he flicked through it. It was much as he expected: bills, booksellers' letters, an invitation to a sherry party at the King's School, a dental appointment for the New Year. He reached next for the postcard reproduction at the end of the high shelf with a detail from a Victorian painting showing four children lounging on a grassy bank. Turning it over, he read: *See you at the weekend—love and kisses, Sadie.*

He frowned. Who was this woman or girl, he wondered, sending such messages to the old man? He thought of the milkman's message in his pocket. Replacing the card, he went to the table.

An old-fashioned typewriter stood immediately in front of the chair; around it were piled papers, reference books and typing paper. Apart from these, there was an ashtray, a bottle of correction fluid and a surprisingly modern stapler. In the midst of all the paraphernalia there was one empty space—a large, comparatively undusty rectangle of polished wood: the place, obviously, from which Rope had removed the Harvey-Watson papers the previous day.

He began to hunt through drawers, then stopped and went back to the table. Something else besides the Harvey-Watson papers was missing. For a moment he couldn't think what, then it came: the manuscript of the book itself. Leaning down, he peered across the cleared surface. Beside the dusty outline of the dead bishop's papers was another, smaller than the first.

For the first time since entering the cottage, he knew what he'd come for—the very thing that was already gone. For a second or two he remained numbly staring at the spot where the manuscript had lain, then, squatting, looked under the table.

Tucked out of sight, just as he'd expected, was a large wicker waste-paper basket. Dragging it out, he began removing the contents, glancing at them and then laying them on the carpet. As he reached further down towards the bottom, his disappointment grew—unexpectedly, there were no discarded sheets of the book—nothing but receipts, circulars, empty matchboxes and one long meaningless list of names. Folding this, he slipped it into his pocket. As he did so, there came the sound of a key being inserted in the front door.

His heart froze. As the key began rattling against the already opened lock, he dropped to his knees and began furiously to hurl the litter back into the basket.

Whoever was outside realized quickly that the door was unlocked; there was the click of the latch and the hurry of feet. Harrison was stumbling to his feet, the waste-paper basket in his hand, as the sitting-room door flew open and he was staring up into the horrified face of Ruth Cratchley.

'Who the bloody hell are you?'

As soon as the girl spoke, Harrison understood: this was Sarah. The Dean had made a slip: she was not Cratchley's niece, but his wife's. Even as he staggered upright, one part of him was marvelling at her likeness to the dead woman's photograph—the same wide-set eyes, the same broad, sensitive mouth. Only the happiness in the eyes was missing and the smile from the lips.

'What the hell do you think you're doing?'

'I was just looking around. The name's Harrison. I'm from the Dilapidations Board,' he mumbled. Putting down the basket, he fumbled for his wallet.

The girl didn't move as he held out the card.

He attempted to smile. 'You're Sarah, I imagine.'

'Why were you looking through my uncle's things?'

'Looking through? I tripped over the waste-paper basket, that's all.'

Her disbelief was obvious. 'How did you get in?'

'I used the keys left with the Archdeacon.'

Anger flushed her face. 'This is still my uncle's home! Christ!' Behind her indignation, he detected the pain.

'As I said, I—'

'Give me the keys and go!'

'Please, if I could just—'

'The keys!'

All the way down the path he felt her eyes on him. As he turned out of sight he clenched his fists. 'Damn! Damn!' he muttered aloud, his face contorting. Then, with a glance up at the now deserted tower, began trudging back the way he'd come.

❀ ❀ ❀

The phone started ringing only minutes after Harrison got home. 'It will be Crocker,' he groaned. Winnie smiled sympathetically as he lifted the receiver. 'Yes?'

'Richard—I've had Sarah Cratchley here.'

'I can explain,' he stuttered, thrown off balance by hearing Ingrams's voice. 'As I tried to tell her, I was just having a glance round. I'm only sorry it upset her so much.'

The Dean's voice was incredulous. 'You've upset Sarah? For goodness sake, how?'

Harrison sighed. 'She found me in the cottage.'

'Cratchley's cottage?'

'Canon Rope gave me the keys; I merely wanted the opportunity of looking at the general condition of the building.'

There was a short pause. 'I noticed you weren't in Matins. I thought perhaps Winifred was ill—in part, that's why I rang.'

'That was very good of you,' murmured Harrison, pink in the face. 'Look, I am sorry the girl was upset. I had no idea she was in Canterbury.'

'Obviously. Anyway, the other reason I was ringing was to say that Drood has been in touch again—Sarah didn't tell you, I imagine?'

'No.'

'Apparently the paperwork has been sorted out and the funeral can now go ahead on Wednesday. I hope you'll be able to make it.'

'Yes, of course.' Harrison glanced at his wife. 'And I think Winnie would also like to be there.'

'Well, at least, it wasn't the Archdeacon,' said Winnie as he replaced the receiver.

'Doubtless that pleasure is still to come. Anyway, I'd better get lunch started.' Gloomily, Harrison went off to the kitchen. As he entered, he caught sight of the picture-cards pinned on the memo board. He returned to the hall. 'Winnie,' he called, 'who would Cratchley know called Sadie?'

There was a laugh from the sitting-room. 'Sarah, of course.'

'What do you mean?'

'It's the diminutive.'

Harrison frowned. 'But I thought Rope said she and Cratchley weren't close.'

There was no answer. *Love and kisses!* it had said on the card, then there was the note to the milkman. Perplexed, he shook his head. If nothing else, one thing was clear: there was a lot that Cratchley had hidden from his friend Canon Rope.

Lunch passed with no call from the Archdeacon. After it had been cleared, Harrison slumped on the settee while his wife read the newspapers.

'Titmouse! Don't I know that name?'

Half asleep, Harrison murmured, 'The Rector of Basset Underhill—what about him?'

'He's here.'

Harrison sat up.

'Good Lord, don't say he's got himself in the Sunday papers!'

Winnie shook her head. 'I was just looking at the list you found in the cottage. M.G.—are those his initials?'

'I think they are.' Getting up, Harrison leaned over his wife's shoulder.

'There—Titmouse, M. G.' She looked up. 'Do any of the other names mean anything to you?'

He glanced through the list. 'Nothing at all.'

'There are over fifty names here with just these eleven ringed—I wonder why?'

Harrison shrugged despondently. 'We'd need Cratchley's manuscript to find that out, and I'm not going to be able to get hold of that, not after this morning's fiasco!'

'We don't need it,' said Winnie, smiling up. 'There's something better than an uncompleted manuscript.'

He stared at her blankly, then suddenly slapped his head. 'My God, you've got it! Of course—the source material itself, the Harvey-Watson papers!' He strode across the room. 'Rope said he'd taken them to the cathedral library. I'll go there tomorrow and get them back.' He paused. 'And there's something else—this funeral on Wednesday: we can buttonhole Titmouse and show him the list. With a little luck, he'll tell us exactly why these particular names are ringed.' He laughed. 'That's if the chap doesn't bore me to death first about his blasted glebe!'

❋ ❋ ❋

'Gone?'

'I'm afraid so, Colonel. They were despatched over an hour ago; they'll be well on their way back to Lambeth now.'

'Lambeth Palace?'

'The papers belong to the Archbishop's archives.' The librarian waved towards the shelves of leather-bound volumes. 'Now, if you are interested in an earlier bishop, perhaps...'

Cursing himself for having delayed his visit to the library, Harrison stepped outside to meet the Dean hurrying down the passageway. Ingrams smiled. 'My dear fellow, you seem to be everywhere these days!'

'I needed to consult some papers.' Harrison coloured. 'This wretched business of the Basset Underhill glebe.' He waited for the interrogation to begin. Instead, Ingrams looked about him and sighed. 'So peaceful back here,' he murmured. 'So different from what's happening inside the cathedral.'

'More sightseers?'

'It doesn't stop.'

'No word from the Museum?'

'Nothing.'

'Perhaps you would like me to come and take a look.'

'Would you?' The Dean looked relieved. 'That's very kind.'

The cathedral hummed like some vast, echoing hive; in the distance, above the murmur of the organ, came the boom and crash of doors. As Harrison and the Dean neared the nave, the sounds grew.

'Good Lord!' Standing beside Ingrams at the top of the chancel steps, Harrison, for the first time, surveyed the restless column of visitors, two or three deep, stretching back half the way to the great west doors.

'All for the sight of a stone slab! Who would have thought it?' sighed his companion. 'At such moments, Richard, I wonder how far we really are from the superstition and fanaticism of the Middle Ages and what a thin veneer our rational civilization is!'

The Dean's lamentations were broken off by the arrival of the Verger. 'I've never known the like, sir.' The flushed round face expressed a combination of wild exuberance and gloomy despair.

Ingrams smiled. 'I'm sure you're doing your best.'

'That's all very well, sir,' began Simcocks, but the Dean was already backing away. 'Another meeting, I'm afraid.'

As he disappeared, the Verger shook his head. 'I'm not sure he quite appreciates our problems, Colonel.'

'I'm sure he does.' Harrison started to walk towards the crypt, then stopped. 'Oh, Simcocks, one thing: the keys to the Bell Harry Tower—I take it they're safe?'

A ghastly expression rose in Simcocks's face.

'What's the matter, man?'

'They've gone, sir—the whole spare set,' breathed the Verger, anguish in his eyes.

'Gone? Stolen, you mean? Good God, have you reported this?'

Simcocks hung his head. 'I was hoping they'd turn up.'

Harrison's temper flared. 'Someone's got the key to every lock in the place and you've said nothing!' He lowered his voice. 'Did you know someone was on the tower during Matins yesterday? Up there, waving as if they'd gone mad!'

Simcocks opened his mouth to speak, but before he could do so, there was a call from behind.

'Mr Simcocks! Richard! Both of you, come at once!'

Ingrams was beckoning from the north choir aisle. At a half run, they followed the hurrying figure. Harrison, glancing up through the lattice-work, glimpsed Lloyd-Thomas gazing down through the organ-loft mirror, the convex glass distorting his lean face to that of a melon-headed ogre. Reaching the north transept gallery, Ingrams stopped outside the clergy vestry. 'The door was open. I just happened to glance in.'

'Open!' Simcocks seemed to choke. With a fearful glance at Harrison, he dashed inside. Almost at once, he gave a cry and reappeared, horror on his face. 'Colonel, it's the nutter again!'

Pushing past, Harrison entered the vestry. On the wall opposite, in huge letters was written the single word:

IDOLATERS

It was crudely done, obviously with an aerosol spray applied in frenzied haste. Below the inscription appeared a design, accomplished in the same red paint. Stepping forward, he tried to make it out, but whether it represented a cross or a dagger dripping blood, he found impossible to decide.

CHAPTER FIVE

The procession turned off the motorway and began winding over the North Downs. As the gradient steepened and they were increasingly exposed to the buffeting of the northerly gale, the slow-moving vehicles shuddered under the hammer blows of the wind.

Harrison, driving his somewhat creaky Volvo Estate, gloomily slipped into second gear. Ahead, the line of elderly cars weaving upwards, nose to tail, the venerable Rolls-Royce hearse to the fore, gave him the sense of being part of some extraordinary late-twentieth-century version of the medieval *Dance of Death.*

The hearse, stately and ponderous, reached the crest of the hill, swayed and seemed to hang for a moment before it finally disappeared. The rest of the procession followed, and there below them was the small cluster of houses round the church tower of Basset Underhill.

Harrison parked opposite the church. As he switched off the engine, he glanced back across the road: a clergyman in biretta and cassock, the wind fluttering his surplice, stood outside the lychgate shaking hands with Sarah Cratchley. Titmouse, he thought, feeling in his inside pocket for the list.

A bell began tolling. The back of the hearse was opened, and from among the flowers within one of Drood's men lifted out an incongruously tiny casket. Preceded by Titmouse, the cortège moved away through the lychgate with Harrison wheeling Winnie at the back. As they rounded the outside wall of the small Norman church, she turned and looked up, wrinkling her nose.

'Horrible smell!' she said. 'What is it?'

'I can't smell anything,' muttered Harrison, thrusting the chair on towards the throng of dark-coated mourners gathered at the lower end of the graveyard. Arriving, they joined one end of the semi-circle round a grave into which a hole had been cut. In front, the casket now sat on a square of garish-green artificial grass surrounded by wreaths.

Harrison glanced at the headstone. Its inscription was simple: *Ruth Cratchley 1910-1971 Beloved Wife*. The rest of the slab was bare, except for a quotation at the bottom: *On Thee do I wait all the day.*

'*Man that is born of a woman...*' began the Reverend Titmouse. He stood before the casket, prayer-book in one hand, while with the other he pressed down on his biretta. His surplice, flattened against his back, flapped ferociously at his sides and wrists.

'*Thou, oh Lord, that knowest the secrets of all hearts...*' His words were again lost in the wind.

Harrison surveyed the mourners: the crowd of clerics in black coats and white collars were like the remnants of some scattered flock of aged birds blown in by the gale. He noticed Rope among them, but there was no sign of the Archdeacon.

He looked around. Outside the semi-circle, a few elderly people were dotted among the stones—presumably some of Cratchley's old parishioners, he thought. An old woman, supported by a white-haired, red-faced man, was weeping.

Turning back, he looked across the grave at Sarah. She stood alone, staring ahead. As he looked across, she glanced up. Her pale face remained expressionless as their eyes met.

Looking down, he noticed a card on one of the wreaths—*To beloved Bob from Dorothy.*

'*The days of man are but as grass…*'

Harrison sniffed deeply. Winnie's right, he thought. There is a deuced odd stink coming from somewhere.

Suddenly the brief service was over; people turned and began moving away up the graveyard. The Ingram twins came through the crowd and walked beside the wheelchair as Harrison pushed Winnie back towards the lychgate. Ahead, Titmouse stood on the pathway near the entrance saying his farewells to the mourners.

'So many here—so heartening! A greatly beloved parish priest!'

'Yes, I'm sure.' Winnie smiled up at the anxiously amiable face.

The Rector turned to Harrison. 'A lovely spot, don't you think?'

'Yes, indeed.' He looked at the priest squarely. 'Rector, my name's Harrison. We have corresponded. I wonder, when everyone's gone, if you could spare me a word?'

Titmouse blinked. 'Not Colonel Harrison?'

'Yes, actually.'

'Oh Colonel, you've not come a moment too soon!' With a glance at the waiting throng, the Rector bent forward. 'I thought I was going mad.' He bent closer. 'I even began to believe I could smell them just now in the graveyard.'

'Smell what?'

A look of amazement rose on the Rector's face.

'The pigs, of course! What else?'

'It's quite terrible!'

Harrison nodded glumly in agreement: the smell permeated the whole house. Standing beside Titmouse, he gazed gloomily at the herd of pinkish animals wading through the wasteland of mud and dung outside the Rectory window.

'When I signed the agreement,' sighed the Rector, 'I thought it would mean a few geese at the most.'

'Your Mr Greenhill will be getting an official communication from the Board,' said Harrison. 'All that,' he said, gesturing towards the slough, 'must be rotting the foundations.'

Titmouse shook his head. 'Useless, Colonel, I fear. As I've explained in my letters, the man's a fanatic, not a person you can do business with.' Returning to his desk, he sank forlornly on to his swivel chair. 'The whole thing is pure spite: the animals will never be moved unless we can apply the full rigour of the law.'

Harrison cleared his thought. 'I will do what I can. In the meantime, Rector, there is something you could do for me.' He drew the list from his pocket. 'Do these names mean anything to you? I noticed yours among them.'

Briefly Titmouse scanned the paper, then burst out in delighted surprise. 'These are Harvey-Watson's ordinands—us Manchester men!'

'Those eleven are ringed—any reason why?'

The Rector burst out laughing. 'My dear fellow, they were the chosen ones—the Lesser Apostles!' Blushing, he smiled. 'Our nickname for Bishop Harvey-Watson's closest disciples.'

'A sort of in-group?'

'An in-group—exactly!' Titmouse beamed at Winnie, then turned again to the list. 'Yes, here you are: Kemp, S. J.—a brilliant fellow and a fine sportsman too. Tragic that he died so early. And Archibald Gowning here—another great scholar.' He smiled up. 'A bishop himself now. A Canadian diocese—the Northern Provinces, I believe.'

A number of powerful motorbikes thundered through the village, leaving a flurry of squeals and grunts in their wake. At the sound, the rapture faded from the Rector's face.

'So these eleven were merely a clerical coterie?' Harrison reddened: he hadn't meant to sound so crude.

Titmouse, however, smiled amiably. 'Men of destiny, Colonel.'

Harrison had an awful vision of the present Bishop of the Northern Provinces moving through a vast Arctic wilderness where wolves howled over frozen tundra and the Aurora Borealis glittered through savage darkness. He grimaced, a sense of futility overpowering him. Where was it all going? What possible connection had Titmouse's so-called men of destiny with Cratchley's assassination? He glanced up, noticing a brown stain running across the ceiling. A second vision arose: he was seeing ecclesiastical roofs leaking across the entire length of the diocese from the Thames to the Channel. Damn Crocker! he thought, remembering all the hours of work spent on the rationalization scheme.

'But why only eleven apostles—not twelve?'

Winnie's question burst into his thoughts. He looked round to see her smiling sweetly at their host. 'Don't tell me, Rector, there was a Judas among you Manchester men.'

Titmouse laughed. 'Good Lord, no! Rather the opposite. It's the John of the twelve that is missing.' He smiled. 'St John, you'll remember, was the especially beloved.'

Winnie was all charm. 'And this especially chosen man, the closest to your Bishop—may we ask who he was?'

The Rector beamed: he was clearly enjoying himself. The pig smell, the leaking, ramshackle rectory, a difficult parish, the ever-growing indifference of young and old to the beliefs he'd preached for forty years were momentarily forgotten as he triumphantly met the eager gaze of his guests. 'Who was Harvey-Watson's John? His personal chaplain, of course! And who was that?' Titmouse's smile broadened; he spread out his hands. 'Why, no other than our future Primate, perhaps— that's if I interpret correctly the hints in this week's *Church*

Times.' Chuckling, he allowed the information to take its effect. 'Yes, Maurice Patrick Campion, the present Bishop of Derby and, I fear, the sharpest thorn in our dear Prime Minister's side!'

The silence that followed was broken by the squeak of the Rector's chair as he rose. 'Well, this has all been delightful, but now, I'm afraid, I must get ready for choir practice.'

'Greenhill shall hear from the Board,' said Harrison, wheeling Winnie through the draughty, paint-peeling hall. 'And I shall also have a word with the architect's office about the obvious leaks in your roof.'

Once Winnie had been helped into the car, Titmouse bent to take her hand. 'My wife will be so sorry to have missed you. She's temporarily retreated,' he added, glancing significantly towards the glebe fence, 'to stay with a sister in Northampton.'

Winnie didn't release her hold. 'You nicknamed these twelve the Lesser Apostles. Was that because they weren't Christ's original twelve?'

Titmouse's face went red. 'Not exactly, no.'

'Why then lesser—lesser than whom?'

'Than the Bishop himself. Harvey-Watson had been one of the true Apostles. I mean, of course,' he added quickly, 'one of the famous Cambridge Apostles of the nineteen-thirties.' He laughed. 'Or should I say infamous!'

Baffled, Winnie shook her head.

'Surely, Mrs Harrison, you must know of the Apostles—the group drawn from the intellectual élite of Trinity and King's?' Breaking off, Titmouse glanced over his shoulder at the row of snouts pressing between the bars of the fence behind him, then, leaning forward, whispered, 'Blunt, Philby, Burgess and Maclean!'

There was a sudden commotion in the pig community. Harrison, pushing forward, had almost to shout over the shrill cacophony of squeals. 'Harvey-Watson was mixed up with that crowd! With a lot of Marxist traitors! Good God, is that what you're saying?'

As quickly as it had been disturbed, peace settled again over the glebe, and the answer to Harrison's outburst was given against a background of low contented grunts and scratchings.

'Harvey-Watson was a don, Colonel—young, brilliant and idealistic—a very suitable member of that illustrious society.'

'Nevertheless,' spluttered the other, 'it hardly seems suitable, a future Anglican bishop mixing with Reds!'

Titmouse gave a pained smile. 'You can't blame Harvey-Watson for the unfortunate loyalties of some of his fellow members, Colonel. And it was, after all, a special time: huge unemployment, the hunger marches, the rise of the Nazi Party in Germany—then, I believe, even Lord Rothschild used to sing *The Red Flag* in his bath. Oh, Colonel, please don't look so shocked!'

'Good God, man! You're not suggesting that Harvey-Watson was a Marxist himself?'

The row of snouts behind them quivered and dilated as Harrison awaited his answer.

'No, not at all.' The Rector paused, then suddenly smiled. 'Although, thinking back, I do seem to remember some talk about a long correspondence with old Joe Stalin.'

A few moments later the Volvo was roaring down the drive. Turning on to the road, it raced down the main street and began the long, tortuous climb out of the village.

❀ ❀ ❀

'I don't believe it,' said Winnie suddenly as the car topped the ridge.

'What Titmouse said?'

'No, my dear,' she said, laughing, 'what you're thinking.'

'What the hell am I meant to think? Look at it! Cratchley

murdered by a lethal injection when he's in the middle of writing a biography of a Marxist bishop—all this at the very time when the man's protégé is emerging as front runner for the Primacy!'

'Oh, come on, Richard! *Archbishop of Canterbury is KGB Colonel*—even the worst of the Sunday tabloids might consider that slightly over the top! At the moment I think the Soviet Union has other worries apart from the Church of England!'

Harrison refused to laugh.

'Cratchley must have stumbled across something which he mentioned to someone else beside the Brigadier. As a result, he was bumped off before he could further open his mouth.'

His wife gave a sceptical snort.

'Damn it, Winnie, at least it's an explanation!'

'It's paranoia, dear darling.'

The car skidded to a halt. 'My God, I've got it, Winnie! The Becket factor—of course! What a blind fool!'

'What now?'

'The meaning of the phrase, woman—it's obvious!' Harrison thumped the steering-wheel. 'It's nothing to do with the digging up of the coffin. That was just a coincidence. It's the idea itself: the opposition of Church and State. What was the quarrel between Henry the Second and Thomas Becket after all but the struggle for power between Church and King—for who, in the end, should actually rule, the King with his Privy Council or the Pope and his cardinals in Rome! For all his folk-hero image, in the end Thomas Becket was an agent for foreign rule!'

Winnie shook her head, bemused. 'Richard, I'm lost. For goodness sake, what's all this got to do with today?'

'Campion is a possible Becket, can't you see? As Archbishop, he could use his position not only against the Government, but the parliamentary system itself. His masters might be in Moscow as Becket's were in Rome. Didn't the fellow virtually say on television that he wasn't a democrat? What poor Cratchley was trying to do was warn Greville of an attempt to undermine democratic authority in this country by rotting the whole system from the centre out.'

Winnie burst out laughing. 'All this because Campion was once chaplain to a man who wrote to Stalin about something! It's absolutely absurd!'

'There's nothing absurd about murder!' Harrison burst out. 'Think of that grave back there in the churchyard, Winnie! Think of those ashes we've buried today—there's nothing funny about that at all!'

Her smile faded. 'What will you do? Tell Greville your extraordinary idea?'

He shook his head. 'Not yet. Before I do anything else,' he said, engaging the gear, 'I've got to get my hands on the Harvey-Watson papers. Then we'll see if it's all paranoia or not!'

CHAPTER SIX

It was still not quite light when, after stopping at London Bridge, the train began rumbling over the bridges and viaducts towards Waterloo East. A neon-lit room slid past, a pattern of silver stars stuck on the window, through which, in the stark, cell-like whiteness within, a solitary girl sat typing. Blowing his nose, Harrison wondered despondently if he'd caught a chill in the graveyard the previous day.

There was a crashing of doors as the carriage shuddered to a standstill. Moments later, Harrison was being borne forward by the surge of passengers. It was bitter cold outside the station; turning westwards up York Road, he walked briskly, his umbrella ringing on the frozen pavement, his head throbbing. Emerging from a subway, he skirted the wall of St Thomas's Hospital, glancing at intervals over the road where in the growing sunlight the frost-coated oaks and cedars soared over the secret gardens of Lambeth Palace. As he plucked the brass bell-rod at the gatehouse, over the river Big Ben began striking the hour.

'Yes?'

The black door had opened a few inches and a young man's face was peering out. Harrison passed over Ingrams's note, then followed the porter across a gravel yard. Skirting an ivy-covered wall, they passed an oak door standing slightly ajar. Within, he glimpsed a pair of green wellington boots and a plastic mackintosh on a hook in a passage. He thought of the deanery: the twins playing badminton in the garden, Ingrams filling his pipe. All the doubts that had haunted his journey rose huge and dark. Winnie was right, he was sick: his theories were nothing but the paranoia of a mind cankered and diseased.

He blew his nose and, with his head throbbing more than ever, followed the figure before him on across the yard.

The library was warm and brightly lit. As the porter went forward to whisper to the librarian, Harrison studied the other occupants. There were just two: one, a plumpish cleric owlishly scanning a parchment roll; the other, a bearded African making notes behind a large pile of books.

'Welcome to Lambeth, Colonel.' The librarian, a grey-haired woman of about his own age, beamed. 'Now, how can we help you?'

'There are some documents I want to study—the Harvey-Watson papers.'

'They'll be in the archives; if you'll wait, I won't be more than a moment or two.'

As she left, Harrison turned again to look at the two readers. The first was now gnawing fiercely at the nail of his little finger as he pored over his parchment. Nearby, the African remained impassively writing, safe behind his wall of books. He tapped his umbrella on the polished floor, then glanced impatiently at the clock: the woman seemed to be taking her time. Going to a window, he looked out down a long lawn. Three lines of footprints showed in the frost; two, close together and running parallel, wove in a series of uneven curves; the third, a little separate, ran directly towards the distant trees. He peered forward: between the boughs stood a solitary figure, then two others appeared among the frozen foliage, moving together, heads down, as if in some slow-motioned, spectral dance.

'Colonel!'

Behind the librarian towered a woman whose straight grey hair was cropped short. Under a horizontal fringe, she wore black-framed spectacles.

'Dr Crisp is our senior archivist.'

A moment later he was being led down a corridor.

'Step inside.'

Apart from a table and single chair, the room was bare. The shutters were partly closed, and in the dimness an Anglepoise lamp gleamed down on three elderly black box-files. 'Ah, good.' Going straight to the table, Harrison bent to unfasten the nearest box, but as he did so, to his utter amazement, Dr Crisp clamped a hand heavily on the lid. 'You are from Canterbury?' It was more an accusation than a question; thunderstruck, Harrison stared at her: for no apparent reason, the archivist was obviously boiling with rage. 'These papers came back from your library this week.'

'Yes, they were being studied by Canon Robert Cratchley, now sadly deceased.'

Death had no perceptible effect on Dr Crisp; she continued to glare. As he stared back helplessly, the thought struck Harrison that perhaps, of his charity, the present Archbishop had adopted a policy of employing numbers of the severely disturbed among his staff. This speculation was interrupted by another outburst from the archivist.

'I have always argued against archive material being lent out. After this, people will have to take the trouble to come here to the Palace and study under supervision.'

He had a terrible intuitive flash. 'My God!' he gasped, gripped by a mixture of horror and exultation. 'You're not saying that some of the papers are missing?'

'That is exactly what I'm saying.'

'How many are gone?'

Bending, Dr Crisp flicked each box open in turn. The light gleamed on her steely helmet of hair as she began reeling off meaningless code-numbers from the typed lists pasted on the back of the three lids.

'Have you copies?' he interrupted impatiently. 'Microfilm?'

'Colonel, this is an ecclesiastical library!'

He thought for a moment. 'I presume you've checked with the Howley-Harrison?'

The reply was ice cold. 'Apparently the files were sent back unchecked. Canterbury, it seems, has other matters on its mind.'

Disregarding her, he went to the window and threw back the shutter. The view was the same as it had been from the library. Beyond the lawn, the three figures were almost in the same positions, one watching as the other two circled slowly beneath the trees, heads sunk, obviously deep in conversation.

'Right,' he said, striding back to the table, 'I shall take everything remaining back with me.'

'You certainly will not!' Dr Crisp thrust herself between him and the table. The two faced each other, glaring.

'I wish to use a telephone,' said Harrison at last.

'The files are not leaving, Colonel.'

He somehow controlled his fury. 'Madam, if those missing documents are ever to be restored to your archives, I need to make a phone call as soon as I can.'

She wavered. 'Very well. Follow me.' He was led to a small office where a young typist smiled up from her typing. Dr Crisp pointed at the phone on the girl's desk. 'You may use that.'

'I must be alone.'

There was a sharp intake of breath from the archivist. 'Susan, wait outside in the corridor.'

As the door closed, Harrison took the card from his wallet and dialled. At the other end, the receiver was lifted at once.

'Brigadier Greville, please?'

There was a click, and then came the voice. 'Yes?'

'This is Richard,' he answered. 'I'm in London. Something has cropped up.' Harrison kept his eyes on the door as they talked. As he rang off, he heard voices from outside the window beside him and looked out.

The Archbishop he recognized at once; he was laughing and gesticulating as he approached, arm-in-arm with a tall figure, walking head bowed. A few paces behind, like some aide-de-camp, followed a young chaplain. Harrison craned forward. At that moment the bowed figure looked up, and for the second time he found himself gazing directly down into the eyes of Maurice Campion.

Seeing the frown of recognition appear on the Bishop's face and the Archbishop's head beginning to rise, he ducked back. As he did so, there was a gasp from behind. He swung round to find the typist staring wide-eyed from the doorway.

'Excuse me,' he muttered, pushing past and hurrying away.

'Sinister old bastard!'

The Brigadier paused before a portrait of a rat-faced Dutch merchant incongruously wearing a jauntily-tilted fur beaver. Grinning, he continued to lead on through the maze of galleries.

'All right, Dickie, get it off your chest.'

Harrison glanced around. The National Gallery was quiet that afternoon, and the room they were in was empty except for the pair of uniformed attendants with their backs to them, looking out into the adjoining gallery. Bending close, he began whispering.

Turning a few seconds later, the younger of two attendants observed the two elderly men close together in a corner, their heads low, the one whispering earnestly, the other listening, eyes closed, his flabby grey face calm as a Buddha's. He nudged and looked inquiringly at his companion, but the other merely shrugged. Next moment their attention was distracted by a party of schoolchildren pouring into the further gallery.

'That's everything, is it?' said Greville as the children disappeared. He led a few feet along the wall. Halting before an eighteenth-century pastoral landscape, he shook his head. 'Not much to it, is there? A bit of tittle-tattle from this Titmouse fellow and a few missing papers.'

'More than a few—a hell of a lot, I'd say.'

Greville shrugged. 'Incompetence? Some muddle somewhere?'

'Cratchley was murdered, damn it!'

'Right, Dickie, so what does it all come to?' said the Brigadier, pacing on.

Harrison took a breath. 'Only that the man who is a possible candidate for the English Primacy was ordained, recruited we might say, by an associate of known traitors. On top of that, he openly preaches against Government military and economic policies.'

Greville laughed. 'My dear fellow, so do half his fellow bishops!'

'Yes, but the office of Archbishop of Canterbury is still influential. Christ knows, Campion's charismatic enough as it is!'

Greville gave a sceptical sideways glance. Goaded, Harrison burst out, 'Damn it, somebody thought it important enough to shove a few milligrams of poison into poor old Cratchley's arse!'

Before them, Bosch's frail Christ stood hemmed in by his nightmarish torturers. The Brigadier pursed his lips. 'All right, Dickie,' he said, nodding, 'let's say we buy it for now. I'll have Campion gone over with a fine-tooth comb; in the meantime, you see what dirt you're still able to dig from these papers.'

'But can we get hold of them?' asked Harrison doubtfully.

'The papers?' Greville grinned boyishly. 'Already in our hands, old boy. Picked up half an hour after you rang. Some old dragon was very upset apparently. And that reminds me...' Reaching into his jacket, he withdrew a plain buff envelope. 'There you are—everything you asked for,' he said, passing it over. 'When will you go?'

'This evening, I suppose.'

'Fine. Now is there anything else I can be doing, Dickie?'

Harrison thought for a moment. 'You could look into Canon Rope's background. The papers have been through his hands.' He paused, then added reluctantly, 'Perhaps you ought to have his phone tapped.'

'Rope?' Greville scratched his nose. 'Wasn't he the fellow that mentioned the so-called bee-sting—the thing that first put us on the scent? Doesn't seem very likely, does it, the same chap involved?'

Harrison nodded miserably. His head was throbbing almost unbearably. The whole progress of the investigation was like moving through a mirrored maze where every step or turn only brought a further distorted image of himself, all equally ridiculous and grotesque. 'Check them all,' he said.

'All?'

Momentarily, Harrison had a vision of Ingrams standing in the garden among his Brussels sprouts, the smoke from his pipe rising like incense. 'Yes, all of them, from the Dean downwards—the whole ruddy caboodle.'

Greville arched an eyebrow. 'Right.' He smiled. 'Come on, you and I need a bit of fresh air.'

From under the portico, Trafalgar Square shone in the sunlight before them. Where the frost had melted, the damp paving glistened like steel; pigeons waded in lakes of light and the high Norwegian fir, bare and undecorated as yet, stood against the dazzling glare.

'I presume,' said Harrison, 'whatever the Church decides, Campion will never get the PM's recommendation?'

Greville shrugged. 'I'm not so sure. There's Palace intrigue to consider.'

'Lambeth, you mean?' said Harrison; again he saw the weaving tracks across the frozen lawn and the ghostly figures moving among the trees. He looked round to find Greville smiling at him.

'My dear friend,' he said, pointing with his umbrella, 'I was meaning the place at the top of that road beginning over there.'

Momentarily, Harrison stared across the square to where, beneath the massive arch in the north-western corner, the grey tarmacadam turned abruptly a dark red, then spun round. 'The Mall, you mean? You're not saying...' He lowered his voice. 'Not Buckingham Palace, surely?'

'Apparently,' said the Brigadier, raising his head as if to address the figure on the soaring column, 'we are very concerned about the problems of the inner cities and the general moral decay; hooliganism, riots, rising crime, the increasing divide between rich and poor, it worries us greatly.'

'Even so...'

'Campion is quite the guru of our Prince of Wales, I'm told,' continued Greville, unperturbed. 'And there's plenty left of your one-nation Tories. They'll root for him. As for your liberals and socialists, nothing they'd like better.'

'All the same, his views on defence! The man's virtually a pacifist!'

The Brigadier snorted. 'There's plenty will turn a blind

eye to that if they think Campion can give them back the England they once had—or thought they had.' He laughed. 'After all, isn't this the age of Glasnost and Perestroika? Do we really need Trident submarines or an army on the Rhine? Damn it, haven't our enemies all melted like snow before the breath of the almighty dollar?'

'My God,' breathed Harrison; a cloud of pigeons swirled up and spilt across the massive plinth and the bronze lions.

Greville thumped his arm. 'Cheer up, old lad! Don't worry! If there's half a grain of truth in your damnfool idea, we'll topple the sanctimonious bastard. If we have to, by God, together we'll have him down, neck, heel and bloody crop!'

Loaded down with umbrella and two large plastic bags, Harrison climbed out of the taxi and paid; his head seemed to throb in time with its diesel. He watched it disappear, then looked about. Almost opposite, monstrous and incongruous among the Victorian terraces, rose a massive block of flats. Further down the gently sloping street the lights of a pub shone beside a hump-backed canal bridge.

Under a streetlamp he re-checked the address, then, weary with 'flu, began walking. He crossed a side road, then, next to a bookmaker's, he found the number he wanted on a small white board attached to the railings. Looking down through the bars, he was relieved to see a light glowing behind the curtains of the basement flat.

Clutching his bags, he unsteadily descended the steep metal steps into a minuscule yard. The smell of dustbins rose to meet him. In almost pitch blackness he felt for the bell. There was a loud buzz as he pressed. Almost immediately the door opened, and there before him, framed in the light, stood the slim shape of Sarah Cratchley.

'Thank God, you've been quick!' she cried, before he could speak. 'Do come in.'

Bewildered, he stepped into the low-ceilinged sitting-room. As he did so, the girl gave an astonished gasp.

'You?' she exclaimed.

He had expected anger; instead, there was fear in her eyes.

'You were expecting somebody else?'

'Yes—the police.'

'What?'

She pointed to where a bureau stood, lid and drawers open, its contents scattered on the carpet. 'I've had a break-in.' Her voice shook.

'I wonder if I might sit down,' Harrison murmured faintly.

She stared bewildered, then her eyes softened. She gestured towards the corduroy-covered divan. 'Of course—go on.' As he slumped down, she regarded him with concern. 'Are you all right? You don't look at all well.'

'It's been a long day,' he mumbled. Glancing at the plastic bags beside him, he added, 'I've spent the afternoon buying a few things for my wife.' He looked up. 'Burgled, you say?'

'Sort of.' She forced a smile. 'Look, you sit there. I think we both could do with a strong cup of tea.'

From the kitchen he heard the sound of running water and the rattle of cups. Dragging himself up, he looked round the room. Apart from the ransacked bureau, all was neat and tidy. A word-processor sat on a white table against a wall, a yellow Anglepoise bowed over it. Going to the bookshelves, he bent down: apart from paperback novels, the volumes were sociological or political works. Only the short row of law books were unexpected; then he remembered that before going freelance she'd been assistant legal correspondent on the *Guardian*.

Going over to the table, he ran his eye over the piles of typed paper. He suddenly stopped, and, dizzy, his head ringing, he looked again at the word-processor and then across to the portable television in the corner. What had she meant— 'sort of'?

'Feeling better?' She smiled as he entered the kitchen. 'The kettle's just beginning to boil.'

'This burglary, what's been taken?'

She shook her head. 'Hardly anything as far as I can see. The word-processor is still there, thank goodness, and my camera's safe.'

'What has gone?'

'Just some jewellery. It has all been tipped on my bed, but they seem to have taken only some of the cheaper pieces. They've even left my aunt's engagement ring.' There was a hint of pain. 'Not to their taste, presumably.'

'Sarah, before the police arrive, there's something I must ask. Where's the manuscript you removed from the cottage?'

She stared at him. With enormous relief, he saw the amazed bewilderment in her eyes. Whatever the nightmare he was falling into, at least he could say with absolute certainty that the young woman in front of him was innocent of her uncle's murder.

She went as if to speak, but instead, pushed past him. He followed her through the sitting-room into a small vesti-bule and then into the only bedroom. As they entered, he noticed at once that the glass door at the foot of the bed was ajar and that there were deep gouges where the jemmy had exerted the pressure to tear the brass bolts through the pine frame.

'Oh God! I put it up there!' Pale, she was pointing up at the broad white shelf over the bed, where, between a row of dolls and framed photographs, was a gap of A4 size.

A loud buzz came from the sitting-room.

'The police,' she said, automatically moving towards the door.

Harrison seized her shoulder. 'Don't tell them about this.'

She stared.

'Trust me,' he pleaded.

The door-buzzer sounded again and, loud and insistent, continued to ring.

'Christ knows why I bothered!' Sarah burst out as the street gate above clanged shut. The visit hadn't been exactly a success: Sergeant Grant of the Islington CID had a manner that managed to combine an almost callous offhandedness with insolent officiousness, to which he'd added a silent though powerful measure of disapproval at finding an elderly man nursing a heavy cold in the flat of an attractive young woman. After a cursory glance at the forced door, and having made scathing remarks on the locks, the door-frames and finally on basement flats in general, he left, virtually boasting that nothing would be done.

Angrily closing the front door, Sarah turned on her remaining visitor, now slumped again on her sitting-room divan. 'Now perhaps you can tell me why someone should break in and steal Uncle's manuscript—and why you should be so interested.'

Harrison looked up, eyes bleary with 'flu. 'Would it be possible,' he asked, 'to first have that cup of tea you promised before my next interrogation?'

'I'm sorry.' She smiled. 'Have you eaten today?'

'I have a somewhat distant memory of a mayonnaise sand-wich.'

'Right,' she said, laughing, 'then we'll eat together.'

He tried to protest, but she had already disappeared into the kitchen. He blew his nose in an effort to clear his head.

'Was that your wife with you yesterday at the funeral?'

'Yes.'

'She looks very nice.' Sarah re-entered with a glass. 'Hot whisky and sugar; it will make you feel better.' She watched as he drained it, then asked, 'Who gave you my address? The Dean?'

He shook his head. For a second or two they regarded each other steadily, then he asked, 'May I use your phone?'

She nodded, returning to the kitchen without a word.

It took much longer to be put through than in the morning, but eventually there was Greville's voice against a background of laughter and noise.

'Yes?'

'It's Harrison; I'm at the Islington flat.' He looked up. Sarah was watching from the doorway. 'There's been a break-in.' Another muffled roar of laughter from the background: the Brigadier was obviously at his club. 'The manuscript's been snatched!'

Except for the background murmur of voices, there was a moment of silence down the line. 'Police involved?' Greville's tone was imperturbable, smooth as a good port.

'They've just left; it's been reported as a break-in—just a bit of cheap jewellery stolen.'

'Good!' A dinner-gong rolled in the distance. 'I'll have to go. You'll be getting those papers in the morning... Oh, and Dickie, old chap, well done! It seems your idea was not such a damnfool one as I first thought.'

Harrison looked wearily up at the watching girl as the phone clicked off in his ear. 'May I now ring my wife?' he asked.

Clearly Winnie had been waiting for his call, for she answered at once.

'Richard, you sound terrible.'

'Just a cold—I'm at Sarah Cratchley's flat.' He glanced towards the kitchen. 'She's had a burglar this afternoon.' He sneezed.

'Poor dear.'

He couldn't tell if her commiserations were for him or for Sarah. 'Did you eat what I left out?' he asked. 'And what about your supper? I won't be back until late.'

'Don't worry, but you don't sound at all well. May I speak to Sarah?'

'Sarah?' he repeated surprised.

'Please.'

Almost from the moment she put the receiver to her ear, Sarah was relaxed and smiling. 'Of course... Not at all... No, I've been very lucky.' Watching the girl's face as she talked, Harrison experienced the sense of being excluded like a child from an adult conversation. She turned and smiled. 'No, that would be fine. Of course he can, there's plenty of room.'

'What?'

The girl gestured for silence. 'Yes, I'll tell him. Right, 'bye then,' she said, replacing the receiver.

'Look,' he began, 'I really can't intrude. I don't—'

She cut him short. 'It's all arranged. You can have my bed; I'll sleep in here on the divan.' She smiled. 'It will be so much better with someone here. I would have been very nervous on my own with the patio door still broken.'

'If you're sure,' he said doubtfully.

'And yes, your wife says not to worry—Margaret Ingrams is going round to collect her for supper, and she'll stay overnight in the deanery.' She got up and smiled. 'Anyway, we need the time—you've got rather a lot of explaining to do.'

After the whisky, the steak and the Beaujolais, Harrison felt better. He and Sarah sat facing each other across a small table on which a low red candle burnt with unwavering flame while he finished telling her of her uncle's mysterious warning to Greville and of the missing documents from the dead bishop's papers.

'One of the many things I don't understand is why you brought the manuscript back before anything else?'

'I don't know—some silly idea of finishing the book myself.' She paused. 'His books meant so much to him.'

'I was told that you weren't that close.'

'Who gave you that idea?' Anger flashed in her face. 'He was virtually my father—he and my aunt brought me up. They adopted me.' Pausing, she seemed to struggle for breath. 'In fact I was going to stay with him that very weekend.'

'So the extra milk was for you.' He flushed. 'I found the note for the milkman.'

She looked down.

'But hadn't there been a quarrel, something about your politics?'

Again her indignation flared. 'Look, I don't know who's been telling you all this. Uncle didn't object to my politics. I told you, I was like his daughter. He loved me.' Through the candlelight, Harrison saw the tears in her eyes. 'Anyway,' she continued, 'my uncle was an unworldly man, an innocent. His life was his books and the Church. Except for those he loved, they were the only real things. Politics and the rest of it, I don't think he took seriously at all.'

'Perhaps there were things in your uncle's life you didn't know.'

Sarah's face seemed to harden. 'But you seem to know a hell

of a lot: what I do, where I live, my politics, even the magazines I work for.'

Without a word, Harrison reached in his pocket for the envelope Greville had given him and held it out. Frowning, she took it and, extracting the contents, began to read. At first her face merely showed amazement, then it flushed.

'This is disgusting! How could they possibly know all this?'

Harrison shrugged. 'The State will always attempt to infiltrate any potentially dangerous groups. As soon as you started going to those Oxford meetings the checking would have begun.'

'It's filthy! Vile!'

'So are bombs.'

'Christ, I'm not a terrorist. Tolstoy and Kropotkin were paci-fists. Can't they bloody well read?'

'Wasn't your Bakunin the father of bomb-throwers?' said Harrison, glancing towards the bookshelves.

'I was never that sort.' There was silence. She looked at him, appeal in her eyes. 'Colonel, this Becket factor, what do you think it means? And this secret Uncle may have found, have you any theory what it's all about?'

He smiled sadly, shaking his head. 'No, my dear. Believe me, nobody has any idea at all.'

Unable to sleep, sticky with sweat, Harrison tossed and turned in the strange bed, his brain churning. He thought of Winnie and worried: it had been years since they had slept under separate roofs. At last, deciding he wouldn't sleep until he'd emptied his bladder, he got up and, wrapping a blanket round his shoulders, went out to the lavatory for the third time since going to bed. Leaning forward to urinate, one hand on the cistern to steady himself, he heard tyres screech in the distance and then a vehicle accelerating past. Harrison stared down into the bowl feeling angry, useless and old.

'Are you all right?' Sarah called as he stepped out into the tiny vestibule between the two rooms. A small globular table-lamp on the floor beside the divan switched on, and there was her face looking out of the darkness. Pulling the blanket round him, he went to her.

'I can't sleep,' she said, looking up.

He pulled a chair over and sat; neither spoke for a time.

'I was thinking about the delay in the funeral,' she said at last.

'Bureaucratic muddle, I heard.'

'Was that all?'

'Of course—what else?'

'I thought perhaps... Oh, nothing, I was just being silly.' She pulled herself up a little; she was wearing what looked like men's pyjamas, and there was something almost painfully appealing about the slim girl's body in the overlarge jacket.

'If anything definite turns up, I'll tell you,' he said.

He felt her hand take his; he glanced down, then, squeezing it, sat without speaking. There came the roar of a speeding car approaching; idly, he wondered if it was the same one back. It raced away past; again the tyres screamed as it swung overfast into a side road. As the sound died, sitting there beside the girl, he experienced a moment of extraordinary wellbeing, and, simultaneously, an enormous pity for the restless ugly world outside.

'Do you remember your parents being killed?'

'I was in the car with them; my little brother as well.'

Footsteps echoed hollowly on the pavement above. 'With your uncle dead, you must feel rather alone. No boyfriend?'

She withdrew her hand. 'Intermittent—isn't that the word they used in my profile?'

Harrison winced.

'There was someone at Oxford,' she continued quietly, 'but he was killed in a climbing accident.' She looked up into the darkness. 'Everyone I love seems to die. Perhaps that's why I haven't been able...' Her voice trailed away. She looked at him. 'They always do die, you know.'

'At least you don't kill them.' Before she could reply, he got up. 'Sleep now,' he said. Switching off the lamp, he began stumbling in the darkness towards the bedroom.

'I'm sorry I was so rude at the cottage.'

'You had a perfect right.'

'Still, I wish I hadn't.'

'Good night,' he said gruffly.

Back in his room, he sank on to the bed and quickly fell asleep. Whether due to what he'd drunk earlier or to a high temperature, his sleep was plagued by vivid dreams. First he was back in Lambeth, wheeling Winnie down the lawn, while around them figures flicked between the trees—sly clerical shades of Crocker, Campion, Titmouse, Rope and the Dean—all as if playing a game of which he understood neither purpose nor rules. Still pushing Winnie, he was suddenly back in Canterbury outside the cathedral. The organ was playing, and a vast procession was winding out of the Great West Door. Suddenly there was Sarah beside them, pointing upwards; he turned to look—there was the figure again, high on the Bell Harry, silhouetted against the sky, but now in the dream, something about the tiny, insect-like shape made him think it a woman, and what he'd seen in his waking life as nothing but a wild, irrational greeting, he saw now as a frantic warning. Terrified, he swung round to find the huge procession almost upon them—a silent, slow-moving mass, irresistibly sweeping on to trample Winnie and himself and leave them crushed and destroyed. Still struggling with a wheelchair that seemed rooted to the path, he woke trembling and sweating with fear.

In the half-light he slipped out of bed. It was icy cold.

Taking the blanket again, he went into the sitting-room: Sarah was asleep, an arm hanging limply to the ground, her face pale. In the bleakness of the winter dawn he stood looking at her—the girl who had become an anarchist to defy the implacable order of a creation that demanded, like the God of Abraham, the blood-sacrifice of those she most loved.

He began to shiver. Turning away, he stumbled back to bed.

CHAPTER SEVEN

Fog had delayed the London train; it was almost ten o'clock before Harrison, having collected his car, was turning off Palace Street into the cathedral precincts. As the Volvo emerged from the Court Gate archway, one of a group of muffled figures ahead broke away and, stepping out, waved the car down. Jaded by his journey and impatient to see Winnie, Harrison wound down the window as Canon Rope stalked round the bonnet and leaned down.

'The Dean's gone!' Eyes gleaming, he rubbed his hands.

'Gone?' repeated Harrison, startled.

'His wife drove him to the station.' Rope leant further forward; from his breath came the tang of whatever antiseptic he used for his dentures. 'There was a packed case on the seat.'

Bewildered, Harrison shook his head. 'Is this something to do with the coffin?'

Rope snorted impatiently; with a glance round, he hissed, 'Colonel, the next Primate is about to be chosen.'

'Impossible!' He stared. 'Damn, it's almost Christmas!'

'My dear fellow, what else can it mean—the Dean slipping away so secretively?'

'I don't understand. What has Ingrams to do with the choice of Archbishop?'

It was Rope's turn to show amazement. 'Surely, Colonel,

you know that the Dean of Canterbury has an automatic place on the nomination committee.' He grinned. 'One of the perks of the post.'

'I didn't know.' Harrison looked through the windscreen towards the deanery. 'He never mentioned a word to me.'

'Our Dean is the most discreet of men.' Rope straightened. 'Anyway, it's all very hush-hush, so…' Putting a finger to his lips, he grinned conspiratorially, then, stepping back, gave a wave before turning to wander away across the central lawn.

Winnie pushed herself into the hall as soon as Harrison called from the door; smiling broadly, she wheeled forward to greet him. 'Ah, the wanderer's return! And how was your night on the tiles?'

'Disturbed,' grunted Harrison, bending to kiss her. Taking his hand, she leant back and studied him. 'What's the matter? You look absolutely terrible.'

'I've just bumped into Rope. He tells me Ingrams has been called to attend the nomination committee or whatever they call it.'

'For the new Archbishop, you mean?'

'Yes, unfortunately.'

A shadow crossed Winnie's face. 'So you did find something, then?'

He squeezed her shoulder. 'Come on, I'll tell you all about it over coffee.'

Winnie remained staring down as Harrison finished his account; on the worksurface the percolator gurgled and plopped. 'So it is real!' she breathed and looked up, her face pale.

He nodded. 'Only too real! And now this blasted committee is meeting before I've got any real evidence at all!'

'You sound as if you've already decided Campion's guilty.'

Before he could reply, the phone rang. 'I'll have to go,' he said, returning to the kitchen. 'That was Mary. The Harvey-Watson papers have arrived. The despatch rider insists on handing them over to me personally.' He turned to go, then paused. 'Perhaps you could ring Margaret when she gets back and find out where Ingrams has gone. Rope may have got it wrong.'

Dressed in black motorbike leathers, the messenger sprawled insolently in the chair as Mary, pink-faced, struggled to concentrate on her typing.

'If you'll bring the files through, I'll sign for them now.'

The young man's swagger, the sense of physical threat he carried so lightly, the casual insolence of manner and voice infuriated Harrison. As the outer door slammed, he felt a wave of sympathy for Dr Crisp, visualizing the librarian bayed and hemmed by the like of that young blond-haired Myrmidon striding away outside. Remembering Winnie's forlorn face as he'd hurried from the house and the face of the sleeping girl in the dawn, his revulsion rose against the grubby world he again served. Sitting down, he opened the first of the box-files. The bishop had clearly been a prolific writer: letters, sermons, newspaper articles, diary-jottings, all lay in bundles, each with its typed label. For a moment he wondered at the devotion of whoever it was, widow, offspring or friend, who had so carefully ordered the mounds of now slightly yellowing paper.

He extracted the first bundle; bound like the rest with a thin strip of pink ribbon, its caption read: *Trinity 1929-33*. Removing the first letter, he smoothed it out and began to read. Almost simultaneously in the far distance there rose a faint rumble like an approaching storm.

The four F1-11 fighter-bombers, flying in almost perfect diamond formation, raced in over the city, then, banking, turned north for their Lincolnshire base. Three thousand feet below them ancient stone and wood quivered invisibly. Neither the sound of the jets nor the clatter of the typewriter from the outer office impinged upon Harrison, however, as the words in faded ink conjured before him a vanished Eden of cobbles, gas-lights, blazers and flannel bags.

> ...when Toby arrives with the divine Sylvia and another Girtonian in tow—all three positively insisting, on me making up a tennis party. *Ergo propter hoc*—dear old Aquinas thrown aside, and next thing, we're racing away in T's awful motor, with our two beauties positively...

The pages turned, and as the 'twenties turned to the 'thirties, Harrison began to discern a growing unease in the young Harvey-Watson's mind. There were references to the worsening economic situation and the rapid rise in unemployment.

> ...one hears of such distressing conditions, especially in the North. What with the wage cuts and the Means Test, one begins to wonder exactly where we're heading...

New names began appearing; there were references to meetings and arguments with Maurice Dobb from Pembroke College, and later, others with a newly elected fellow to Trinity, a certain Anthony Blunt. There was a long letter to an elder brother at the Foreign Office expressing Harvey-Watson's disquiet after speaking with David Haden Guest, just back from Göttingen with talk of anti-Semitism and of gangs of Nazi thugs in the streets.

A sudden shriek came from outside; there was a pounding of feet. Going to the window, Harrison was in time to see the probationer choristers, Simon Barnes at their head, racing each other back from choir practice. With a grunt, half disapproving, half relieved, he returned to the papers.

There was no mention now of croquet or tennis—and, like so many sprites, all the Hermiones and Sylvias had quite disappeared. More new names, new associates, and then, out of a letter to a friend, there came an army—a grey army of half-starved men in mackintoshes and broken boots.

> ...proudly in the drizzle, heads high, came these men of the Tyneside. Watching them pass, I knew that we—our class, our Church and State—have much to be forgiven for. My dear Peter, you would hardly believe that in the *Varsity Weekly* the hunger-marchers rate a two-column photograph on an inside page while the main story is a preview of a wrestling match at the city baths! I'm angry and certainly feel a greater sympathy than ever with Cornford, Bell and the rest of our Marxist friends.

Excited, Harrison reached down for the next letter, but felt only the desktop; looking down, he saw nothing remained of the bundle but the thin strip of binding ribbon. He checked the catalogue number of the letter with the list on the lid: all the final papers of that bundle were missing. He struck his desk in exasperation.

'Colonel, is everything all right?' Mary was staring from the doorway.

He forced a smile and waved vaguely at the scattered documents. 'So much paperwork! It quite gets on one's nerves.'

The girl looked perplexed. 'Well, I only hope he appreciates all this trouble you're taking. A whole day in London and all for a few pigs!'

As Harrison stepped out of Dark Entry on his way home, a movement in the Archdeaconry garden caught his eye: a van was parked in the drive and two men in overalls were lifting a large black-and-white cylinder out of the back. For a moment he watched them, then, frowning, walked on.

'Is Crocker having anything done to his house?'

Winnie looked up from her plate. 'I doubt it—why?'

He shook his head. 'Nothing, really.'

As he recommenced eating, Winnie studied his face. 'You've begun to go through the papers, I take it?'

He nodded, still chewing.

'Well, aren't you going to tell me what you found?'

Harrison laid down his knife and fork. 'Titmouse was quite right: Harvey-Watson was mixed up with them all—Philby, Burgess, Maclean, Blunt—the whole blasted crew!'

'What do you mean—mixed up?'

'What I say. He mixed with them all. During his time at Cambridge, he obviously swung completely to the left.'

'Became a Marxist, you mean?'

He shrugged. 'I imagine so.'

'Imagine?'

'He must have been! Trouble is, whoever has been through those boxes has taken just the letters I need.' He took another bite at his chop. 'He must have been with them, why else are the papers gone?' Frowning, he contemplated the congealing remains on his plate. 'You know, Winnie,' he said, looking up, 'I felt I almost had him, not just Harvey-Watson, but the fellow behind—that Bolshevik bastard, whoever he was, who was busy recruiting them all!'

Winnie looked distressed. 'Oh, Richard, you should hear yourself! You sound worse than Simcocks!'

'Look,' he said, glowering, 'did you speak to Margaret as I asked? Did you ask her where Ingrams has gone?'

'I spoke to her, yes, but she didn't tell me.'

'Wouldn't, you mean?' He got up. 'That's it, then,' he said. 'The nomination committee is meeting, just as Rope said.' He went to the door. 'I must ring the Brigadier at once.'

Winnie sighed. 'At least finish your lunch! Nothing is going to happen quickly.'

'On the contrary,' he snapped back, 'the whole thing is beginning to race and I feel I'm rapidly losing control.'

❀ ❀ ❀

Brigadier Greville rang back late that afternoon. 'You were quite right, Dickie.' His voice was unusually grave. 'God knows why the selection has been put forward—they've seized up like clams down at Lambeth.' A heavy sigh rolled down the wires. 'Well, we'll just have to hope that they don't recommend Campion if your absurd theory is true. How about you? What's happening?'

'I'm still ploughing on.' Harrison closed his eyes: his head ached after nearly two hours more of Harvey-Watson's voluminous scrawl.

'Well, anything?'

Harrison's indignation flared. 'How could there be! Someone has been through these papers with a fine-tooth comb. They've even torn pages out of his diaries!'

'You sound tired, old chap.' There was a hint of scorn in the Brigadier's tone. 'Not too disturbed a night, I trust!'

Harrison ignored it. 'What's happening at your end?'

'Don't worry, we've got our own little fine-tooth comb out: the boys are going through everything—political friends, associates in the unions, foreign connections and all the rest. That reminds me, you asked me to check out this fellow, George Rope.'

In the gathering twilight Harrison sat as the Brigadier reeled out his list. 'Durham University, graduated 1932. Two years at the School of Oriental Studies, London, then a long spell with the China Inland Mission. Came back to the UK in 'forty-nine.' The voice continued remorselessly. 'Apparently, he always spends the last two weeks of August at the Seahaven guest house, Torquay, where the only thing the landlady can say of him is that he enjoys his food.' Greville paused. 'Need I go on?'

'Nothing of interest at all?' Harrison's heart was dust.

'Not unless you regard a letter to *The Times* on the subject of Ming vases as of enormous significance.'

'I had to check,' muttered Harrison miserably.

'Quite right.' The voice oozed warmth suddenly. 'Don't worry, we'll check them all. You just keep digging on through those files just as fast as you can.'

After Greville had rung off, Harrison sat motionless, the receiver still humming and crackling in his hand. A sudden click and silence from the instrument broke his reverie: replacing the receiver, he looked at his watch. Nearly quarter to four: the whole day had gone getting back from London and going through the first box-file. Apart from a frustratingly inconclusive talk with the cathedral solicitor on the subject of the Basset Underhill glebe, he hadn't touched a bit of diocesan business for days.

Blankly he stared down at his paper-strewn desk. Since lunch, he'd moved on through nearly a decade of the bishop's life—the leaving of Cambridge for the East London curacy and the supervision of the University's Bermondsey Mission, his own parish in 1935 and then the Secretaryship of the Bishop of London's Poor Relief Fund the following year. When Greville had rung, he had reached Harvey-Watson's installation as honorary canon of St Paul's in 1939.

He glanced through his notes: there were Harvey-Watson's reactions to Hitler's rise, the Spanish Civil War, the Moscow show trials, the Munich Agreement and the German-Soviet Pact—dread, shame, shock and, with the declaration of war, curious relief. It was all so predictable, every reaction just what might have been expected from any concerned English person of the day. With an exasperated sigh, he threw down his notes. Just then, a deep sound began to intrude on his senses. He frowned, not understanding for a moment, then his mind focused: it was the Bell Harry tolling. Of course, he thought, it was time for Evensong, and this was the single bell of the final summons.

The bell had stopped ringing before Harrison reached the calefactorium door. Hurrying to the transept steps, he saw that the entire length of the rope dividing off the martyrdom stones was now heaped with wreaths and bunches of flowers. Just as Ingrams had predicted, a Becket cult had obviously begun. For a moment he paused, thinking of the graffiti in the vestry and the figure behind the gates, then continued up to the nave.

Light gleamed ahead in the choir; from within came the sounds of the service. Harrison hurried up the chancel steps fully intending to take his usual seat. However, as he entered the archway under the huge sculptured screen, he halted as if before an invisible barrier.

Before him, candles and lights shone on purple and polished wood. He stood as if dazzled, then, as a priest began reading the lesson, he edged back. As he did so, there was a quick rustle directly behind. Startled, he spun round in time to see a figure dash from him, flitting like some weightless sprite back into the gloom of the nave.

Shaken, he stood frozen, staring into the shadows where that breathless ghost had vanished. His heart steadied; whoever it was must have followed and been standing right behind him, yet, amazingly, he'd not heard a thing.

For some reason he was certain that it had been a woman—and there had been something in the wild, erratic movement of that flight that convinced him that she was the same person who had fled from the crypt gate the week before.

Almost before he was conscious of doing so, he began running tiptoe down the steps in the direction in which the figure had disappeared. In the south-west transept he paused. He had heard no crash or boom of a door: he was quite certain that the person was still somewhere close. He looked behind the bookstalls and peered down the nave. Nothing moved. Running up the few steps to the south choir aisle, he began peering among the monuments, alcoves and side-chapel entrances. After a minute or two he gave up: for the second time, whoever it was who haunted the cathedral seemed to have escaped. Then a thought struck him. Turning, he hurried back down to the transept.

Even before he reached them, he saw that the chain and padlock of the crypt gate was missing. He looked round, but there was nobody to call. From the choir, a hymn began as he pushed through the gate and stepped down to the inner door. It gave easily under his hand. He pushed it open slowly, peering forward. All was darkness below. He hesitated a moment, then, lowering his head, crept down the steps.

In the low, hollow interior, the only light came from the lamplight shining dully from the path outside. Silently he moved forward, then stopped: from somewhere in the darkness came a low, choking groan.

The sound was more animal than human; stock-still, his heart pumping hard, he listened. The sound died, then rose again, gasping, choking as if for breath, then again falling away. It was coming from behind the hessian screen. Cautiously, one step at a time, he began moving towards the hinged gap. Reaching it, he leant slowly forward to look in.

So dark and shadowy was the space within that for a few seconds he couldn't make out anything at all. Gradually, however, as his eyes adjusted, in the centre of the paving before the still darker patch of the canvas appeared a shape. As Harrison, hardly breathing, strained to see, it quivered, moving slightly from side to side, then again began to emit the same choking groan he'd first heard.

The sound died; the movement stopped; silently, the shape seemed to grow upwards from the ground, doubling, then trebling in size. Edging back from the apparition before him, Harrison fought back the impulse to retreat, but then his heart slowed and he partly relaxed—it was a human shape that stood before him, and whoever it was had risen from a crouch to stand erect.

The figure began swaying to and fro easily. Again, from it, came the same unearthly choking sob as before. Reaching up at the pillar beside him, Harrison felt for the switch on the junction-box leading to the bulb over the coffin. He found it and, bracing himself, pressed down.

In the brilliant light, the Archdeacon jerked round. Except for his red-rimmed eyes, his face was ghastly pale—a mask of wretchedness, thin and bony, out of which the eyes shone with a glittering strange intensity. His mouth moved, but no words came. Instead, half turning away, he stood, a rigid silhouette, black-cassocked and silent, in front of the dark stretch of tarpaulin and the bare hanging light.

Harrison was immeasurably shocked. 'I'm so sorry!' he muttered, his fingers frozen to the switch. 'I thought there was an intruder.'

Crocker's throat convulsed as if straining to swallow; his prominent Adam's apple bobbed and jerked in his scrawny neck. 'That's all right, Colonel.' He struggled for self-control. 'I came to go to Evensong, but then...' He broke off and, spreading out his hands, he raised both arms and then let them fall back to his side.

There was something of such despair in the gesture that Harrison, much as he wanted to, felt unable to leave. He remained where he was, gazing at the tall figure before him.

'What's happened, Archdeacon?'

Crocker lowered his head. 'Not what has happened, Colonel, it is what is happening.' His neck convulsed violently, then he spoke again, his voice unnaturally calm. 'Rather, I should say, it is what will happen—what must!'

Harrison looked down at the dark patch on the floor, remembering the figure flitting before him into the shadows. 'I don't understand. Do you fear for the coffin?' He paused, a thought came. 'Or is it for the Church, Archdeacon? I mean the possible choice of new Archbishop?'

Crocker looked away. 'It's my sister, Colonel. She has taken a very severe turn for the worse.' Again the Adam's apple twitched and jerked. 'I had hoped,' he continued, 'that my prayers had been answered, that the discovery of...' The Archdeacon lowered his face. 'The poor darling's suffering is very great.' Crocker's voice died in a harsh croak; his face twitched and a shiver ran through him.

'My dear fellow!' Without thinking, Harrison stepped forward and placed a hand on the Archdeacon's shoulder. As he did so, he noticed with shock the frailness, almost hollowness, of the gaunt frame beneath the cassock: he was reminded of the corpse of a bird. 'Come on,' he said, 'I'll walk you back as far as Green Court.'

Evensong was still continuing as they left. As they descended into the martyrdom transept past the heaped offerings round the Becket memorial, Harrison turned to tell Crocker of the figure that had fled from him, but, seeing his face, said nothing.

As they reached his garden gate the Archdeacon stopped and looked up at the lighted window on the first floor. 'Our mother died of the same thing. It was Dorothy who virtually brought me up.' His voice was calm and quiet. 'After she's gone, I won't want to stay on too long.'

'Leave Canterbury, you mean?'

Crocker shook his head; Harrison saw with surprise that he was smiling.

'No, Colonel, that wasn't quite what I meant,' he said.

'How's the steak?'

'Wonderful, darling,' replied Winnie.

The Bugle-Horn was a modern hotel, a place of piped music and imported oak. Driving into the car park to meet a neon-lit Santa Claus waving above the words *Yuletide Greetings* had sent both their hearts plunging. In fact, they were soon enjoying the velveteen luxury of the dining-room where the candlelight glinted and glistened on the sheen of the low-slung, garish Christmas decorations.

Winnie hadn't been greatly surprised when he'd told her they were eating out: treats and scrupulous over-attention had always been his way of disguising the deserts between them. Indeed, since Cyprus, cut flowers and chocolate boxes had had something of the funerary token about them. Wearily, she'd listened to his attempting to book a table on a Friday night close to Christmas—finally, in desperation, phoning that gaudy monstrosity he'd spotted that morning when driving back from the station.

She'd been wrong, however, about the evening out. To her surprise, she found it no mere token, but a reaching out, an attempt, as it were, to recover lost ground. Something had happened; something had brought him back to her. She let him talk on, waiting to find out what it had been. In the car he had spoken of the sense of disgust he'd felt prying through the intimacies of the bishop's papers, of his need, yet inability, to join the congregation at Evensong; he'd recounted his shock of turning to see the figure dash from behind him, of the vain hunt, and then of that terrible confrontation in the crypt. Finally, now over their meal, he told her how, looking up at the light in the window after Crocker had gone indoors, he'd determined that nothing, not the investigation nor Greville and all his works, would separate them again. So it was love that had brought him back, she mused to herself, and once again, indirectly, the mysterious coffin was involved. She smiled to herself.

'What's amusing you?'

'Sorry, I was miles away. What were you saying?'

'Just that, whatever the outcome, I only hope this selection process is settled soon. With Crocker the way he is and that wretched woman running loose about the place, we need Ingrams's steadying hand.'

There came a roar of muted laughter from behind: through the frosted-glass partition dividing one end of the restaurant from the rest, shadowy shapes were moving. The laughter and noise increased: obviously a large private dinner-party were sitting down for their meal.

Harrison glanced round, then turned back to stare gloomily down at the candle between them. 'I'm sick of it already, Winnie, all this poking at shadows!' He gave a deep sigh. 'It's useless anyway! Whatever was in the files, must have all been removed.' He raised his wine-glass and drank, and then, quite unexpectedly, grinned. 'Anyway, as far as I'm concerned, the blasted Harvey-Watson papers can stay in the office safe until Monday. Let's you and I get out together somewhere this weekend.'

Reaching out, his wife squeezed his hand. Behind the glass came a raucous shout and the thumping of fists.

'Perhaps,' said Winnie suddenly as they were finishing their coffee, 'you should tell the police about the person you saw.'

'Perhaps you're right.' Harrison started to get to his feet. 'How about a liqueur? You order them. I'm going to find the gents.'

As he had expected, the men's lavatory was pink tiled and pink lit, and there was a faint scent of perfume in the air. Slightly unsteady, with a feeling of wellbeing, he stood before the urinal. Turning away, he went to walk to the washbasins on the opposite wall. As he did so, the door opened, and then, almost simultaneously, there came an exclamation of surprise.

'Colonel Harrison!'

Swinging round, he gaped at the apparition before him: incongruous in the pinkish gloom of the lavatory stood a kilted Highlander in full regalia, but with what appeared to be a miniature fez tilted rakishly on his head.

'Good God!' he burst out, recovering his senses. 'It's Gillie, isn't it?'

Greville's assistant managed a smile; he reached up towards his outlandish headgear. 'A wee hootnanny, Colonel. I'm here with the South London Caledonian Society. Our annual weekend-away pre-Christmas bash.'

'Really,' muttered Harrison, hardly listening. Obviously the fellow was in Canterbury on duty, but the highland dress and the preposterous party-hat—the attention to detail was wonderful!

'Well, I had better be moving; the others will be waiting.'

Remembering the Brigadier's urgency that afternoon, Harrison glanced towards the empty cubicles. 'I'm afraid,' he muttered, 'you've caught me playing hookey.' It was useless: blank incomprehension was the only expression to appear on the Scotsman's face. 'I shall be getting on with the work tomorrow.'

He attempted a comradely smile. 'It's for my wife—it's our wedding anniversary,' he lied.

Gillie retained his baffled look: his heart was clearly of the same impervious granite as that of his homeland. 'We all need rest, Colonel.' Glancing down, he plucked lightly at a pleat of his kilt and smiled. 'If nothing else, we owe it to our wives.'

Winnie looked up concerned as her husband rejoined her. 'Whatever's the matter? What's happened?'

'I just ran into that bloody man Gillie. You remember—Greville's assistant. He was with him when they came to the house.'

'Yes, but whatever is he doing here?'

Harrison sighed. 'One thing I didn't tell you,' he said, 'I asked the Brigadier to check all the cathedral clergy.' Seeing her pained expression, he said quickly, 'Look, I had to. If nothing else, there's been murder done!'

Winnie began to say something, but at that moment, from beyond the glass partition, there came a low drone which rapidly rose to an unearthly wail.

'My God!' murmured Harrison, looking round, 'I have never known anything like it!'

His wife laughed. 'Darling, they're only bagpipes.'

'I know that!' He leaned across the table. 'I'm talking about the trouble they're taking—the sheer quality of the cover.' Seeing the baffled look on her face, he leant further, whispering, 'They've got Gillie dressed up as a highlander. He's with them in there!'

She glanced doubtfully in the direction of the wailing pipes. 'Are you sure?' she asked, looking back.

'Of course I'm sure! I told you, I met him...' His voice was lost as the bagpipes rose in crescendo. Shadowy figures grew suddenly large behind the glass, lurching and swaying grotesquely. Next moment the partitions slid back, and, with a pair of pipers leading, a stream of tartaned men and women began dancing into the main body of the restaurant, linked one to the other in a conga.

Husband and wife watched as the weaving line snaked among the tables, then Harrison leant forward and hissed: 'There's Gillie, the chap with the fez.'

Winnie looked at the ungainly figure swaying in the dance, glancing at intervals to laugh back at the equally lanky grey-haired woman holding him round the hips. 'Surveillance, darling?' There was a twinkle in her eye as she turned. 'Well, if it's true, the man deserves an Oscar for his performance.'

Saying nothing, Harrison shrugged unhappily; doubt and uncertainty were swirling within him, as if goaded and driven on by the wild keening of the pipes.

CHAPTER EIGHT

Throwing aside the colour supplement, Harrison looked across the breakfast table at Winnie who sat bowed over a copy of the *Observer*.

'Anything interesting?'
'Nothing much,' she said quickly, turning the page.
He frowned. 'What is it? Let's see.'
Silently she passed over the paper.

A large photograph of Maurice Campion wearing a miner's helmet dominated the double page. Above in large letters was the legend: EMERGENT THIRD FORCE. Beneath, the sub-title read: DERBY'S MAVERICK SETS OUT ON THE CANTERBURY ROAD. Appalled, Harrison began to read.

In the depths of the Hertfordshire countryside a secret committee is meeting. The result of their deliberations may well profoundly affect the future of Britain. In a sixteenth-century manor house, protected from prying eyes by a high wall and thick shrubberies, five Anglican bishops, an assortment of deans, archdeacons, minor canons and plain reverends, together with a group of the laity (all male), including a retired Air Marshal and the chairman of a merchant bank, have the task of drawing up a short-list of two names. All must be ordained, have only one wife (or less!) and, in the words of *The Book of Common Prayer*, not 'given to wine, no striker, not greedy of filthy lucre'. The two names, in order of preference, will be sent to Downing Street where the Prime Minister will approve one. This will then be forwarded for the Queen to formally choose 'her true and beloved first minister of State and Primate of all England': in other words, her new Archbishop of Canterbury.

'Secrecy!' snorted Harrison. 'God Almighty—either the *Observer* has a mole or someone at Lambeth leaks like a sieve! Just listen to this, Winnie.'

Although under five per cent of Britain's population are practising members of the established church, the choice of primate could have far-reaching effects for, according to reliable ecclesiastical sources, the most likely name to top the list soon to drop on the Downing Street mat will be that of Maurice Patrick Campion, 58, best known and most controversial of the present English bishops.

'Hear that?' he exclaimed, his voice incredulous. 'They even know which way the voting's going!'

Winnie continued placidly buttering her toast as he read on.

The Prime Minister's reaction will certainly be one of dismay, but hard though it may be for many in the Government to stomach an open advocate of unilateral disarmament and staunch supporter of the corporate state as future Primate, Campion's charismatic appeal and his powerful denunciations of pornography, violence and greed have won him wider respect and popularity than any Anglican bishop for over a century. Bishop Campion, however, possesses something rarer than mere popularity: he has spiritual authority—it is this, together with the support of almost the entire Church and a sizeable section of the public, which may, in the end, force the Premier's hand.

With an exclamation, Harrison sprang to his feet. 'Off to Matins, dear?' said Winnie, smiling.

'Matins?' He stared at her. 'There's no time for that now! I must go on with those papers.'

She sighed. 'Oh, how I wish we hadn't seen that ridiculous man on Friday.'

'Gillie, you mean?' Harrison glared from the door. 'Let me tell you, Winnie, there's nothing ridiculous about Gillie— nothing at all!'

Slamming the study door, he went to his desk and drew forward the third and last of the box-files. He glanced at the carefully labelled title: *The Manchester Years. 1949-58*, then began lifting out the thick wedges of paper. Finally, he took a notebook from a drawer. Opening it, he stared down despondently: apart from the title he'd written, *Years 1940-48*, the pages before him were blank.

The previous morning, after a night haunted by visions of Gillie and the Brigadier, he'd hurried over to collect the Harvey-Watson papers from the office safe. The day had then gone in reading through the second box, expecting any moment the phone to ring with Greville scornfully inquiring after his evening out.

Instead of a young don's reaction to the poverty and politics of the 'thirties, the second box had contained merely the details of an aspiring cleric's life—committee reports, memoranda, together with the increasingly predictable sermons and articles—liberal, optimistic, all tinged with the democratic and socialist tenor of the war years. Spurred on only by his dread of the Brigadier's call, Harrison had read on, following Harvey-Watson's almost inevitable career moves, from canon to archdeacon and on to suffragan bishop of Kensington, and then, finally, at the bottom of the box, to the parchment with royal seal and signature appointing 'Our well-beloved and trusty William John Harvey-Watson' to the bishopric of Manchester. Not one letter or document had been removed from the entire box: indeed, throughout the whole tedious day the only relief had been that after March 1948 the Bishop's thick scrawl was replaced by neat professional type.

With the sound of the cathedral bells announcing Matins in his ears, Harrison began reading. Invisible above the overcast, the sun climbed towards its zenith, Matins began and finished, the narrow streets and alleys of the city filled with movement and life, and in the nave the queues for the crypt grew longer as the final years of the nineteen-forties passed before him. Then, as he read into 1951, he jotted a note. He went on reading, but now, as the minutes passed, his pen moved with ever-increasing frequency over the pages of the notebook.

❖ ❖ ❖

'Well?' said Winnie, pushing into the room. 'No lunch today?'

Harrison looked up and, saying nothing, held out the notebook. Her smile faded. Taking it from him, she glanced through the pages, then looked up inquiringly.

'Extracts from Harvey-Watson's diary,' he said, taking the book back. 'Just listen. "A young man of discretion whom I can trust, a true brother and comrade." That's Harvey-

Watson talking of Campion. He'd become his chaplain a couple of months before. Now this: *"Maurice has the vision and already looks beyond any parochial or national interest to that wider good which, despite apparent set-backs, works its inevitable progress through human history."'* Harrison sat back, smiling triumphantly 'There you are, my dear—inevitable historical progress! Karl Marx, pure and simple. And there's plenty more of the same. Obviously Harvey-Watson had found a fellow spirit in Campion—a comrade, as he says, who actually shared the vision!'

'Whatever that was,' said Winnie quietly.

'What do you mean?' He glared at her. 'It's clear as day, damn it! *"Beyond national interest"*, *"the wider good"*—what the hell does all that sound like?'

Winnie gave a wry smile. 'Christianity?'

Harrison went to speak, but then, getting up, looked out through the window. Over the cathedral the cloud spread imperceptibly grey. He shook his head and turned to face her. 'You refuse to see anything, don't you?' he said.

'Anything that's not there, yes.' She smiled. 'I don't think even Brigadier Greville would condemn a priest for actually believing in his calling.'

Harrison slumped back in his chair, staring down at the still unread pile of papers. 'All right,' he murmured bitterly, not meeting her eyes, 'go on—tell me, it's useless, that I'm a fool, that I'm wasting my time grasping at shadows!'

Winnie drew an envelope from her pocket and laid it before him.

'What is it?'

'A Christmas card for Sarah Cratchley. I've enclosed a little note, thanking her for putting you up. Perhaps you could sign it as well and put on the address.'

Harrison gazed down at the envelope. It lay, clean and white, beside the faded grey-yellow of the bishop's papers—the present against the past; the living moment against the eternity of death. All at once he struck the desk and got up. 'Come on, damn it,' he said, 'let's go out and have lunch.'

Winnie burst out laughing. 'Eating out again—what would the Brigadier say?'

'Confound the Brigadier!' Laughing, he ruffled her hair. 'I must get away from these papers and get some fresh air in my brain. If not, I'll go crazy!'

Two hours later the Volvo was parked at Whitstable, its bonnet facing out over a grey flat sea. The two of them sat with the engine running, the heater on, listening to music on the radio. Winnie looked round at her husband; he was staring across the level beach to where a couple walked arm-in-arm on the water's edge. 'What are you thinking about?' she asked.

'Somebody called Dot.'

'Who's that?'

'Harvey-Watson's secretary. That's what he called her—"my beloved, reliable Dot". She was with him from 'forty-eight onwards; moved up to Manchester when he went and stayed with him, I imagine, until he died. It was she who compiled the papers.'

'Dedication?'

'Oh, at least that,' he answered thoughtfully.

'Wasn't he married?'

'Harvey-Watson? Oh yes.' Harrison gave a short laugh and, smiling, took her hand. 'Amazing, isn't it—the tenacity of love!' Turning away, he looked down the beach where the couple now stood in the distance, two thin dark silhouettes against the misty expanse of sea. 'Poor devil!' he murmured quietly.

'Who do you mean? Harvey-Watson or his secretary?'

He shook his head. 'Neither—for some reason, I was thinking of poor old Crocker. I'm not sure quite why.'

Harrison groped his way down the frosty path to his gate next morning. All about Green Court lights gleamed. It was early, and apart from himself, no one else was moving. Pausing, he looked across to the archdeaconry where, around the edges of the drawn curtains of the first-floor room, there came a faint orange glow. Wind blew icily through Dark Alley; it cut at his face as he fumbled for the office keys. Impatient to be at his desk, he hurried up the steps to the door of the main office and, entering, switched on the lights.

'My God!' The sound died in his throat.

It was as if a minor hurricane had blown through the offices of the Diocesan Dilapidations Board: chairs lay over-turned, files had been torn and thrown from the shelves, drawers were ripped out, their contents scattered over the carpet. Upturned in one corner was the office typewriter; in another, smashed on its side, was the photocopier. Even the Christmas decorations had been torn down and thrown into the midst of the confusion.

If anything, the devastation was even greater in his own office—even his heavy desk was overturned and ink had been poured over the welter of papers and books covering the floor. He looked to the safe. It stood wide open. Numbly, he pushed his way over and, crouching on the litter of strewn papers, peered in: all three shelves of the cavernous interior were empty. Quickly gathering the documents scattered in front, he stood up and checked what he had: three architec-tural reports, the Brewery share-certificates and the Basset Underhill deeds. Then he noticed the petty-cash box at his feet. As he picked it up, he immediately felt the weight of the coins and notes inside.

It took him a few moments to find the phone. As he re-inserted the plug in the socket, he heard with relief the crackle of life from the earpiece. Leaning against the wall, his hands trembling, he dialled. As before, his call was answered at once.

'Tell the Brigadier when he gets in that they've now had a go at the Harvey-Watson papers themselves.'

Ringing off, he went to stand at the window. Outside, the pale winter sunlight was beginning to illuminate the passage below. He shivered. Whoever they were, these dark enemies, they were a lot closer to him than he'd thought. There came the sound of steps. Lloyd-Thomas hurried past, music-bag in hand. As the organist's footsteps died, a thought came which sent a rush of cold to his stomach. In a moment he had the phone in his hand and was dialling fast. He heard it connect and start to ring.

'Come on! Come on!' he urged, his face contorting. At last he heard his wife's voice.

'Winnie, are you all right?'

'Of course. Whatever's the matter? What's happened?'

'The files, are they still on the study desk?'

'I expect so. I haven't moved them if that's what you mean.'

'Check, Winnie—now!' He waited, gripping the receiver as if clinging from a cliff-face, then her voice was back.

'Yes, they're still there.'

Below, he heard the office door open. 'Winnie, for God's sake hide them somewhere.' The sound of the feet had nearly reached the top of the stairs. 'Put them in the airing-cupboard, underneath the clothes.'

'But, darling...'

From the outer office came a scream. There were more feet on the stairs. 'Just do it!' he snapped, slamming down the receiver.

Turning, through the open door, he saw his secretary's face

staring aghast at the chaos, and behind her, peering over her shoulder, the cadaverous features of the Archdeacon.

Inspector Dowley was a beefy man with a coarse, ruddy complexion, whose thick-set, rather pear-shaped body, seemed more suited for wading through farmyards or breasting winter uplands than sitting in a suit, conducting interviews on a somewhat narrow, straight-backed chair. As Harrison studied the florid, heavy face across his desk, he was struck by the thought that generations of the Inspector's forebears might well have come annually to the monastery with their rent, perhaps to the same building, even to the very room they were in, to stand awkwardly in patched tabard and hose while contemptuous clerks languidly scanned the manorial rolls.

'So—' the Inspector scraped at his chin—'you came back here on Saturday morning because you needed some files?'

'Yes.'

Mary intervened. 'The Colonel has been working all hours to sort out Reverend Titmouse's glebe.'

'Quite so, miss.' Dowley turned. 'And that, sir, I presume, would explain why an ex-military gentleman like yourself may not have taken the precaution of re-locking the safe?'

'I suppose so.'

Dowley looked at him steadily. 'What I don't understand, Colonel, is why, if you were working on this matter of the glebe, you left the Basset Underhill deeds in the safe.'

Damn him, thought Harrison, the man was no fool.

'Well, Colonel, so why not the deeds? And what were these other documents you removed instead?'

'I'm afraid I am not at liberty to say. It's a highly confidential matter concerning the highest authorities of the Church.'

'Really? The highest authorities of the Church!' The voice was dust-dry. 'And I thought it was just a matter of a few pigs!'

Colouring, Harrison stared back at the bull-face across the desk. Out of the corner of his eye, he noticed that Mary looked close to tears.

'Perhaps, Miss Simpson,' said the Inspector, 'now that the fingerprint lads have finished, you'd like the sergeant here to help tidy up next door while the Colonel and I continue our chat.'

With a final anxious glance back, Mary went out. As the door closed, Dowley sat back, scratching his neck.

'Would you call yourself a religious man, Colonel?'

Astonished, Harrison stared at him, then bristled with fury. 'I attend cathedral services, if that's what you mean.'

'Regularly, I'm told.'

'Look, what is all this about?'

The blue eyes coolly returned his stare. 'In the words of your Head Verger, Colonel, we appear to have a nutter on the loose. Now someone has ransacked these offices, apparently taking nothing with them, in spite of the fact there was a good deal of cash in the safe.'

'I don't see what that has got to do with my church attendances.'

The Inspector smiled briefly. 'According to the Verger, you were not at all keen on us being called in when the graffiti first appeared. Today again, I understand, you were reluctant to allow Dr Crocker to call us.'

'I didn't want any fuss.' Outside the window, came the voice of the choirboys returning from practice; from the outer office came the rumble of furniture being moved.

'Next, we learn you came here alone on Saturday morning, but didn't remove the deeds you were meant to be studying.'

'As I explained, I—'

'On top of this, we've been reliably informed that you were discovered one evening in the cathedral crypt, having disturbed the coffin.'

'This is intolerable!' Red in the face, Harrison began to rise.

'And on Friday,' continued the other, unperturbed, 'the Metropolitan Police asked us to check on you.'

'What?' The colour draining from his face, Harrison sank back on his chair.

'You were reported found in the burgled flat of a young lady in Islington when, according to your secretary, you were meant to be at Lambeth Palace looking into this glebe matter.' There was a pause. 'Now, sir, what a gentleman gets up to in his own time is his affair, but if there's anything you want to get off your chest, now is the time.' Dowley bent forward confidingly. 'What has it been—some upset, domestic trouble, overwork?'

Harrison took a deep breath. 'I have nothing to say.'

Dowley eyed him steadily for a few seconds. At last he rose. 'All right, Colonel, that will do for now.'

❀ ❀ ❀

Winnie refused to take it seriously: 'Oh darling,' she laughed, 'they can't really believe you're some religious maniac! You daubing those awful slogans—it's too absurd!'

Harrison scowled. 'It's that gossip Simcocks I blame. Wait till I get my hands on the bloody man!'

'Why didn't you tell the Inspector about the person you saw in the cathedral?'

'I've told you,' answered Harrison resentfully, 'the fellow they sent is absolutely paranoid: if I had said I chased after some woman through the cathedral, it would have just confirmed his belief that I'm off my head.'

'Or just plain over-sexed.' Winnie grinned. 'Did he really think you've got a young mistress in London?'

'It's not funny at all.'

'Oh, come on! If I were you, I'd take it all as a great compliment!'

With a snort, Harrison returned to poking at his lunch; after all the emotion of the morning, he found he could now hardly eat a thing. Suddenly he looked up. 'Winnie,' he said, 'where are the papers?'

'In the airing-cupboard as you asked. Oh, you're not going to look at them now! Can't you at least...' Her voice died as he hurried out into the hall.

Removing the blankets, Harrison gazed at the box-files. As he did so, he felt a stir of excitement: no longer did they represent a futile obsession or an insane pursuit. For these three battered boxes, his office had been broken into and ransacked: the chaos that had met his eyes that morning was the tangible proof that, despite what had already been pilfered, there still perhaps lay within the last of them a trace at least of whatever it was for which Cratchley had to be killed.

Despite Winnie's objections, he insisted on locking the front door with the mortise as he left. He walked briskly back to the office. He was eager now for the search, and determined that before he slept that night, he would have combed the remaining papers.

Climbing the office stairs, he paused near the top: the door above him stood slightly ajar and from beyond came a male voice. 'Dowley's back!' was his immediate thought, but as he listened, he quickly realized it was not the Inspector who was speaking.

'Terrible, Miss Simpson, terrible! It doesn't bear thinking of—not in these hallowed grounds!'

He positively bounded up the remaining steps. 'Ah, Mr Simcocks! What a very pleasant surprise!'

The balloon head spun round; the Verger struggled to rise. Mary looked up from rearranging the scattered papers. 'Mr Simcocks has come with a message, Colonel.' Amusement twinkled in her eyes. 'A confidential message I'm not allowed to hear.'

'Confidential!' Harrison's gorge rose at the word.

Simcocks beamed. 'It's from the Archdeacon, sir.'

'Indeed! Then perhaps you might like to step in and give it me here,' said Harrison, leading into the office. 'Now,' he said, closing the door behind his victim, 'before anything else, perhaps you'd be good enough to explain why you found it necessary to gossip about me to the police.'

Simcocks's eyes and mouth gaped; his face and whole scalp glowed a bright unnatural red, as if, at that moment, some strange chemical had been added to his blood.

'In particular,' continued Harrison, 'I'm at a loss to understand why you found it necessary to inform them of my evening visit to the crypt.'

'It was after those messages on the walls. They asked me about anything unusual.'

'Let me tell you, Mr Simcocks, that as a result of your indiscretion, this morning I have had a most disagreeable interview with a representative of our local constabulary.'

'I thought it for the best,' stuttered the hapless Verger.

Despite his fury, Harrison felt a spark of sympathy for the man: after all, if nothing else, he had been doing his duty. 'All right, then,' he said, relenting at last, 'you'd better give me your message.'

The Verger shook his head miserably. 'I'm so sorry, sir.'

'The message, man!'

Simcocks's eyes rolled slightly as he tried to summon his thoughts. 'Oh yes, it's about the gentlemen from London.'

'Gentlemen from London. What nonsense is this?'

'The museum men, sir. They're down in the crypt. The Archdeacon wants you to join them.'

'The British Museum archæologists, you mean?' New resentment flooded up. 'What, here now—unannounced, with the Dean still away and less than a week before Christmas? God Almighty!' He sighed. 'All right, Mr Simcocks, inform the Archdeacon I'll join him directly.'

The sudden arrival of the experts from the British Museum had much the same effect on Canterbury Cathedral as lumps of fresh dung falling into an apparently barren desert: within minutes of their arrival, excited sightseers were scurrying through the porches of the almost deserted building, and, despite the Archdeacon's expressed desire for secrecy, by the time Harrison reached the south-west transept, a seething mass were clustered before the crypt gates.

The screened-off area was now brilliantly lit from within, giving the hessian-covered frames a semi-transparent effect, so that the silhouettes of those behind appeared through the coarse woven fibres like figures in a vast shadow-theatre, monstrously elongated and unearthly grotesque. Going to the gap in the screening, Harrison looked in at the scene.

Arc lights had been rigged, and there, in the centre of the floor, its canvas covering now removed, the top of the coffin lay under the harsh glare of concentrated light. Two strangers, obviously the archæologists, knelt at either end of the lid. Between them, they were stretching out a tape-measure while a female assistant jotted down details. It was Crocker, however, who dominated the scene. Illuminated in the glare of the lights, he stood, Simcocks beside him, gaunt and motionless, hands joined before him, the lenses of his spectacles fixed on the coffin. Harrison marvelled at the change from the last time he'd found him in the crypt: then he'd been a weeping, wretched creature wracked by grief, now there was a serenity about him—and standing there in that brilliant light, he exuded confidence, authority and belief.

Joining him, Harrison glanced back over his shoulder. Squinting against the glare, he made out Keates, Pennyfeather and Dill. Further along, a group of clergy were clustered around the Precentor, among which, somewhat to his surprise, he saw Canon Rope. As their eyes met, the elderly cleric grinned and waved. With a nod, Harrison turned back to Crocker.

'What's happening, Archdeacon?'

'Ah, good, you are here, Colonel. As you see, the preliminaries have begun.'

The short exchange was conducted in the quietest of whispers, for the whole occasion had a strangely solemn and intense air, as if, before them, instead of the possible bones and dust of a seven-hundred-years-dead saint, lay the very bleeding body of Thomas Becket itself, the head smashed open, the vestments still sticky with brain and blood.

At last one of the archæologists, a tiny man, heavily bearded, with a great mane of black hair, rose to his feet.

'Let me introduce you,' said Crocker, moving forward. 'These, Colonel, are Doctors Kettle and Kemp. And this—' he gestured round—'is our invaluable Colonel Harrison, who will, I'm sure, arrange whatever practical assistance you need.'

'Is the find of interest?' asked Harrison, shaking hands.

'Undoubtedly!' Dr Kettle, a large, genial man, beamed at the questioner while his diminutive colleague nodded.

'And its age?'

'Ah!' Kettle stared up at the vaulted ceiling. 'I would hazard a guess at the eleventh century.'

There was a buzz of excitement from the group round the Precentor who had been straining forward to hear the verdict. Crocker, however, merely smiled complacently.

'Well,' said Harrison, 'I'm sure Mr Keates and his men will be only too keen to help with whatever has to be done.'

Dr Kettle smiled towards where the men's faces were mercifully blanketed by the dazzle of the lamps, then glanced at his so far silent companion. 'I believe Dr Kemp would like the digging to be begun at once—by tomorrow we should be ready for the hoist.'

Soon Harrison was enjoying the sight of Keates himself, along with Dr Kettle, the girl assistant and the two men, carefully scooping away the earth around the coffin with trowels. One by one, most of the onlookers left. Promising to return for the raising next day, Harrison too made his excuses and left, leaving the Archdeacon and the Verger to their motionless vigil before the figures kneeling in the heat and dazzle of the lamps. Before he had reached the crypt steps, however, a voice called his name from behind. Reluctantly he turned to see the animated face and toothy grin of Canon Rope emerge from the gloom.

Remembering Rope's earlier contempt for the find, Harrison had been surprised to see him in the crypt at all. He was even more amazed now to see the enthusiasm on the elderly face.

'History is being made, Colonel!'

Harrison glanced up at the illuminated screens, over which stretched, like a huge goblin, the shadow of the Archdeacon, and next to it, the shorter, more troglodyte form of the Verger. 'I suppose so,' he murmured, turning back to the steps.

He emerged to find that the crowd in the transept had grown. All the space around the bookstalls was now densely packed and the passage to the nave was blocked by early arrivals for Evensong who had been drawn by the excited buzz of the crowd. There was a tug at his sleeve. 'Come on, let's use the south choir aisle,' hissed Rope, drawing him towards the flight of stairs to their left.

At the top, Harrison paused to look gloomily back down over the cluster of heads. He found himself once again longing for Ingrams's return.

'Ignorant sheep!' Rope walked on. 'All this fuss about a pathetic box of bones!'

'But didn't you just say something about history being made? I thought you'd caught something of the Archdeacon's enthusiasm.'

'Hertfordshire, Colonel, that's where history is being made—not down in that gloom with Crocker and his cronies!'

'Hertfordshire? The nomination committee, you mean?'

Pulling him aside, Rope leant forward. His teeth gleamed. 'They've done it! It's over—the decision's made!'

Harrison's stomach seemed to go hollow. 'Not Campion, surely?'

Rope grinned like a wizened monkey. 'Top of the list, old boy.'

'Good God!' murmured Harrison flatly. Numbly, he stared through the railing beside him at the effigy of the Black Prince. Although he'd been half expecting it, the news was still a shock. He felt suddenly trapped, fenced about as completely as the dead young man lying before him, hands upraised, in his iron cot.

How did Rope know about the committee's decision? What ecclesiastical drums, he wondered, had carried the message to Canterbury? Before he could ask, the Canon was walking on. He hurried to catch him up, but as he reached him, Rope halted and pointed through the lattice-work.

'Look—the throne of blood!'

He was pointing to where, below the high altar, stood the Augustine throne. Squat and heavy, it lay before them, its dull marble glowing slightly in the slanting rays of late afternoon sun. 'Ah, there the antick sits!' murmured Rope. 'Some by fire, some by the axe, some by the sword, some by the knife. All murdered! All killed!'

'Archbishops? Surely not!'

'Oh yes—first Alphege at Greenwich, pelted to death under a shower of ox bones, then Becket, of course, Sudbury next, his head lopped over the Tower wall, Cranmer roasted alive in the Oxford ditch; finally, Laud under the headman's axe.' The sinking sun, striking through the stained glass above, had darkened, and suddenly the dun-coloured marble of the chair was bathed deep crimson in the dying light. Turning, Rope grinned round. 'See! As I say, a throne of blood!'

'It came upon the midnight clear,
That glorious song of old,
Of angels bending near the earth,
To touch their harps of gold.'

The candlelight glowed on the semi-circle of faces; breath swirled like smoke before the lanterns and Bread Yard rang with the voices. Harrison pressed Winnie's shoulder; she looked up at him, smiled, and, reaching up, touched his arm. They had been just finishing supper when they heard the singing begin. He had wheeled her out to listen as he'd done every year.

'For man at war with man hears not
The love-song which they bring:
O hush your noise, ye men of strife,
And hear the angels sing.'

The words caught at his throat; the faces and the lantern-light blurred. He felt a mixture of emotions: nostalgia for childhood; pain for his own unborn children; wonder at his continuing capacity for hope. He was back suddenly at his prep school, sitting with his companions on the main staircase before

the open front door, holding candles and singing to the passers-by
and the semi-circle of adults looking up from the decorated hall
below. He felt his wrist squeezed: he looked down to see Winnie
nod towards the singers. A small figure had stepped forward.
Peering, he saw it was Simon Barnes.

'Venite fideles, venite adoremus...'

There was just light enough for Harrison to see Winnie's
face. He caressed the nape of her neck, and as the solo
finished, he whispered, 'If you like, we could invite the brat
round for a bite on Christmas Day.'

'Did you mean that about Simon?' Winnie asked later as
he helped her to bed.

He smiled. 'Why not? The poor wretches aren't allowed
home until Boxing Day. Awful for any kid, a chorister's
life.'

She squeezed his wrist. 'Do you really have to go
through the rest of the papers tonight? You look completely
worn out.'

'I'd better,' he said, disengaging his wrist.

'Don't be too late—promise.'

'Right.' Bending, he kissed her cheek.

He felt nothing of that sense of expectation he'd had at
midday: it was late, he was tired, and the emotions stirred by the
carols still clung, distancing him from the nebulous hunt after
whatever ancient secrets might lie under the battered cover of the
last of the box-files.

Taking it to the study, he switched on the desk light and sat
down. Time passed. Through the darkness, the cathedral clock
chimed eleven and then twelve.

For the most part, it was heavy going: sermons, committee reports and numerous letters. Weary as he was, however, Harrison began noticing among the petty details of diocesan business the first references to doctors' visits and hospital appointments, then to the stomach pains, the vomiting and ever-growing sense of physical weariness as the cancer that was to kill Harvey-Watson remorselessly spread.

And always now there was Maurice Campion.

As the bishop sickened, the older man's dependence on the younger had clearly steadily grown. In the notes and letters between them there was now a touching intimacy and affection which read like that of father and son. Harrison, his eyes growing heavier and his brain increasingly dull, read on—then suddenly, blinking, he jerked fully awake. In his hand was a hand-written note dated 12th November, 1952. Holding it directly under the lamp, he re-read it with amazed incredulity.

> My dear Maurice,
>
> Uspensky has contacted me at last. He's asked for a meeting, and I want you there. As matters stand, it could be dangerous for many of our friends, but you, dear brother, know that secret reason why I wish this matter soon to be set in hand. I want you to arrange a safe house where our entire group can meet. I cannot over-emphasize the need for the utmost discretion.

Below was Harvey-Watson's signature, a long straggling sweep of a scrawl.

Laying it down, Harrison remained staring at the faded scrap of paper. Among the bishop's worries about church upkeep, the recruitment of clergy and the steady decline of congregations, the message was devastating; with its talk of danger, secrets and safe houses, and with its reference to that mysterious Russian name, among the day-to-day diocesan affairs it lay, a smoking revolver among children's toys.

Recovering himself, he ran his hand over the still unread mound of papers; he lifted them slightly, feeling their weight. Exhaustion forgotten, expectation now thrilling through him, he drew down the lamp more and bent back to his reading.

There were more notes, all to Campion, all guarded and circumspect. There were more Russian names, however: Kelnikov, Polotsky, Vovchok. There were now many documents missing. He read faster, jotting in his notebook as he went. Then suddenly he found himself staring down in almost disbelief at the latest letter in his hand:

> My dear Maurice,
>
> Dot has arranged our flight tickets to Stockholm for the 14th and we now have our papers. Doubtless, you'll be amused to hear that we shall be travelling under the guise of plumbing engineers! Our friends will make contact with us at the hotel. I pray I will have the physical strength to be with you both.

Getting up, he began pacing the room, his hands clasping and unclasping. Halting, he glanced at his watch: it was almost two. He went to the desk and picked up the phone.

'Yes?' The voice was alert.

'A message for the Brigadier. Tell him...' Harrison paused. 'Tell him, the Becket factor is proved.'

Replacing the receiver, he stood before the drawn curtains. Gradually he calmed, and as he did so, his sense of triumph faded. Frowning, he re-read the letter; then, returning to the window, pressed his forehead against the cold pane. Seconds passed; then, straightening, he went back to the phone.

The same voice as before.

'Harrison here—I just rang. I wish to change the message.'

'Yes?'

He breathed deeply. 'Scrap what I said. Just tell the Brigadier I need to see him, that it's imperative we meet as soon as we can.'

CHAPTER NINE

Daylight stole imperceptibly over Canterbury, gradually grey-ing the freezing darkness and drawing out of invisibility first the cathedral towers, then the roofs of the surrounding city. Almost reluctantly, the frozen lawns and frost-laden trees of the precincts emerged from the dimness, and now, from his office window, Harrison could see down the length of Dark Entry. Shaking his head in an effort to throw off the drowsiness cloying his brain, he bent again to the text.

> ...or other devolution of the Lessee's interest in the Lease
> or Grant of Letters of Administration or Probate and of
> the name quality and place or places of the Assignee or
> Assignees Underlessee or Underlessees...

The words swam before him, more incantation than sense. His frustration grew: the legal position of Church holdings in Basset Underhill seemed shrouded in at least as much ambiguity as the dead bishop's secrets. Pushing back the deeds, Harrison looked up at the Bell Harry, dark against the grey, overcast sky.

Harvey-Watson, together with his secretary and chaplain, had been involved in clandestine business with the Russians—that much was evident, but of the exact nature and extent of the treachery he still had not the slightest idea. What he'd seen was but the froth and flurry of a surface; the depths beneath remained as impenetrable as before. Indeed, far from illuminating those dark recesses, the dying man's letters had merely added another mystery—one that had taken him back to the phone a second time, and which now again began to gnaw at and torment him.

A phone rang in the outer office. He looked at his own expectantly. Nothing happened: there was only the brief ring as Mary replaced her receiver. A moment later, however, there was a knock at the door.

'It's Mr Simcocks, sir. Apparently they're ready.'

'Ready?'

'The coffin, Colonel.' The girl's face was excited. 'They're about to lift it.'

Outside, the chilly air revived him. He walked briskly, relieved to be turning his back, however temporarily, on both Titmouse's tangled affairs and the apparently fathomless mysteries of the Harvey-Watson papers.

Although it was early, the crowd in the south transept was already large. As Harrison approached, he saw with sudden misgiving that heavy cables now trailed across the pavings into the crypt. Hurrying to the steps, he stared down into a bowl of light. Clearly, television had arrived.

Hot under the blazing glare of the lamps, the screened-off section was a mass of spectators. Through a ring of cameramen and photographers, Harrison saw the Archdeacon and Verger standing exactly where they'd stood when he'd left the day before.

He pushed across.

'Archdeacon, whoever allowed these cameras in?'

Crocker smiled serenely. 'I managed to prevail on the Precentor.'

'But surely the Dean...' Harrison's voice died as the buzz of conversation faded around him. Dr Kettle had stepped forward, hand raised.

Since the previous afternoon a frame of wooden beams had been constructed over the shallow pit. From this hung a chain block-and-tackle. Craning forward, Harrison saw that the soil and rubble round the coffin had been cleared, and that a couple of broad webbing-straps now encircled its girth as slings, both already connected to the hook of the lifting gear. Dill and Pennyfeather clambered beneath. A nod from Kemp, and immediately the continuous circle of chain began rattling through the iron blocks. The webbing-straps rose and grew taut. As the strain was taken up, the speed on the vertical chain slowed to a steady series of clinks. Under their medieval-looking engine, Pennyfeather and Dill, heaving down on the chain as the slings grew bar-tight, could have been a pair of rack-masters about their grisly work.

There was a loud creak from the webbing-straps.

Simcocks grinned anxiously round at the Archdeacon, his face red and perspiring in the glare. Dill and Pennyfeather strained, veins swelling in their foreheads. The straps gave a cry. Glancing round, Harrison noticed that Crocker's eyes had closed.

Another loud groaning creak, then, as if trying to shoulder itself free, the great slab shuddered and perceptibly rose. The clinking became regular again as the lid of the coffin crept steadily up until its curiously ambiguous emblem was level with the floor.

The clink of chain continued, and inch by inch the previously invisible walls of the casket slid into the dazzling glare. Photographers' bulbs flashed; the cameras swung and whirred, then there was a slight gasp from the spectators as there gradually emerged a finely worked bas-relief chiselled in the coffin's almost smooth side.

The clinking stopped. The pendant coffin swung slightly a yard clear of the floor, its carved coat-of-arms and mottoed scroll now fully and starkly revealed.

A nod from Kemp, and the chains ran back again through the men's hands. With Keates and the two archæologists pushing outwards, the coffin sank until it rested on two pairs of stout metal trestles positioned in front of the now empty pit.

Crocker stepped forward and scanned the carving. '*Surget Veritas*,' he pronounced in a whisper. He turned back to the cameras. '*Surget Veritas*,' he repeated loudly, face triumphant. 'Let the truth arise!'

For a moment he remained before the flashing bulbs, then, turning back to the coffin, fell to his knees. Almost simultaneously, Simcocks slumped down. Acutely aware of the cameras, Harrison stared round in numbed disbelief as others began following suit. Then suddenly, with enormous relief, he heard from behind a familiar voice.

'Ah, good, I see you've managed to get our little find safely raised.'

Turning, he saw Ingrams pushing his way forward.

The sudden intrusion brought the kneelers stumbling to their feet. In silence all watched as the Dean, going to the coffin, bent to study the carving. He straightened. 'Yes, Archdeacon, quite right: *Surget Veritas*—let the truth arise. But as for the design—three swans and a tower.' He shook his head. 'That, I'm afraid, means nothing to me at all.'

Crocker, pale-faced, reeling slightly, stared back at him dazed.

'Good to see you, Richard.' Coming over, Ingrams held out his hand. 'Winifred well, I trust.' Harrison mumbled a reply, but the Dean was already looking away towards the shadowy outer recesses of the crypt. 'I've brought you a friend. We shared a taxi up from the station.'

Through the gap in the screening a dimly seen figure now stepped into the light.

Ingrams beamed. 'An old companion-in-arms, I believe.'

Harrison hardly heard him: he was staring at Greville's grinning face.

'The fellow must have been mad!' muttered Harrison, looking across to where two huge pantechnicons parked before the west front were being reloaded. 'Going down on his knees like that! Lord knows what more trouble it will cause!'

'Come on, Dickie—no use brooding.'

Frost still lay white on the lawns around them as Harrison and the Brigadier walked together towards the distant trees. The sky was darker now and the wind was cold.

'Right!' The Brigadier swung round, his face eager. 'So the Becket factor is proved! Let's have it, then!'

'I told your fellow to scrub that message. I said I just wanted to see you.'

'Well, I'm here.' The other's smile had gone. 'Shall we get on with it?'

Only when Harrison had finished speaking did Greville look up. 'Safe houses, clandestine meetings, trips to Scandinavia under assumed names!' The Brigadier stared across the lawns. 'What the hell was going on?' He looked round. 'In a way we're as much in the dark as before.'

'Darker, I would say. It's why I cancelled the first message, why I wanted to see you. I can't see how those two notes could have been missed. They're too compromising, too explicit.'

The Brigadier thought for a moment. 'Dickie, were they typed?'

'No, hand-written. Why?'

The other shrugged. 'I just wondered...'

'You mean, were they planted?' Harrison shook his head. 'Not a chance. They're signed and, as I say, both in the bishop's handwriting.' He sighed. 'I suppose it could have been a balls-up.

Either that, or whoever went through the files didn't have time to finish the job properly.'

The Brigadier nodded. 'Near the bottom of the last box, you say?'

'Yes.' Harrison nodded. 'That's got to be the answer. After all, why break into my office after them? They must have realized they'd missed something. Again, there's Cratchley's manuscript. Why didn't they steal it straight away? Why have to go to the bother of breaking into Sarah's flat? Something definitely disturbed them.' Harrison looked around the almost deserted grounds. 'Something must have cropped up here that prevented them from quite finishing the job.'

'Yes,' murmured the Brigadier, 'we've been lucky.' Suddenly he smiled. 'And lucky to have you here, Dickie.' He slapped the other's arm. 'Don't look so gloomy, old chap. You've done an absolutely marvellous job! You've given us the end of a string. Now I'll have my boys wind it in.'

'But what do you think is at the end of it? What possible interest could Moscow have in an Anglican bishop?'

Greville sucked his teeth. 'I don't know—as a sleeper, possibly.'

'Sleeper?'

'You know, like these johnnies now slipping their home-made viruses into computer programs so that later, at some predetermined time, the damn things can bob up to destroy the whole system. Undermine from within, hasn't that always been the Soviets' way? Plant a few traitors in the Foreign Office, a few in MI6, a couple in Porton Down, in the BBC and all the rest of it. In other words, infect the whole shooting-match!'

'But all the same, the Church of England?'

'Why not? It's part of the Establishment. Anyway, how did Stalin grab eastern Europe after the war? Remember those elections of 'forty-five and 'forty-six? He had some of the Catholic Democrats in his pocket, planted years before. When the time came, they voted the way they were told.' Greville breathed heavily. 'What a coup: an atheist system with its own pet Archbishop of Canterbury putting in his spoke just often enough to confuse and demoralize the public, making them doubt in the end the morality of every elected Government we get. You see the way: destroy democracy by endlessly carping at and criticizing it.'

'But now? What's the point? The Soviet economy is collapsing. Aren't they on the retreat? Their armies are pulling out. Don't we see them on television chopping up their tanks?'

'Don't be a fool, Dickie! They're chopping up scrap-iron—kit that's twenty years out of date. You should see what comes across my desk: they're building submarines nearly as big as the *Bismarck*; they've got tanks steaming off the production-lines with armour-plating that we've nothing to touch.' Pausing, Greville smiled wearily. 'They may make damned awful motor-cars, but never forget, old friend, they're still the best bloody chess-players in the world.'

Harrison nodded. He thought a moment. 'One little thing—what was Gillie doing at the hotel?'

'Gillie?'

'Yes, your successor. What was he doing in Canterbury?'

A look of uncertainty hovered momentarily in the Brigadier's eyes, then he shook his head. 'Forget him,' he said. 'The main thing now is to finish the job.'

The restaurant of the Old Swan was a dark, low-ceilinged room, heavily timbered, with oak panelling and crudely-cut overhead beams. From their warped irregularity and the variety of redundant joint-cuts, these latter had clearly come from still earlier buildings or from ancient hulks.

'You're a lucky devil, having a safe niche here,' said the

Brigadier, leaning back to light a second cigar. His eyes had grown misty. 'What I'd give for the quiet life.'

It was well past lunch-time. Apart from a young couple talking gravely together and a waiter reading a newspaper, Greville and Harrison were alone. They sat facing each other while from below came the sound of piped carol music playing to the shoppers milling in the street outside.

Greville drew on his cigar and leaned across the table. Harrison stared through a haze into his red-veined, slightly bloodshot eyes. 'A bloody lifetime spent poking into sewers!' He grimaced, his heavy jowls quivering. 'Damn it, I'm sick to my soul of it all!'

Harrison looked down at his brandy glass, certain he was being softened up for whatever new demand was about to be sprung. Even before he'd got home to tell an anxious, scornful Winnie of the Brigadier's lunch-invitation, he'd determined to serve no longer. He'd put them on the right track: his duty was done, his debt paid. For his own sake as much as for Winnie's, the investigation would now have to go on without him.

He steeled himself. 'What do you want of me?' he asked.

'Want?' The Brigadier looked up surprised, then smiled ruefully. 'Nothing, just your final report.' He drank what remained of the brandy and, leaning back, smiled ruefully. 'My dear Dickie, what more did you expect?'

'But I thought...'

Greville shook his head. 'All good things come to an end—I'll be out myself soon.' The voice was gentle, almost brotherly. 'You've done your duty. Leave the rest to us. You're a civilian now. You're out. Be glad.'

'This report?' Harrison's heart was ash.

The Brigadier waved his cigar dismissively. 'The usual thing: a balanced appraisal of what you've read—a useful supplement to my final report.'

Harrison swallowed. 'What about Cratchley's murder? Do you want that included?'

The other shook his head. 'Stick to Campion and Harvey-Watson. All we need is your general assessment of the security implications.' He paused for a moment. 'Mind you, it might be useful if you could tie Campion's past to what he says today. I'll have some press cuttings from his recent sermons and talks sent along. Draw what connections you can. All right?'

'Fine,' answered Harrison hollowly.

The Brigadier leaned forward. 'But be fair, Dickie, won't you? An absolutely balanced appraisal, you understand? Don't rush to pre-judge the man.'

'Of course not.'

'Come on!' Greville grinned. 'Don't look so down! You've done well. Who knows, there may be a little something for you in the next Honours List.'

Turning away, Harrison stared through the window: there was a forlorn melancholy now to the hurrying crowds under the cloud-laden sky. He felt a frightening emptiness. He looked round. 'What will be done next?'

'With the investigation?' Greville took a leisurely drag on his cigar, then carefully tapped out the ash. 'Usual thing—go through the files ourselves, check these names you've given us, follow up the leads.'

'You'll talk to Campion, I suppose, give him the chance to explain?'

'Of course.'

'Then?'

The Brigadier eyed him narrowly. 'Dickie, he may not be guilty of anything.'

'Secret meetings with Russians at the height of the cold war! Safe houses! False names!'

The other shrugged. 'We'll find out. Now, another armagnac?'

'Not for me.'

'Don't be so bloody silly!' As the Brigadier turned, raising a hand for the waiter, Harrison saw him for a moment in profile: an old man, grey, sagging flesh heavy from his skull, dragging on, bearing always the great business of State. He felt an enormous admiration. 'Will you get Cratchley's killer?' he asked.

Greville took another lungful of smoke. 'If it's important.'

'And the traitor here? The one that set them on to the old man, the one that's watching me?'

The other smiled. 'All in good time, don't worry.'

Harrison sipped his brandy, aware he'd never now know the truth behind Harvey-Watson and Campion's meetings with the Russians, never know who Uspensky, Kelnikov, Polotsky and Vovchok and the rest had been—and, until the announcement of the name of the next Archbishop, not even know if the case against Campion had stuck. He looked up. 'I'd like the killer caught.'

'Why?'

Harrison flushed slightly. 'You once said something about us owing God a priest.'

'Seferiades? Christ, can't you forget that bloody man?' Greville flushed. 'We had to compromise him, didn't we? The Greeks were banding against us. He was one of their main pivots. We didn't know they'd butcher him.'

'Of course we did.'

The Brigadier wearily closed his eyes, then suddenly opened them and glared across the table. 'So what? Good God, we were doing our duty as we saw it.' His voice was cold with fury. 'We can't all of us sit back, masturbating our girlish consciences! Some have to have the guts to act by what little light there is—yes, and fail if we have to, then fight again. In Italy and Yugoslavia I saw things, did things, you'd hardly believe. And now again, bombs in Piccadilly, kids torn apart, the whole apparatus of tyranny! How do you think any of that buggery is going to be stopped? One bloody man, politically involved! There's millions of innocents been killed, still being killed, will go on being killed!' He paused, leaning forward, 'If you're going to fight evil bastards, in the end you've got to be prepared to hate your own soul, my friend!'

As if frozen, Harrison stared back as Greville continued. 'Look at Cyprus today.' The Brigadier wiped the spittle from his lips. 'Split, divided, and how many dead? I'd have killed any of them, anything. Losing is my only regret!' His hands shook as he lifted what remained of the cigar to his mouth. He sucked, and then, through the smoke, stabbed down the butt, grinding and twisting it in the ashtray between them. He glared up. 'Let those who can't fight their corner leave it to those who can! Go away, Dickie! Go back to your cottage, back to those bloody roses round the door!'

Harrison slowly got to his feet.

'Your report,' said the Brigadier, not looking up. 'I presume I'll still get it?'

'Of course.'

At the door he glanced back: Greville sat slumped at the table, staring down at his glass, his hand still pressing the sodden cigar-butt into the ashtray.

It had grown quite dark. Low, yellowish cloud covered the sky and a northerly wind was blowing. As Harrison stepped into the open air, he shivered. Buttoning his coat, he walked briskly through the crowds back to the Buttermarket. In the gathering dusk the municipal Christmas tree glistened with fairy lights beside the dark mass of the war memorial; a Salvation Army band, fingers stiffened with cold, struggled through *Away in a Manger.*

The nave was almost empty. It was that time of day when, between the fading of daylight on winter afternoons and the beginning of Evensong, there was a lull in the daily stream of visitors. Now, with the coffin raised, the crypt doors were locked, and for the first time in weeks the vast interior of the great church was bathed in a solemn stillness as dusk descended over the city without.

Harrison strode up the central aisle. Ahead the dim lights of the choir beckoned. Barely acknowledging a greeting from a junior verger, he mounted the chancel and entered.

Facing him was the golden, spread-eagle lectern; behind loomed the dark outline of the Augustine throne. Ascending to his customary seat, he sat gazing down over the tiers of stalls at the white marble presbytery floor, his thoughts reeling sickeningly around what he'd just endured in the upper room of the Old Swan.

It was not so much the Brigadier's contempt itself that had shaken him, but its extent, and the savagery with which it had finally burst. Throughout their relationship he had always sensed the scornful distrust, tinged strangely with pity, lurking beneath the apparent warmth. Between the smiles, the encouragement, the physical touch, one part of him had sensed a scorn as unmistakable as those ghostly indentations on the palimpsests in the Howley-Harrison Library, where, beneath the inked Latin on the re-used vellum, the pagan Greek of the original writer still appeared—imprints which not all the feverish scraping of the monks had ever been able fully to erase.

And there was the self-contempt. He'd left Winnie to join Greville confident, almost joyful, to refuse further service; now instead, here he was, sickly miserable at being cast from that sordid, twilight world he'd laboured so long to escape.

He closed his eyes.

'*O most merciful and loving father...*' The words died on his lips. Despair engulfing him, he opened his eyes. What he saw made him sit forward: a figure was looking up at him from the shadowy entrance next to the Chichele tomb—he or she was standing in exactly the place where Campion had stood those weeks before, and there was something about it that reminded him of that ominous shape that had flitted before him from under the organ-loft.

The figure moved; as it stepped into the light, with relief he saw it was Ingrams. The Dean hesitated, then climbed to join him. 'I hope I'm not disturbing you, Richard.'

Harrison shook his head.

Ingrams lowered himself into the adjoining stall. 'I've just been to see poor Dorothy,' he murmured. 'Apparently you've been a great support.'

'Crocker said that?' He was surprised and oddly pleased.

A cassocked chorister entered and began distributing sheet music among the choir stalls. Ingrams glanced at his watch. 'What about a breath of air? We still have a few minutes before Evensong.'

Together they descended into the martyrdom transept. There Ingrams paused to survey the array of flowers spread before the Becket memorial. 'Look at it! What do I do?' There was exasperation in his voice. 'And now all this today! It was bad enough letting the television in, but Crocker kneeling down like that—whatever possessed him?'

'I wouldn't worry.' Harrison smiled reassuringly. 'I think you defused the situation beautifully.'

'You haven't heard, then?'

'Heard what?'

'The graffiti in the Lady Chapel. We've had the police in again. The paint was still wet when it was discovered. They think it was done just after the raising was shown on the midday news.' The Dean sighed heavily. 'Richard, you should have seen what was scrawled up—bizarre, insane obscenities!' Frowning, he gestured towards the flowers. 'With all this on one hand and that on the other, to say nothing of the break-in into your office I've just heard of, I admit I'm more than ever frightened what the outcome will finally be.'

'Will the coffin be opened before Christmas?'

Ingrams shook his head. He walked to the calefactorium door. 'I've postponed it until the new year. Who knows—by then, passions may have cooled.' Opening the door, he gave a tiny gasp and looked back, his face shining. 'Look, Richard, it's snowing!'

Beyond the gloom large flakes were thickly drifting down. The cloister garth was already blanketed. Ingrams stepped out into the passage and, stretching out into the darkness, caught a couple of flakes. He held them out, his face radiant. 'Wonderful!' he exclaimed. 'A white Christmas! The twins will be delighted; they've been praying for one for weeks.'

Seeing the joy in the other's face, Harrison felt his own spirits lift; just as the snow was transforming the grey scene around them, so the Dean's simple goodness and warmth fell like a benediction upon him. 'Yes, indeed,' he said, 'God willing, it will be a truly peaceful and blessed Christmas for us all.'

Unexpectedly, Ingrams laughed. 'Well, it will be peaceful for me unless I get my phone fixed. There's been something very peculiar about it since I've been back.' He laughed again gaily. 'If I didn't know better, I'd swear the Church Commissioners were having me tapped!'

CHAPTER TEN

The snow fell for hours that first evening, and then again next day, so that before dusk the entire south-east of England in a line from the Wash to the Solent had been hushed and virtually stilled by a heavy and widespread blanket of white. The wind remained in the north and the snow persisted. As a result, far thinner than usual crowds trudged the muffled, snowbound streets, and though the traffic still moved through the ancient city, its sound was curiously muted, so that town and cathedral crept, as it were, towards the time of the Nativity in almost unremembered tranquillity.

Harrison daily scanned *The Times* for news, or even a hint, of the impending appointment of a new Archbishop, but there was nothing. Whether or not due to pressure from Greville or his masters, the decision, or at least its announcement, was, like the opening of the coffin, clearly being postponed until the new year. Campion himself, however, remained in the news: there was coverage of his visits to a number of temporary Christmas refuges for the homeless; he made headlines with a savage denouncement of the order for the latest of the Trident-class submarines.

With the crypt closed and the snow lying deep on the roads, the pilgrims vanished from the cathedral; the flowers withered before the Becket memorial and were removed; no more threatening graffiti appeared. The disinterred coffin itself remained undisturbed, while above it the choir practised the festival anthems and the altar vestments were changed from the sombre purple of Advent to the white and gold of Christmas.

By Christmas Eve, Harrison had caught up on the work delayed by his fevered involvement in the investigation. With an easy conscience, therefore, he sat drinking his morning coffee when his secretary entered with a large envelope.

'This has been just delivered by hand,' she said.

He waited until she'd closed the door before opening it. As he did so, disappointment momentarily pinched: what he had in front of him were not the cuttings on Campion he'd expected, but only the returned Basset Underhill deeds he'd sent to the cathedral solicitor for his comment. He read the covering note.

> I'm afraid we can find nothing to prevent the present glebe leaseholder keeping any animals whatsoever. It is, after all, designated agricultural land. The only remedy the Rector might have would be an action for nuisance—or possibly something under the Public Health Act. We suggest a commonsense compromise between both parties. Surely, this can't be impossible.

He sighed inwardly. A commonsense compromise—if only! How had Titmouse described—what was his name, Greenhill? A puritan fanatic—not a man one could do business with. Greenhill? He frowned. The name rang a distant bell. Getting up, he went to the door. 'Mary,' he called, 'can you lay your hands on the rationalization report?'

He turned the pages quickly. There it was: Frederick Greenhill agreeing in principle to cooperate in the sharing of the running costs of the church hall in the parish of St Mary the Virgin at Sheepcote. He checked name and address between deeds and report, then reached for the phone. As he waited for it to be answered, for an awful moment he visualized a snowbound farmyard, frozen machinery, a cold-eyed puritan farmer.

'Hard Slope Farm.'

He swallowed. 'Ah, Mr Greenhill. This is Colonel Harrison of the Canterbury Diocesan Dilapidations Board speaking.' He took a breath. 'I wonder, if between us, we might clear up a slight misunderstanding...'

The midnight service was over. The cathedral bells pealed over the darkened city as Harrison pushed Winnie out through the porch. In the moonlight the snow-smudged towers gleamed against the stars; behind, silhouettes flickered before the open door.

'Happy Christmas, darling.'

'Same to you.' Winnie strained up to touch his lips.

As he wheeled the chair on, Harrison chuckled aloud. Winnie leaned round. 'What's so funny?'

'Those confounded pigs. Who'd have thought that Titmouse had never mentioned the matter to Greenhill!'

'But why hadn't he?'

Harrison snorted. 'As far as he was concerned, Greenhill was one of the enemy—an Elder of the Strict Baptists. Titmouse expected animosity, therefore everything poor Greenhill did, no matter how innocent, seemed a deliberate attack on his world.' Laughing, he shook his head. 'Absurd, of course, but there it is: pure paranoia!' He laughed. 'The result, I presume, of living too long in that stifling, enclosed world of his!'

'And he's going to move the pigs?'

'Greenhill? Yes, at once. He seemed genuinely upset when I told him the distress his animals were causing.'

Figures moved before and behind them, and as the bells fell silent, through the freezing darkness, the cloisters echoed with the murmur of voices and tread of feet. Hearing the sounds and seeing the shadowy shapes moving with them, Harrison felt a sudden exhilaration: he and Winnie were not lonely, disparate individuals locked in the isolation of separate identities, but were part of a great community, a vast whole, encompassing past, present and future, the dead, the living and the yet to be born. Joyfully he thrust the chair on, visualizing the glow of churches and the ringing of bells over all Christendom that peaceful Christmas morning.

Ahead, Green Court glowed with light. All round the quadrangle windows were lit, illuminating the moving figures. Automatically, Harrison glanced towards where the light also glowed in Dorothy Crocker's room, and wondered what she thought, hearing the crunch of all those feet in the frozen snow and the festive greetings echoing to and fro on this, her last earthly Christmas.

Ingrams and his family stood outside the deanery talking to Canon Rope and Major Coles, the King's School bursar. As Winnie and Harrison approached, the twins broke away to greet them, followed by their mother.

'I hear you're having one of the younger choristers to share Christmas lunch,' said Margaret. 'Well, you must both come over for tea at the deanery afterwards.'

'Ah, Richard,' said Ingrams, coming forward, 'I'm glad to have seen you.' He pulled out a bulky envelope. 'This came by special messenger.' He held it out. 'Sorry to be thrusting diocesan business on you first thing on Christmas Day.'

'Not at all.' Uncomfortably aware of Winnie's eyes on him, Harrison hurriedly thrust the package into his inside pocket.

'Why didn't you tell me?' she said later as he helped her to bed.

'It didn't seem important.'

'Then why that furtive look when you took the package from Matthew?' She looked away. 'You'd have thought it was a love-letter.'

'I'm sorry.' He looked tenderly at the thin face on the pillow. 'I didn't want to distress you: you were so pleased I was out of the whole thing.'

'But you're not out of it!' She swung back to face him.

'I am, Winnie—completely, whether I like it or not. All I've got left to do is write this wretched report.' He went to the door. 'Now I'm going to make the cocoa.'

'Richard!'

He turned.

'You will be careful, won't you?' Her eyes were fixed on him.

'Careful?'

'What you write.'

He laughed. 'You sound like Greville.' He smiled reassuringly. 'Don't worry, I'll be perfectly just.'

Waiting for the milk to heat, he went to the window. In the moonlight the cathedral rose huge and black; unearthly shadows lay over the trodden snow. There was an eerie desolation to the stillness. For the first time in days, he thought of Cratchley: the gleaming vault above; the darkness about him; the sudden sting of the needle. What dark and malevolent hand had it been? And what alien force lurked still, invisible yet? Fear suddenly chilling him, he reached into his jacket to feel the reassuring solidity of the package pressed against his chest.

From the sitting-room came the high-pitched voice of their guest, followed by Winnie's laughter. Pausing momentarily to adjust the pink paper crown, Harrison walked on into the kitchen. Slightly clumsy from the wine over lunch, he filled the percolator. As he waited, he went to the window.

Outside was the same scene that he'd gazed at those few hours before. Now it was transformed: the shadows were gone; the snow gleamed in the courtyard and, in the distance, the cathedral towers soared, honey-brown speckled white against an azure sky.

The percolator spluttered and gurgled; the aroma of coffee pervaded the air. The morning had been lovely, Winnie and he waking with the sunlight bright through the patterned curtains above the bed; they'd prepared lunch, talking together as if the polio, Cyprus and the barren years had never been and they were back in the little Battersea house in the first years of the marriage.

From across the passage came the sound of laughter.

Incredibly, there had been a resurrection; unlooked for, unbelieved in, love had risen. Separately, Winnie and he had tramped the desert between the two murdered priests until, miraculously, at the worst of times, in the dead of winter, with another killing and the return of the Brigadier, love had been reborn. He thought of the coffin, not as some unwelcome interruption, a security problem, a catalyst of either fanatical devotion or fear—but as he'd seen it first, a crude, simple casket that had risen from the dust coincidentally with his own buried love.

Absurdly happy, he turned off the gas. Picking up the steaming percolator, he carried it into the sitting-room.

Winnie smiled round as he entered. 'Darling, I have just heard the silliest thing.'

Harrison grinned at the boy sitting across from his wife. 'Some invention of yours, Simon?'

The boy flushed. 'No, sir, I didn't make it up.'

'It's about Simcocks,' interposed Winnie.

'Really? What about him?' Harrison bent to place the percolator on the coffee-table beside Winnie.

'Simon says he's seen a ghost—Careful, darling! You've spilt the coffee.'

Harrison mopped at the liquid with his handkerchief. Recovering, he looked round. 'This ghost? Where was it supposed to be? Somewhere in the cathedral?'

Barnes shook his head. 'No, sir, in Dark Entry after the midnight service last night.'

'Outside, then?' Harrison felt an enormous relief.

'The older chaps are saying old Fatty, I mean Mr Simcocks, fairly bolted—ran for his life.'

'Indeed.' Momentarily, Harrison had a vision of the Verger—sweating, preposterous, legs pounding like pistons, ludicrously fleeing from the same ominous shadows that he'd seen in the moonlight. Not daring to meet his wife's eyes in case he laughed, he looked down at the boy with mock gravity. 'No, my lad, this won't do—I can believe in many things, but not in our Verger running!'

Emboldened by Winnie's laughter, Barnes exclaimed, 'But he did see her! Really, sir!'

'Her?'

'Yes, sir, Nell Cook! The person walled up for killing a priest. He's quite definite: a woman's ghost chased after him along Dark Entry and she had a knife in her hand!'

❋ ❋ ❋

'Got rid of your charge safely?' asked Ingrams, helping Harrison off with his coat as Winnie was wheeled to the drawing-room by Margaret and one of the twins.

'Young Barnes? Yes, he's off to the party the Headmaster's wife is giving.'

'You know, Richard,' said Ingrams wearily, hanging up the coat, 'I sometimes think our cathedral is something of a Moloch—so many childhoods sacrificed to its service!'

Harrison's resolve to speak faltered: the Dean looked

exhausted; he'd already preached or officiated at three services since midnight. It seemed wrong to burden him further, especially on a Christmas afternoon.

'Well, shall we join the ladies?' Ingrams began to lead up the hall.

Harrison went to follow, then stopped. 'Dean, I wonder if I might first borrow a book?'

Ingrams stared in surprise. 'Now, you mean?'

'If I might. I need something to browse through during the holiday.' He paused blushing, then almost despite himself, he heard himself blurt out, 'I really wanted to look through something of Cratchley's.'

'Indeed!' His host looked bemused. 'All right, come and see what I've got.' Leading into the study, he went straight to a shelf. 'Any particular title?'

The other shook his head.

Ingrams pulled down a volume. 'You could try this.'

Harrison glanced at the title: *Archibald of Calcutta—The Light of South India. 1885-96.* He flicked through the pages, pausing at a faded photograph of a tall, gaitered figure in shirt-sleeves with episcopal collar and cross—presumably the light of South India himself—who appeared about to take a swing with a croquet-mallet before a group of admiring clergy, both Indian and Anglo-Saxon.

'I think the others will be wondering where we are,' said Ingrams, going to the door.

Harrison snapped the book closed. 'I'm sorry, Dean, but I must speak to you about this business last night.'

'Simcocks's ghost you mean?' The Dean chuckled. 'One shouldn't smile, but I fear all this excitement of late has rather inflamed our Head Verger's natural propensities.'

'You don't think there's anything in it, then?'

'Surely you don't believe in this ghost nonsense, Richard?'

Harrison looked out through the french windows to where,

just visible, a small snowman stood lop-sidedly in the gathering gloom. 'I've seen her,' he said.

'Nell Cook?' The Dean's voice was incredulous.

'No, but the woman that Simcocks took for her—the person who's been haunting the cathedral since the coffin was unearthed, the same person who stole Simcocks's keys and scrawled up all that graffiti.'

The Dean's face was grave. 'A madwoman—is that what you're saying? And you've seen her, you say?'

Harrison nodded. 'She bolted from me one evening when you were away. She had been standing right behind me under the organ-loft during Evensong. When I turned, she ran.'

'Did you recognize her?'

He hesitated, then shook his head.

'Your office break-in? Do you think that was her work?'

Harrison shrugged. 'Anything's possible.'

The Dean went to his desk and stared down. 'I suppose the poor creature's harmless?' he said, looking round.

'I'm not sure. The boy Barnes says she had a knife. Of course, that may be just childish exaggeration.'

'What do I do?'

Harrison surprised himself at the immediacy of his answer. 'Get in touch with Inspector Dowley: he's a rough diamond, but a damned good policeman, I think.'

The Dean nodded. He walked to the window. 'There's something else that's now worrying me even more. It's this commemoration service we hold in the evening on the anniversary of the Becket martyrdom. You must know about it. It's held in the crypt every year on the twenty-ninth of December—in other words, next Saturday. It's usually quite a small affair, but this year...' The Dean broke off and then looked earnestly at his guest. 'Richard, could you possibly attend? I'm sorry to ask, but after what you've told me, I have an absolute dread of what may happen.'

'Of course. I'd be delighted to come.'

'My dear fellow, how very...' Ingrams's voice faded. The phone had begun ringing in the hall. Delight lit the Dean's face. 'Excuse me,' he murmured, hurrying out. In a few moments he was back, beaming with pleasure. 'A Christmas present from British Telecom! That was the operator. Apparently, they've managed to sort out the fault at long last.'

'Fault?'

'I thought I'd mentioned it. They've just installed a new exchange.' Ingrams smiled. 'Half the phones around the place haven't been working properly for days. Didn't you know? Come on, let's go and tell Margaret the good news.' Harrison followed into the drawing-room. It was only when he was seated that he noticed with some surprise that he still had Cratchley's biography of Bishop Archibald clutched in his hand.

More snow fell that night. Apart from the usual Boxing Day sherry party at the King's School, Harrison and Winnie remained snug in their cottage. Time passed pleasantly, Winnie spending the greater part of the day painting and sketching while Harrison worked on his report for the Brigadier.

Oddly enough, he found the task a positive relief. Ever since hearing of Cratchley's death, he'd felt his life haunted by what was essentially nebulous and obscure; he had moved, so it seemed, through a dark cloud of unknowing, in which phantoms, vague and intangible, moved in dimensions beyond his reach. Now, however, with his notes and the cuttings before him, he felt back in the world of the concrete where reason and judgement could be applied to fact, and where, with patient logic, he could systematically assess the final balance of truth.

The writing of the report gave other relief: occupied

with the material before him, his forebodings stirred by the news of Simcocks's bizarre encounter on Christmas morning gradually faded. Working, he was safe from the disquieting images of the waving shape on the tower, the knuckles on the crypt bars, the fleeing figure rushing before him: those terrifying symptoms of an ancient irrational force which, invisible as plague bacillus, were stirring again within the ecclesiastical walls.

Free to deal with the actual, he spent the greater part of each day at the desk where, just over three-quarters of a century before, his father, then a young staff officer to General Hamilton, had prepared a report on the likelihood of a successful landing at Cape Hellas in the Dardanelles. With the same careful adherence to fact as his father before him, he wrote his own report on the security implications of the Harvey-Watson papers.

Just as the engineer officer of 1915 had stuck rigidly to known water depths, the elevation of cliffs and the apparently reliable reports of the lack of Turkish fortifications and troops, so Harrison painstakingly listed the missing documents in the bishop's papers, presenting through Harvey-Watson's own words the long-dead bishop's reactions to the poverty and politics of the 'thirties. Without comment, he noted Harvey-Watson's membership of the Apostles and his association with known traitors at Cambridge. Finally, referring to the secret meetings, he listed the names of the mysterious foreign associates of the late bishop.

Having dealt with the dead, he turned to the living, stressing the undoubted bond between Maurice Campion and his bishop and the part played by the young chaplain in the arrangements of the secret meetings at home and abroad. He mentioned Campion's journey to Sweden with the dying Harvey-Watson and his secretary. Lastly, with the aid of the cuttings, he compiled a synthesis of Campion's continuing attacks on the

Government's economic, social and defence policies, paralleling these with the views of his late mentor and friend.

Working and re-working the wording until he was completely satisfied with each statement, it took him three days to complete the task. With a certain pride, he re-read it, then took up his pen to sign in the space he'd left above his name.

He bent forward, but even as the nib touched the paper, a doubt struck him. Raising his eyes, he looked at the innocuous standard phone beside him. For a moment or two he continued to contemplate its ivory-coloured surface, then, getting up, went to the sitting-room, the still unsigned report in his hand.

Winnie looked up inquiringly as he entered.

'I would like you to read this before I sign it.' Without comment, she took the papers. Turning her chair to catch the fading light, she began to read.

'Well?' he asked as she finished.

'My dear, you can't put your name to this.'

'You don't think it fair?'

'Perfectly.'

'And I've stuck to the facts.'

'As far as you know them, yes.'

'Of course! As far as I know them—what else?' He glared at her. 'Christ, woman, we have to work with the little light we have! No one is going to know the complete truth—not on this earth!'

Silent, Winnie outfaced him.

'I've dealt only with facts.'

'Facts?' The manuscript rustled in her hand. 'These meetings Harvey-Watson and Campion took part in, you don't know what they were about. You don't know what was in the missing papers—everything's surmise! These men—Uspensky, Kolnikov, Polotsky—you don't even know who they were.'

'I can guess!'

She glared back. 'All right, who were they, then?'

'Enemies!'

'Of course! And not long ago you were scoffing at poor Reverend Titmouse!' She dabbed angrily at her eyes.

'Damn it, where haven't I been fair?'

'Yes, but it's the total effect, don't you see?' She leaned forward, gripping his hand. 'You're condemning Campion and he's not able to answer. You're attacking a man's reputation—two men's—and one of them's dead and can never defend himself.'

Turning from her, Harrison looked out to where the snow gleamed red under the setting sun. 'Of course, you are right,' he said. 'Titmouse was bloody ridiculous, but this is different, Winnie. We saw Cratchley's ashes buried; they're there now, buried in the Basset Underhill churchyard. That's real, not surmise.' Taking her hands, he looked directly into her face. 'My dear, all I've done is to try somehow to reach out for that truth he was murdered to hide. If you've got any other explanation for his murder and the missing papers, say it now.'

Winnie looked away.

Back in the study, Harrison laid the manuscript on the desk on which his father had put his name to that recommendation that led directly to the landing of the 29th Division—a landing which, according to an airman overhead, turned the sea absolutely red for fifty yards back from the beaches, appalling and blighting forever the life of the desk's original owner watching from the agonizing safety of a battleship lying a mile offshore.

For a moment longer Harrison hesitated, then, leaning over, wrote his signature and flicked the document closed.

The phone rang next morning as Harrison and Winnie were having breakfast. 'That was Ingrams,' he said, returning to the kitchen, 'reminding me about this commemoration service tonight. Apparently, he's agreed to Crocker conducting the service, but has insisted on preaching the sermon himself.'

'I'd like to go with you,' said Winnie.

He looked at her in surprise. 'It could be tricky,' he said doubtfully.

'Getting me down the steps?'

'Not that. Ingrams hopes the snow will keep people away—I'm not sure. The thing could be very embarrassing.'

She smiled. 'I'll survive.'

If the Dean had really expected the snow to keep away the crowds that night, he was to be disappointed: even before they had reached the crypt entrance, Harrison and Winnie heard the excited murmur and buzz rising from below. With a sense of foreboding, Harrison followed behind as the wheelchair was manhandled down the steps.

The interior of the crypt was extraordinarily impressive. Emerging through the low door, Harrison had the impression of entering a completely medieval world. The low-arched chamber was entirely lit by candles. In their uncertain light, the dim shapes of the congregation sitting between the massive pillars, muffled in coats and scarves, could easily have been those of the very monks who had struggled in vain to save the about-to-be commemorated martyr from his assailants' swords.

Ahead, between the rows of folding chairs, two candles, like sentinels, burnt serenely either side of the crucifix on the open altar of Our Lady Undercroft chapel. Above, hanging in golden chains, a tiny red lamp glowed faintly. The mystical effect was, however, somewhat spoilt for Harrison by the sight of Lloyd-Thomas perched incongruously at a small harmonium, the Welshman's grim face looking more disagreeable than ever in the gloom.

Taking his seat next to Winnie's chair in the front

row, Harrison glanced towards the closed dark wall of the screening, then turned round to survey the congregation. Some sat unmoving, silent and poker-faced, while others, equally motionless, knelt bowed on their hassocks. The majority, however, were oddly restless—whispering, pointing and nudging each other, some even turning and animatedly speaking to those behind or leaning forward across the chairs to address those in front. Harrison's heart sank: the atmosphere reminded him of nothing so much as that before a regimental boxing-match.

The congregation grew more restless; with the arrival of each newcomer to swell the ranks of those packed at the back, the excitement grew. From the rear, someone said something inaudible to those at the front; there was a scattered burst of applause. Harrison glanced round apprehensively to catch Winnie's eye as murmurs of dissent steadily grew.

All at once, Lloyd-Thomas began to sway back and forwards on his stool. As the thin, reedy notes of the harmonium filled the crypt, the congregation grew quietly expectant. There came the rustle of vestments and the soft tread of approaching feet.

First passed a cassocked verger bearing a cross, then appeared Crocker, resplendent in gold and white. There was a slight pause, then came Simcocks leading the Dean who was dressed in alb, green chasuble and white-furred hood. Despite himself, Harrison's thoughts returned to those rumbustious Aldershot nights, for the two clerics in their gorgeous vestments looked disquietingly like a pair of robed prize-fighters being conducted into the ring.

'*Brethren, be sober, be vigilant; because your adversary the devil, as a roaring lion, walketh about, seeking whom he may devour...*'

There was silence apart from the voice echoing in the dimness; the murmurs of dissent that had resumed as the harmonium ceased playing had died again the moment the Archdeacon turned.

Crocker's appearance was extraordinary: gaunt and tall, he faced the congregation, hands upraised. It was his face, however, above all, that silenced the crypt: even those who had come to scoff or protest at the veneration of a Roman saint in the very bowels, as it were, of Protestant Anglicanism found themselves temporarily overawed by the terrible countenance now directed towards them.

Instead of softening Crocker's features, the candlelight emphasized the bone and sinew beneath the skin; above the gorgeous white of the vestment, ghastly pale and hollow-cheeked, that face could almost have been an animate version of the chiselled death-mask of the emaciated corpse sculpted on the lower tier of the Chichele tomb. God knows what the wretched fellow has been going through, thought Harrison, visualizing the vigils at his sister's bedside.

Strangely enough, where the flesh had diminished, the spirit appeared to have grown: there was quite extraordinary intensity to the shrunken face and to the eyes behind the steel-rimmed spectacles.

'O God, make speed to save us.'

'O Lord, make haste to help us,' responded Harrison's neighbour enthusiastically. For the most part, however, the congregation remained sullenly silent. Indeed, if it hadn't been for the Dean's determined lead, the responses might well have died altogether. Also, now Crocker had turned his back, audible opposition began again, spurred on and inflamed by the Archdeacon's curiously ornate plain-song.

'Flummery!' called a voice as Crocker sang his way through the *Nunc Dimittis*.

'Popery!' growled the man immediately behind Harrison's back.

If Crocker was aware of the gathering storm at his

back, he showed no sign. Unwavering, he chanted on, hands raised in supplication, the bony arms and wrists protruding from his wide-sleeved vestments. *'I believe in God the Father...'*

In deference to the Creed, the dissenters fell silent. Crocker's chanting seemed to slow, and as he reached the words *'The Holy Catholic Church'* the third word rang with peculiar emphasis. A pause followed the phrase as if the Archdeacon was determined to allow it to fully sink in. Then followed *'The Communion of Saints'.* Again the phrase was dragged out, the emphasis now falling on the final word. What's the confounded fellow playing at? thought Harrison in an agony of apprehension: it was as if Crocker, like Becket before him, was deliberately goading his enemies on.

'Almighty God, by whose grace and power thy holy saint and blessed Martyr, Thomas Becket—' There were simultaneous murmurs of protest. Momentarily, Crocker faltered, then continued loudly— *'triumphed over suffering and despised death, grant that we, enduring hardness and waxing valiant in fight, may with the noble army of martyrs, receive the crown of everlasting life.'*

A hymn-book flew fluttering to land at the Archdeacon's feet.

'Scandalous!' cried Harrison, glowering round in the general direction of the thrower. Winnie clutched his wrist in warning; it was too late: to his horror, his word was taken up by the man behind. A moment later the word was echoing and re-echoing around the crypt, along with 'Superstition', 'Idolatry', 'Popish practices' and the like. Mercifully, Lloyd-Thomas struck up with, *For all the Saints.*

As the hymn ended, the Dean came forward to deliver the address. Having removed his outer vestments, he stood on the lower altar step dressed in plain white alb, girded at the waist by a worn leather belt.

At first, neither Harrison nor Winnie could hear what he

said as his quiet, almost conversational tone was drowned by the murmurings and muttering that had resumed with the ending of the hymn. However, these gradually died away as Ingrams calmly continued.

'...to commemorate a good shepherd who died for his flock and to honour a man who was not afraid to stand up to the force of tyranny.' The simple words and the tone in which they were delivered had a miraculously soothing effect on the crowd. 'It is the spirit of this brave man we remember and praise, not his bones or dust, wherever those poor things may lie.' Ingrams paused, as if defying anyone to deny what he'd said. In the short silence, Harrison noticed that Crocker sat, head slumped forward, eyes closed.

'And it is especially right,' continued the Dean, smiling round, 'and most gratifying that so many have braved the winter weather to come here tonight, for in this coming year a new shepherd must be chosen for the flock.' Again Ingrams, pausing, smiled round warmly as if addressing children. 'I want every one of you to pray that our new Archbishop will have the same courage and strength as Thomas Becket had in defending and guiding the Church committed to his charge. And for a moment, I want you all to think about what our new shepherd must defend: he must defend that spirit of toleration which has always been the glory of our own dear Anglican Church; he must defend the rights of those who, subscribing to the Thirty-Nine Articles, find under its wide umbrella whatever form of worship best suits and helps them in their worship of Almighty God.'

Harrison, glancing around, saw heads nodding in agreement. He's got them eating out of his hands, he thought, looking back at his friend with affectionate respect.

'Now I want you to ask yourselves why we of this cathedral church wish to commemorate Thomas Becket annually.' Pausing once more and smiling, Ingrams looked round the congregation. 'What, dear friends, exactly is the Becket factor?'

Harrison strained to catch each quiet word.

'The Becket factor is surely integrity—the integrity of any man or woman who, seeing a duty, is prepared to face criticism, ridicule and even death to see it done.' The speaker paused, running his eyes over the dim blur of faces before him. 'May we here tonight all have the courage to do the same.'

'Richard! Winifred!' cried Ingrams in delighted surprise as he emerged from the vestry. 'You waited for me. How very kind!'

'We had to congratulate you,' said Harrison.

'Yes, Matthew,' added Winnie, 'it was a lovely address.'

'Thank you both.' The Dean appeared tired. He looked around at the now shadowy outlines of his vast charge. 'Well,' he murmured with a sigh, 'now we must leave it to God.' Whether he was referring to the effect of his sermon or merely to the cathedral itself, he didn't explain. Instead, wrapped in thought, he walked in silence while Harrison wheeled Winnie towards the western porch.

'Matthew, how was Stephen Crocker after the service?' asked Winnie.

'Difficult to tell—though he was kind enough to thank me for the address before rushing back to Dorothy.' He shook his head. 'At the moment, I'm afraid our poor Archdeacon is moving through very difficult dimensions from the rest of us.'

As the chair was pushed out into the night, Winnie looked round. 'Feel it?' she said. 'The temperature's risen.'

Indeed it had. As the three of them moved through the quiet precincts, from the surrounding blackness came the heavy drip of melting snow. To Harrison, the sound seemed oddly appropriate—almost a symbol of what had happened in the crypt: the warmth and humanity of the Dean's sermon, he felt, had thawed the ice of intolerance and suspicion, dissolving all the pent-up anger and fear that had polluted the precincts ever since the coffin's emergence.

'I want to thank you both again for coming tonight,' said Ingrams, halting at the deanery drive. 'Bless you both. I much appreciated your support.' He paused, looking round the silent precincts. 'Walking back now, I've made up my mind to have the coffin opened with the least possible fuss. After tonight, I'm more fearful than ever of the passions it may unleash.'

'Surely not!' said Harrison. 'Not after your sermon!'

Ingrams shook his head. 'Whatever frantic spirit has been stirred by this find will not, I fear, have been appeased by any poor words of mine.'

As if to confirm the Dean's statement, a shriek, quavering and terrified, rang out from the darkness behind them.

'God save us!' cried Ingrams.

'Stay with Winnie,' shouted Harrison, already beginning to run in the direction of the sound. His feet slid and slipped on the slush. As he reached the pitch black entrance to the Selling gate-house, he stopped, partly from exertion, partly from fear. Straining, he listened, peering ahead, his heart pounding hard. Behind him, he could hear Winnie and Ingrams anxiously calling.

He began moving cautiously forward again. Keeping close to one wall, he moved towards where the one light shone in the passage just beyond his office. He stopped and listened—nothing. He was about to move forward again when he heard a low moan. Peering forward, he made out a movement in the pitch blackness at the foot of the wall. Crouching, he advanced. The shape moved again: something or somebody was apparently attempting to crawl on its stomach the last foot or two to his office door.

Harrison reached out. As his fingers touched, the shape writhed away from him, letting out a half-strangled moan.

'I say, are you—' began Harrison, bending forward. An arm suddenly reached out and clutched his neck.

Instinctively, he jerked back, pulling up as he did so the head and shoulders of the man clinging to him. 'Good God!' he gasped as he saw Lloyd-Thomas's face rise from the dark.

The organist's face, either from the effect of shadow and light, or from the horrific expression upon it, was hideous as a gargoyle's. Still clutching fast, he simultaneously attempted to pull himself up and gargle something into Harrison's ear.

'It's all right—hold on,' gasped Harrison, gripping under the other's armpits. Straining, he raised and attempted to prop him against the wall. This was nightmarishly difficult, however. The organist's legs sagged and the slush seemed to have so soaked his coat that Harrison, struggling to hold up his weight, could feel his hands slipping against the dampness. Was it a stroke, he wondered, brought on by the strain of the service? Desperately he shouted up the passage for help. As he did so, Lloyd-Thomas gargled something again into his ear.

'Hang on, old chap. Help's on its way.'

The other shook his head frantically: his eyes rolled and he choked and gargled again: this time, Harrison heard the word distinctly.

'Stabbed, you say?'

Lloyd-Thomas, his head falling on to Harrison's shoulder, made no reply. Letting go of the slumping body with his left hand, Harrison held it up towards the light: against the glare, it looked as if he was wearing a black glove.

Turning, he shouted frantically. As he did so, Lloyd-Thomas's legs appeared to give out completely. Grabbing again with both arms, Harrison strove to hold him up. It was useless: slowly Lloyd-Thomas slipped down to the base of the wall, where he slumped grotesquely forward, arms outspread like a stringless marionette.

CHAPTER ELEVEN

Superintendent Collins was a smooth man, all charm and courtesy. His ingratiating manner and polite, informed admiration of Winnie's watercolours grated on Harrison. There was at least, he thought, a lumpish substance, an earthy integrity, to Inspector Dowley, at present perched somewhat awkwardly on a narrow, straight-backed chair by the sitting-room window.

Harrison was puzzled why a senior policeman had arrived merely to check the details of the statement he'd made after the ambulance had rushed Lloyd-Thomas away. After all, the case was merely a stabbing and the victim was already apparently out of intensive care. He glanced over the oiled head of the young Superintendent to the older man, but, impassive as a boulder, Inspector Dowley's face gave nothing away.

'Very nice, Colonel,' said Collins, at last looking up, 'you obviously know how to make a report.' He smiled. 'As you can doubtless guess, after your recent break-in, the Inspector here insisted on running a check on you. You are now, of course, no longer under any suspicion whatsoever.'

Harrison looked through the window. Canon Rope was crossing the yard on his way to Evensong. What did Collins mean? Had they found out his work for Greville? Did they know of his past?

The Superintendent's voice broke into his thoughts. 'In the

light of this recent attack, there are one or two further questions, however, I would like to ask about the break-in. There is
the possibility that there was something the intruder failed to
find. Apparently, you told Inspector Dowley something about
collecting some confidential papers from the safe that weekend.
Could anyone have been after those?'

Harrison shrugged. 'Anything's possible.'

The Superintendent stretched out his legs.

'You know we found the weapon?'

'I heard, yes.'

'It was only a few yards from the place of the attack, thrown
into the cloister garth—just a kitchen knife, a cheap Czech
import.' Collins paused. 'Very amateurish, the whole thing: the
weapon itself, then throwing it away like that and the assailant
not even bothering to wear gloves.'

Why, wondered Harrison, was he being given these
details?

'We were lucky enough to get a very good set of prints from
the handle,' continued Collins. 'And that, Colonel, is really why
we're here. You see, it appears that they exactly match those
found on your office safe door.'

'The same prints?' Harrison stared. 'You're sure?'

'Absolutely.' Collins tapped the toes of his shoes together.
'So,' he continued, looking down his long legs as if addressing
his elegant footwear, 'we have to assume that the same person
who raided your office also stabbed Mr Lloyd-Thomas. The
question is—why?' There was a short silence. 'The first theory,
the one preferred by the Inspector here, is that we have a
maniac loose.' The Superintendent looked round. 'According
to the Dean, Colonel, you may have seen this person before
the break-in, but, for reasons of your own, didn't choose to
tell us.'

Reddening, Harrison glanced up to see Dowley's blue eyes
fixed upon him.

'I did see someone, yes.'

'A woman apparently.'

'That was my impression.'

'And then there is the other theory.'

'Well?'

'I'm afraid this one is a little more frightening.' Collins smiled. 'I mean to you personally, Colonel.'

'Go on.'

'There's something we haven't told you. Apparently, the victim was carrying a music case when he was attacked. We found it thrown in the garth along with the knife.'

'You mean the attacker was after something,' said Harrison, 'something he or she thought was in the music case? I don't see what connection that's got with me unless...' His voice died.

'Exactly! Unless the attacker was after the thing he'd failed to find in your office.' The Superintendent smiled sympathetically. 'If it's true, I'm afraid, Colonel, that means the intended victim was not Lloyd-Thomas at all, but you.'

❀ ❀ ❀

From the kitchen, Winnie heard the policemen leave; she waited, expecting her husband to join her. Instead she heard him return to the sitting-room and shut the door. She bent again to the letter she was writing, but after a moment laid down her pen and wheeled herself into the hall.

'Whatever are you sitting here in the dark for?' she said, surprised to find him sitting motionless in the dusk.

'Leave the light, please.'

'What's happened?' Her voice grew suddenly alarmed. 'It isn't Mr Thomas, is it? He's not worse?'

He shook his head. 'Apparently, they've found a good set of fingerprints on the knife.'

Winnie frowned. 'But isn't that good?'

'The trouble is they exactly match the set found on my office safe.'

'They think it's you?'

He shook his head. 'I was with you and Ingrams, remember.'

'Then I'm lost—fingerprints in your office and then on the knife?' Suddenly she was frightened. 'You're not saying that someone was trying to kill you?'

'No, unfortunately.'

'Unfortunately! Whatever do you mean?'

'Just it would be easier than all this damned uncertainty.' Springing up, he strode across the room. 'This break-in business, it's just like the Dean's phone: I was absolutely certain it was being tapped, and it wasn't; I was sure that someone had been after the Harvey-Watson papers, and now I'm not.' He swung round. 'I'm frightened, Winnie—frightened I see things just because I expect them; either that, or I'm not seeing what really is there.'

'Look,' she said, wheeling forward, 'if it's the report you're worried about, why send it in at all? No one can make you. You don't want to damage an innocent man.'

'I said I would, so I must.' He shook his head. 'It's just I want more time to get my thoughts into some—' He broke off. The phone had started to ring.

For a moment, husband and wife looked at each other as the bell, loud and insistent, rang through the cottage, then Harrison made for the door. When he returned, however, he was smiling. 'It was only Ingrams. He wants us to go for dinner tonight and see in the New Year. I said we would. I hope you don't mind.'

'Of course not. That will be lovely.'

The warmth of the Dean's tone and the unexpected invitation superficially soothed Harrison's disquiet. Nevertheless, at a deeper level, his unease persisted. Later, when Winnie was preparing for the evening out, he returned to the study and, unlocking the centre drawer of the desk, drew out the report.

He read with steadily growing relief. Given the change in Harvey-Watson's political sympathies and his dangerous associates at Cambridge, the assessment of the bishop's political leanings was fair. As for Maurice Campion, his undoubted intimacy with Harvey-Watson, let alone his part in the secret meetings and the clandestine journeys abroad, meant that the same question-mark that hung over his dead mentor's loyalties must also hang over his. The exact nature and extent of the deep game the two men had played at the height of the cold war would, he thought, undoubtedly appear in the Brigadier's final report. In the meantime his own supplementary observations could stand: whatever the truth about the office break-in or the ridiculous muddle over the phone, on what little material evidence remained in the rifled papers, Campion's candidacy was clearly compromised.

New Year's dinner at the deanery was not to be a great success. As Margaret answered the door, a look of relief lit her face. 'Thank goodness you're here!' She leaned forward. 'I hope you don't mind, but we've also invited Canon Rope.' Seeing her guests' involuntary looks of dismay, she added quickly, 'The poor man's so alone now.'

Ingrams and Rope got up as the new arrivals entered the drawing-room. The Dean seemed subdued, but Rope came forward at once, all grin and polished teeth. 'Ah, Mrs Harrison,' he exclaimed, bending to shake hands, 'the Dean and I were just discussing your ravaging beast.'

Winnie looked startled, but Rope continued, 'Ravaging beast—you remember, surely? Your own expression for our Lord

Bishop of Derby.' With a spasm-like rub of his hands, he smirked like some wizened mischievous Puck.

Ingrams coughed. 'I think, Canon, until the question of the Primacy is finally settled we ought not to—'

'Quite, Dean!' interrupted Rope. 'Downing Street is taking a quite unconscionable time, is it not?' He grinned at Harrison. 'Your smoke-filled rooms, Colonel, yes?'

'I think,' said Margaret, intervening, 'it's time we ate.'

Rope's face shone with renewed enthusiasm. Rubbing his hands with anticipation, he followed his hostess as she wheeled Winnie out. Harrison, with Ingrams scowling beside him, brought up the tail of the little procession filing across the hall.

Dinner began in silence. Harrison, sitting at the Dean's right hand, looked down towards Rope, wondering again what had been the exact nature of the relationship between the benign if eccentric Cratchley and the self-absorbed, unlikable little gossip who now sat scooping and gnawing at his melon like some feasting marmoset?

'Matthew, how is the patient?' asked Winnie.

'Lloyd-Thomas?' The Dean forced a smile. 'Much better, I'm pleased to report—really quite his old self again.'

'Did he get a sight of his assailant?' asked Harrison, visualizing the Welshman's gloomy face on the hospital pillow.

Ingrams shook his head. 'Whoever it was, stabbed from behind. He heard the sound of running feet and then the knife was in his back.'

'Oh, awful!' murmured Winnie.

'And odd,' murmured Margaret, 'the same thing happening in the same place as it happened to poor Bob Cratchley.'

'Whoever the poor tormented creature is,' said her husband, 'I only pray that he or she is soon caught and given help.'

'Quite,' murmured Harrison.

'I must say, Mrs Ingrams,' interposed Rope loudly, as if

he hadn't heard a word, 'this melon is absolutely delicious!' He grinned around the table, then, bending, recommenced scraping the rind.

Thereafter the meal remained a muted affair with the Dean for the most part sunk in gloomy abstraction. However, as they were finishing the final course, he broke into one of the even longer than usual silences that had punctuated the meal. 'Richard, how are you getting on with the late Archibald of Calcutta?' He smiled at Winnie. 'I must admit to being surprised at your husband's sudden interest in minor Victorian bishops.'

Before Harrison could reply, Rope intruded. 'Cratchley's book? You're reading it, Colonel?' He tittered. 'You amaze me! I wouldn't have thought there was much of interest in those devotional offerings of his.'

Harrison heard the Dean sigh softly as the Canon returned to spooning up what remained of his crème caramel.

Over coffee in the drawing-room, Margaret and Winnie, with Rope in attendance, talked together while Harrison, sitting with Ingrams on the settee, tried to draw him into a discussion on the proposed restoration work on the gate-house. The television had been turned on with the volume low in anticipation of the midnight hour, and as his conversation with the Dean lapsed, Harrison found himself looking at the screen. Obviously some celebration of Hogmanay was being broadcast: couples in tartan were performing a highland reel. Idly he watched, admiring the graceful lightness of dancers and dance, when all at once he was seeing again Gillie dancing through the dining-room, the incongruous party-hat on his head. The Brigadier had looked surprised when he'd mentioned it. Had he been as wrong about that as he had been about the phone-tapping and the office break-in?

'My dear fellow, why the frown?' Ingrams was regarding him anxiously. 'Is everything all right?'

'I'm sorry, I was just remembering poor old Lloyd-Thomas.'

'Yes, indeed.' The Dean nodded. 'You know, I've been thinking, Richard, wouldn't it be better to postpone the opening of the coffin until his assailant is caught? Anyway,' he said, lowering his voice, 'I may have to be up in York for a few days.'

Unluckily, at that moment the wail of bagpipe music on the television suddenly ceased. Rope looked round. 'York?' His eyes shone. 'You're off to see Haverwell?' He rubbed his knees. 'Smoke-filled rooms with our number two on the list!'

'Come on, everyone,' said Margaret, hastily getting up. 'It's about to strike midnight. Matthew, would you please fill everyone's glass.'

Across Green Court came the first boom of the clock. Ingrams raised his glass. 'To a peaceful New Year.'

'Peaceful?' Rope's dentures gleamed. 'In light of your committee's nomination, Dean, that may be just a little too much to hope.'

❊ ❊ ❊

'Oh, you're not going to read!' protested Winnie sleepily as the bedside lamp went on.

After the evening at the deanery, Harrison felt unable to sleep. For half an hour he'd lain in the dark, staring up at the ceiling, his thoughts revolving around the enigma of Gillie's visit, the phone-tapping and the office break-in; indistinct, nebulous shades, his doubts swirled before him, phantom-like wisps beyond his grasp. At last, unable to bear it longer, he reached for a book.

Ordinarily, he could dip into *The Road to Oxiana* and lose himself almost at once; now, however, Robert Byron's pre-war Persia and Afghanistan couldn't hold him. After a few minutes he gave up. Instead, he looked at the other books piled on the bedside table. There, unopened since he'd carried it away from the Deanery, was Cratchley's life of Bishop Archibald.

Gazing at it, he thought of Rope's caustic quip. What had he called his dead friend's works—devotional offerings? The expression had grated at the time, but looking now at the dull brown dust-jacket, he could only too easily imagine how accurate the assessment had been. Nevertheless, almost despite himself, he reached out and extracted the unalluring volume from the pile.

The writing was surprisingly good; there was a crispness and pace to the style, a deftness of touch that, combined with a slightly quirky humour, carried Harrison over the first page. As he read, behind the words he seemed to perceive the writer's face—Cratchley, with that curious lop-sided little grin, Cratchley hurrying past with his customary affectionate wave. Suddenly it was unbearable: the writer too close, the murdered man too real. Closing the book, he stared ahead, seeing Cratchley among the shadowed spectators, pointing upwards; he could almost hear the enthusiasm in his voice, almost see his enraptured smile, and then, as if from nowhere, the mysterious figure sidling from the blackness, needle outstretched.

To escape, Harrison flipped the book open again. And there again was the photograph of Bishop Archibald standing before his admirers, croquet mallet in hand. In Victorian stock and gaiters, the shirt-sleeved figure appeared as quaintly anachronistic as when he'd glanced at it first. However, now as he studied it, he noticed something in the corner he hadn't seen before—a small blob of white. Holding it close to the lamp, he saw what it was—a dog, a small terrier of some sort, looking towards the bishop in rapt and excited anticipation.

The little dog changed everything: the absurdly quaint figure in flannel shirt and gaiters in the heat of the Calcutta summer a hundred years before was suddenly someone loved, a living being, a man like himself. For the first time, Harrison studied the long-dead cleric's face with sympathetic interest. As he did so, memory stirred: the face before him bore a striking resemblance to another he'd recently seen.

Across the silent precincts, the clock struck two.

It was no good—he couldn't think whose face. He turned to the front to see if there was another photograph of the bishop. As he did so, he caught sight of the dedication.

> *To my dear wife and helpmeet, grand-daughter of Ronald Henry Archibald.*

'Of course!' he exclaimed aloud, sitting up: the likeness was to the photograph of Ruth Cratchley he'd seen in the cottage and, similarly, to Sarah.

'Are you all right?'

Winnie's face had emerged from the duvet. Half-asleep, she blinked at him anxiously.

'Look at this,' he said, flipping back to the photograph. 'Who does it remind you of?'

His wife gazed blearily at the picture held under her nose and shook her head.

'Sarah Cratchley, can't you see? Bishop Archibald was Ruth Cratchley's grandfather.'

'Really,' murmured Winnie, re-closing her eyes.

But Harrison was not giving up. 'Cratchley dedicated the book to his wife. Remember Rope's phrase tonight—devotional offerings? What he meant was that Cratchley's choice of subjects had an emotional connection, that those he chose to write about were connected to his friends and those he loved. After all, why else write about an obscure nineteenth-century bishop?'

'So?' came the weary voice muffled under the duvet.

'So it brings up the question neither of us has asked: why did Cratchley ever choose to write about Harvey-Watson at all?

What was the old fellow's connection with his subject? In other words, to whom was he going to dedicate the book?'

'Does it matter?' Winnie's voice was hardly audible now.

'That,' said Harrison determinedly, laying down the book, 'is what I hope to find out tomorrow.'

On Winnie's insistence, Harrison delayed ringing the deanery until mid-morning to allow their hosts of the previous evening time to recover. With growing impatience, he sat in the study after breakfast. At last, as the hall-clock struck ten-thirty, he picked up the receiver.

It was Margaret who answered. He thanked her for the dinner-party, then asked if he might speak to Ingrams. He was shocked to be told that there had been a telephone call early that morning summoning him to York, and that she was just back from having taken him to the station.

Harrison's disappointment was intense: apart from Canon Rope, the Dean was the only one he could think of who might be able to tell him for whom the book was being written. As he had no intention of searching out Rope for a possible answer, there was nothing to do for the moment but try to be patient.

For this, the last day of his holidays, Winnie had arranged a visit to one of her friends from art-school who now lived in Essex. The time passed pleasantly enough, but as soon as they were home, Harrison called round at the deanery for news.

It was worse than he'd imagined; the Dean had phoned Margaret only an hour before to say that he was unlikely to be back before the weekend at the earliest. Disconsolately, he returned to Bread Yard, more than ever wishing he'd over-ridden Winnie's objection and rung Ingrams first thing as he'd planned.

Next morning, diocesan work recommenced. At once, Harrison's life was occupied with the results of the cold snap over Christmas. Letters came in droves, the phone rang almost continuously; it seemed that every rectory, vicarage, church and parish hall in the entire diocese had burst pipes, reinforcing his impression that all ecclesiastical structures had a unique predisposition for leaks. On the third day of Ingrams's absence, however, the question of Cratchley's particular choice of subject returned to his mind when he met Rope in Green Court on his way back from a hurried lunch. Whatever his reservations, he decided to broach the matter at once and hurried forward to meet him.

Rope seemed more aquiver with excitement than usual.

'Well, Colonel,' he burst out before Harrison could get out a word, 'battle royal is joined, and our own Dean is in the very heat of the fray!' He seized Harrison's wrist. 'Poor Haverwell! He is being mightily pressed to back down. If he does, it's a *fait accompli*: the PM will be left with just the ravaging beast!' He rubbed his hands. 'Before long we shall have blood on the floor!'

Looking down at the old man writhing before him in apparently fiendish delight at the controversy tearing his Church, Harrison felt an overpowering repugnance. Excusing himself, he walked on to his office, deciding that the question of Cratchley's choice of subject would, after all, have to await Ingrams's return.

Saturday came and there was still no sign of the Dean. Next morning he was in the middle of poaching eggs when the paper-boy rang; Winnie went to the door; a few moments later he heard the sound of her chair returning.

'You'd better look at this.' She was in the doorway, holding up the copy of the *Sunday Times* with the bold headlines: CABINET SPLIT OVER CHOICE OF ARCHBISHOP: PM UNDER CHURCH PRESSURE.

For a moment he stared as if mesmerized by the words, then, taking the paper, he began skimming through the front page.

> Maurice Campion, the controversial Bishop of Derby, variously described by the Home Secretary at the party conference last summer as 'an Etonian Ayatollah' and 'a pontificating busybody', appears increasingly likely to become the 104th Archbishop of Canterbury. According to our religious correspondent, powerful pressures, both from within the Church and outside, are pushing a reluctant Prime Minister into recommending his name to the Queen. Reliable sources suggest that Campion's candidacy for the Primacy has already caused, in the words of a senior minister, 'an unholy row' among Cabinet members. The final decision has apparently been postponed for the present, but with persistent rumours that the Archbishop of York may ask for his name to be withdrawn, pressure on the Government is likely to prove irresistible.

Throwing the paper aside, Harrison swung round. 'You know what this means, Winnie? If it's got this far, then Greville's boys haven't been able to come up with anything substantial against Campion or there just hasn't been time. Either way, if he still thinks the fellow's a risk, he'll want to use anything he's got.'

'Including your report?'

'Exactly, and before you say anything, Winnie, if and when he demands it, I have no justification for holding it back.'

For a second she looked as if she was about to plead, but instead, saying brusquely, 'My egg's getting cold,' she pushed to the table.

Outside the morning greyed. By the time Harrison left for Matins, drizzle was falling. In Green Court he saw the pale face of somebody he took to be the Archdeacon gazing from Dorothy Crocker's bedroom.

His grim mood persisted throughout the service, the sight of the Dean's empty stall intensifying his longing for Ingrams's return. Winnie was in the sitting-room when he reached home. From her face, he knew at once that what he'd been dreading since he'd seen the paper that morning had happened.

'Greville?'

'He left a number: it's on the pad.'

'Right,' he muttered, turning for the door.

'Richard!' She looked at him beseechingly. 'Can't you at least wait until after lunch?'

He steeled himself. 'I'd rather get it over with.' She heard the murmur of his voice from the study and then heard him ring off. A few moments later he was back.

'Well?'

'I said I needed more time. I've got to the end of the month at the latest.' He came over and took her hands. 'If I'm going to get to the bottom of this matter by then, I'm going to need all the help you can give me.'

Winnie smiled. 'When you were in church,' she said, 'it occurred to me that it's time we spoke to Sarah again.'

Before ringing, Harrison and Winnie checked their copy of *Crockford's* to see if the clerical directory could provide a clue to the connection between her uncle and Harvey-Watson. The result was disappointing: Cratchley had been an Oxford man; after ordination he'd taken a curacy in the Bristol diocese, then had served the war years as a naval chaplain—where, presumably as such, he'd met the Brigadier in Alexandria. After the war, his ministry had been spent entirely in the Canterbury diocese. Thus, at least according to the sparse facts provided, there was no direct link between Cratchley himself and either the diocese or bishop of Manchester. Whatever connection there was, therefore, must have been indirect: some third party or intermediary obviously lay between the two dead clerics.

Lunch over, with Winnie beside him, Harrison rang the Islington flat. Sarah answered almost immediately. Though clearly surprised to hear from him, she seemed genuinely pleased. When he asked how she'd been, she told him she was just back from staying with friends on the Continent. There was a gaiety to her voice that had not been there before, and with some reluctance, therefore, he moved to the subject of her uncle's book.

She could tell him virtually nothing: she had no idea why he had chosen Harvey-Watson.

'Can't you remember anything at all?' asked Harrison, his disappointment acute.

There was a pause while she thought. 'When he came to stay last September,' she said, 'I remember showing him on the map how to find the way to somewhere he needed for his research.'

'Lambeth Palace?'

The girl laughed. 'He knew his way there. No, this was to somewhere in West London, some really out of the way place in Acton. I think it was a Church; I'm almost sure it was.'

'Really.' Harrison glanced at his wife who was listening, head close to his. 'Check our London *A to Z*,' he whispered. He turned back to the phone. 'Sarah, you don't remember the name of this place?'

'I've got an idea it began with a B—a woman's name: Saint Brenda's or Saint Beatrice's, something like that.' Sarah paused. 'I remember there was a choice between catching a train from Paddington or a long walk from the tube—in the end, Uncle decided to take the tube.'

'You don't know which tube station it was?'

'No—but I do remember him saying that it would give him the chance to walk through Bedford Park.'

'The estate?'

'Yes.'

Winnie had the *A to Z* open. Her finger moved across the page. 'Turnham Green tube station is just south of Bedford Park,' she whispered.

Harrison nodded.

'Could it have been Turnham Green, Sarah?' he asked.

'I think so, yes.'

Husband and wife's eyes met triumphantly.

'You don't remember, I suppose, the road or why he was going there?'

'I'm sorry, Colonel, I just wasn't that interested.' There was a sudden choke to her voice.

Harrison felt the receiver being drawn from his hand; next moment, Winnie was brightly introducing herself. Leaving the women to talk, Harrison returned to the sitting-room to stare despondently out at the leaden sky. He was as far as ever from tracing the link between the writer and the book. The phone rang off; a few moments later, Winnie pushed herself into the room.

'Look,' she said, holding out the opened *A to Z* as she entered, 'north from Bedford Park the nearest mainline station is Acton Central and it's on the direct line from Paddington.' She drew a ring on the page. 'If it was only a short walk from the station, the church has got to be in this area here.'

Harrison shrugged. 'If we found it, would it help?' he said. 'Presumably, the vicar or whatever it is will be just some old geezer like Titmouse from Harvey-Watson's Manchester days.'

'Cratchley thought it worth the visit. Anyway, what other idea have you got?'

'I shall ring his publishers tomorrow,' replied Harrison,

thinking of the idea only as he spoke it. 'He must have discussed the book with them.'

Having to wait until the following day meant more delay, and when Harrison did ring the SPCK next morning, it was only to learn that Cratchley's particular editor, a Mr Ellis, had retired and was now living in Ross-on-Wye. To make matters worse, his successor was unhelpful; she had never met Cratchley and was reluctant to pass on the retired editor's number. On the other hand, when Harrison at last got through, Ellis was very forthcoming: he'd had a great regard for Cratchley, whose work, it appeared, had been highly esteemed in certain quarters. However, over the particular choice of Harvey-Watson, he could only remember the Canon ringing to say how excited he was by his latest choice of subject. When pressed, he recalled Cratchley mentioning a friend who had put him on to Harvey-Watson; he didn't know who the person was, but he'd gained the impression that he or she lived in close proximity to the writer, for he distinctly remembered Cratchley saying how grateful he was at being able to do the bulk of the research without having to leave the precincts at all.

If anything, the conversation only increased Harrison's frustration: now that his idea of a missing link was confirmed, and knowing that whoever it was who had given the murdered man the idea for his fatal subject actually lived among the cathedral community, his yearning for Ingrams's return intensified the more. However, as Winnie pointed out when he vented his frustration over lunch, there was no guarantee that Cratchley had confided in the Dean at all. In the meantime, she again suggested they follow up the one lead they had: the West London church the dead man had visited.

Supper over, that evening the two of them sat together at the kitchen table to trace the church in the area around Acton Central station with the aid of the London phone directories Winnie had persuaded the local library to send round. The search continued for an hour without success: under the Church of England listings there was no church dedicated to a female saint in walking distance of the station, and none at all beginning with the letter B.

'Let's try Roman Catholic,' suggested Winnie.

'There's not such a place!' Harrison burst out after another half an hour's fruitless search. 'Sarah must have got it wrong.'

'What about doing it the other way?' suggested Winnie. 'Let's look at the map to see if we can spot anything on that.'

It took only a matter of moments to find, just north of the station, a small cross denoting a place of worship.

'It must be the one,' said Winnie, 'but how do we find its name if it isn't under either the Anglican or RC listings?'

'That's easy.' Harrison began flipping through a directory. 'I'll ring the local police—they'll know.' He scribbled the number and got up.

'You're going to do it now?'

'Why not?' From the kitchen, she heard him ring, then ring off; he re-entered the room smiling. 'St Barbara,' he announced.

'Barbara? But why isn't it listed under the Anglican churches?'

Harrison laughed. 'Because, my dear love, this place in Acton isn't a church as such, and it certainly doesn't belong to the Church of England.'

'Well, what is it then and who does it belong to?' Instead of answering, Harrison picked up the directory L–R and flipped through almost to the end. 'There it is.' His thumb lay across the bottom right-hand corner. Immediately below it appeared the words: *St Barbara Church ho. (Archim).*

'*Archim*—what does that stand for?'

'Archimandrite.' He smiled. 'It's from the Greek, *archi*—first, and *mandra*—an enclosure or monastery. In other words, it meant an abbot originally. This place in Acton where Cratchley went is the fellow's residence!'

Winnie frowned. 'But I don't see. What was Harvey-Watson's connection with the Greek Orthodox?'

Harrison smiled mysteriously. 'Not Greek, my dear.' He lifted his thumb from the directory page revealing the words: *The Russian Orthodox Church in Exile.* 'Yes,' he said, enjoying her surprise, 'Cratchley went to London to meet a Russian.' He rubbed his hands. 'If nothing else, we at least seem to have found the Soviet connection!'

The cathedral clock struck the hour. As the last boom faded, Winnie stirred and, rolling on to her back, stared open-eyed at the ceiling. 'I just don't see it,' she said.

'What?' Harrison murmured sleepily.

'The Soviet connection. The Russian Church here in Britain is made up of White Russians, or at least the descendants of those who fled the Revolution. They're the last people in the world to be carrying out the Kremlin's wishes, whatever those might be!'

'They're still Russians.'

'Yes, dear,' murmured Winnie wearily.

'Anyway, Soviet connection or not, the question remains: what the hell was Cratchley doing visiting a Russian anyway? What has a confounded Archimandrite got to do with a dead Anglican bishop, for God's sake?'

'Just that, I suppose,' answered Winnie, laughing.

'Very funny!' He sighed. 'If only we knew who in the precincts is the person connected to Harvey-Watson! When the hell is Ingrams ever going to return?'

'I don't think you'll have to wait long for that.'

'What do you mean?'

'Margaret told me today that Dorothy Crocker is much worse: apparently, she's fallen into a coma. The doctor wants her moved to the hospital. The Archdeacon, of course, won't hear of it.'

Harrison was silent for a few moments. 'Strange, isn't it,' he murmured, 'she sent that wreath to Cratchley's funeral, and very soon people will be sending wreaths to hers.'

Winnie didn't reply.

'Anyway,' he continued, 'what's all that got to do with Ingrams getting back?'

'The Archdeacon has sent a message asking Matthew to be here when she dies.'

'I see.'

Oddly enough, the likelihood of the Dean's imminent return and thus the opportunity of at last perhaps finding the missing link didn't excite Harrison now. At that moment he was thinking of Crocker's pale, tormented face in the crypt; he thought of the dying woman, remembering her, tall, grey-haired, digging in the archdeaconry garden.

'Richard, why did she send it?'

'Send what?'

'Her own wreath to Canon Cratchley's funeral? Why didn't she just have her name added to her brother's?'

'I don't know,' murmured Harrison. 'Let me sleep.'

'No, wake up!' Winnie's voice was urgent. 'Have we been looking in the wrong direction? Because Canon Cratchley's book was about a bishop and the Church, we automatically think that it had to be a man who inspired the idea, but there are also plenty of women who work for the Church.'

Still half asleep, Harrison lay, his mind returning to the Basset Underhill churchyard, to the gusts of the wind, the smell of the pigs, the ring of white flowers on the winter grass. Then all at once he was completely awake and sitting up.

'My God, Winnie, you've got it! That's it—Dot—the diminutive of Dorothy!' He was bolt upright now. 'What a damned fool I've been! Of course, Dorothy Crocker was Harvey-Watson's secretary!'

He switched on the bedside light and sat, his mind racing as the implications flooded in. 'Then it must have been Dorothy who originally sorted and filed the papers! That means she knows it all: what was in the papers that have been removed! The truth about Harvey-Watson and Campion! The entire Russian involvement!'

Jumping out of bed, he went to the window and looked out at the courtyard; beyond the encircling walls, he could imagine the orange glow of light in the archdeaconry window. Heart chilling, he looked back to the bed. 'In a coma, you say?'

Winnie nodded. 'And she's not expected to come out of it.'

Harrison beat his palm with his fist. 'It's taken me all this time to find where the truth is, and now—' his voice rose in anguish—'just when I've found it, it's already beyond my reach!'

CHAPTER TWELVE

Harrison went straight to the archdeaconry after breakfast next morning. He'd slept only by fits and starts and, perhaps due to fatigue, there seemed an odd unreality to everything as he stood under the porch that dank, overcast morning and rapped on the door.

Feet echoed on marble; the door opened, and the Archdeacon faced him. If Harrison had slept badly, Dr Crocker looked as if he hadn't slept at all. Lean, unshaven and ghastly pale, his eyes puffy and bloodshot, he emerged from the gloomy portals of the house a Lazarus newly summoned from the tomb.

'Colonel Harrison?' Bewilderment and disappointment combined in his face for an instant. 'Forgive me, Colonel, when I heard your knock, I rather hoped it was the Dean.'

'How is Miss Crocker?'

The thin mouth twitched. 'Mercifully unconscious—her sufferings, I pray, are finally at an end.' He struggled for a smile. 'But thank you for coming to inquire. It was most kind.'

'I won't disturb you further.' Harrison backed away; clearly, his faint hope of questioning the dying woman was futile. However, Crocker stepped forward. 'Please, Colonel, I would be most grateful if you could join me for a cup a coffee.'

Reluctantly Harrison followed him down the high-roofed hall, noticing in the drab dimness a number of austere steel-engravings, a few wilting plants and a dusty college trophy-oar hanging on a dark-painted wall. Two women were in the kitchen, obviously nurses or helpers of some sort. When coffee had been made, they went upstairs while Harrison, cup in hand, followed the Archdeacon into his study.

It was bleakly cold in the room. As they drank their coffee, inexplicable sounds of movement came from above, where, behind closed doors, death held sway and the floorboards creaked to the feet of invisible initiates holding its vigils and performing its rites.

Harrison, head heavy from lack of sleep, gazed blankly at the primly neat desk beneath the window with its pile of unopened letters, the empty brass vase and the folded copy of *The Independent*. A bluebottle, drowsy with winter, began humming at the window. Disturbed by the insect, the Archdeacon glanced up, and seeing his guest's eyes on the paper, smiled bleakly.

'How ridiculously trivial and distant the whole world seems to me at this moment, Colonel.'

'Quite,' murmured Harrison, his eye catching sight of the headline on *the Independent's* front page: HAVERWELL BACKS DOWN: CHURCH UNITES BEHIND CAMPION'S SELECTION.

He cleared his throat. 'I've never actually spoken to your sister, Archdeacon, though I've often seen her, of course.'

Crocker nodded. 'She was a very private person.' He hastily corrected himself. 'I mean, Dot is very strong; since she was a girl, she has always been very self-contained and determined.'

The familiar diminutive came like a needle. Harrison glanced automatically at the ceiling. He'd been correct—the woman above was indeed the unlikely third of that extraordinary triumvirate that had secretly conferred those years before with Uspensky, Kolnikov and the other mysterious representatives of Stalin's Russia.

'I'm sure your sister has many friends,' he remarked, glancing at the Archdeacon who was staring across the room.

'Friends?' Getting up, Crocker gazed out at the desolate garden outside. He turned back to Harrison, a melancholy smile on his haggard face, and shook his head. 'Her friends have mostly crossed over long ago.'

'Crossed over?' A vision rose momentarily of border-posts, barbed-wire and barking dogs.

'Yes, Colonel, into that world of light to which she herself is journeying now.'

'Of course.' Harrison swallowed. He shook his head to clear his brain. 'Canon Cratchley? Was he one of those friends?'

The Archdeacon turned back to the window. 'I would hear them laughing together. God help me, I resented it.' He looked round. 'Robert Cratchley was a warm, loving man, and Dot, of course, was fascinated by the book he was writing. It had been her own idea.'

'The Harvey-Watson biography? She suggested it?'

'Yes.'

'Did you know him?'

'The bishop?' Crocker shrugged slightly. 'Not well, but I met him, of course.' He returned to his chair. 'Dot worked for him for many years. She only came here to act as my housekeeper after the great man died.'

'Great man?'

Crocker flushed. 'According to Dot.'

'You didn't like him?'

The Archdeacon stared fixedly towards the window for a moment, saying nothing, then looked round. 'Dot had a great deal of affection for Harvey-Watson. I suppose I felt excluded. I was resentful.' He paused slightly. 'You see, Colonel, my sister virtually brought me up. She was all to me, mother, sister and friend.'

Harrison cleared his throat. 'I must be getting to the office. Miss Simpson will be wondering where I am.'

In the hall, Crocker put out his hand. 'It was very good of you to come.' Instead of letting go, he held on to Harrison's hand, his Adam's apple convulsing for a moment or two as he appeared to struggle with himself. Calming, he looked directly into the other's eyes. 'Colonel, I wonder if you would like to see her before you go.'

There was a terrible appeal in the eyes behind the steel-rimmed glasses. Why exactly Crocker should wish to show him his unconscious, dying sister, Harrison couldn't imagine, unless in that stiff, possessive man was an overwhelming desire in these final hours to share at last with somebody the woman who had obviously been the crutch and jewel of his life. At that moment, there in the drab hall, he felt something akin to love for the gaunt lonely figure before him. 'Yes, Archdeacon,' he heard himself say, 'I would very much like to see your sister.'

Dorothy Crocker lay still. Her breathing was laboured, but the pain that for months had ravaged her face had finally released its hold; her features had relaxed, and, looking down at the unconscious, grey-haired woman, Harrison saw behind the mask of a dying elderly woman the face of the young woman and the girl and, further back still, even that of the child.

He heard the door open. A nurse entered and whispered to the Archdeacon. A look of relief crossed his face. He turned to leave, but as Harrison went to follow, he gestured him to stay.

The door closed and all was silent except for the laboured short breaths from the bed.

Raising his head, Harrison looked out across the garden: the clouds were thinning; through watery sunlight, tiny figures moved to and fro on the pathways of Green Court. For a few moments he remained looking out, then turned back to contemplate the unconscious form on the bed.

In appearance, Dorothy Crocker was typically English, pale in complexion, rather horse-faced, with heavy, somewhat masculine features. She had obviously never been beautiful, but even now, in her shrunken, wasted features, remained those marks of that strength and determination which her brother had mentioned.

A writing-desk stood in a corner; next to it, a small bookcase. Harrison glanced through the contents: a history of the Mothers' Union stood next to Elizabeth Goudge's life of Christ. Turning away, he noticed behind the oxygen cylinders by the bedhead a low table on which stood a crucifix and two mounted black and white photographs. Going over, he picked one up.

It was a close-up shot of brother and sister, both in tennis dress and carrying rackets. Stephen Crocker looked about eighteen, Dorothy a few years older, both with such grave expressions as if even then each glimpsed the lonely, hard track ahead. Harrison glanced back at the emaciated face on the pillows, then gently replaced the photograph. He picked up the second: a full-length shot of three figures on a beach, sea behind. In the centre was Dorothy in a flowery 'fifties dress, flanked by two men in open-necked shirts. Across the bottom was written in the same neat hand as the contents lists on the box-file lids: *H W, Maurice and yours truly—Vaasa 1953.*

Returning to the window, Harrison held the photograph to the light, conscious all the time of the laboured slow breathing continuing on with machine-like regularity.

The face of the young Campion was remarkably similar to the face appearing now almost daily on the nation's television screens: there was the same hawkish handsomeness, the same aristocratic poise. But it was the third, far older figure of the group that held Harrison's attention as he gazed for the first time at the man he'd hunted and pursued through the files.

If his chaplain had something of the eagle or hawk about him, Bishop Harvey-Watson undoubtedly belonged to the earth: he was a short, stocky man whose heavy ox-like face looked directly into the camera, the probing intelligence bright in his eyes.

Conscious always of Dorothy's breathing, Harrison looked round at the bookcase, the plain orange curtains at his side, the equally plain crucifix, and then again at the ravaged grey face propped high on the pillows. Glancing back to the photograph, he once more stared at the young woman, smiling with such open and evident devotion at the older man at her side.

The nurse waiting outside the door looked surprised as he hurriedly left. Descending to the hall, he made straight for the front door, hearing the murmur of voices from the study as he passed. Only when he was outside did he pause and stare up at the cathedral towers looming against the misty indeterminate sky.

He took a step forward, then again paused, his hands knotted as if to check his racing thoughts: so, after all, Dorothy had spoken; a voice had risen from the grave.

Dorothy Crocker had spoken all right: the strong, unbeautiful face, the room, the books, above all, that expression on the face of the young woman in the photograph looking round at Harvey-Watson, had spoken with an eloquence and a clarity that her lips could never have achieved. Unambiguous and utterly convincing, her whole life, her very being, had been in that room: guileless, simple and strong, there had been decency, even innocence, in all that she was and had done.

The implications were huge and absolutely devastating in their effect: his whole theory on the case, all the certitude underlying the report in his desk, had collapsed. Dorothy had originally compiled and ordered the Harvey-Watson papers: everything, therefore, had passed through her hands, and thus, by implication, had met with her approval—the approval of that same decent strong soul who had encouraged Cratchley to write his book. The conclusion was inescapable: the files had been as innocent as the dying woman's love for the long-dead married man.

But why then had the papers been rifled? If the original source material had been innocuous, why had the manuscript been stolen from Sarah's flat? More questions sprang by the moment as he walked on in a daze. If it had all been so innocent, what had been the reason for Cratchley's strange warning to the Brigadier? Above all, why had the old man been murdered at all? He halted. He had answers to nothing: he was back again at the beginning without explanations or certainty at all.

There was a call from behind. Turning, he saw Ingrams wave from the front door and hurry towards him. He remembered the murmur of voices from the study. So that's why the Archdeacon had left the room: at Crocker's urgent request, the Dean had at last returned.

'Thank goodness I've caught you!' Panting slightly, Ingrams reached him. 'I didn't realize you had left the house.'

'I had to get back to the office,' he murmured.

'Of course. It was very good of you to spare the time for Stephen. He is most appreciative.' Glancing back, he shook his head sadly. 'I fear our dear Archdeacon is in a very poor way.' The Dean looked tired and strained; his hair was ruffled, his dark suit crumpled and creased. 'I'm afraid,' he continued, 'I have a favour to ask. I know how encumbered you are, but Stephen has just made a request, a plea rather, to which I could only accede.' Ingrams looked troubled. 'He has asked that the coffin be opened before Dorothy dies.'

'I see.'

'I wish I did!' Ingrams sighed. 'Still, I have promised that if the Museum can arrange it, we'll have the coffin opened tonight.'

'Tonight!'

'Tomorrow will be too late,' said the Dean. 'Look, Richard, could you possibly arrange with Mr Keates to have his men in the crypt at about seven tonight with their tools?'

'Of course.' Harrison thought for a moment. 'We'll need the city pathologist in attendance.'

'Is that really necessary?'

'It's the law if there's any dead body involved. But don't worry, I'll phone the authorities and explain the whole matter. I'm sure they'll oblige us if they can.'

'My dear fellow, where would I be without your good sense and worldly wisdom?' Ingrams smiled affectionately. 'Well, I'd better return to poor Stephen and Dorothy.' He turned to retrace his steps, then stopped. 'You will impress on the men the need for absolute secrecy.'

'Of course.'

Ingrams nodded, and with a slight wave, resumed his walk back towards the silent house.

As before, the screened-off area was brilliantly lit. Blinking against the glare, Harrison led his small party to where the coffin rested on its trestle supports as if lying in state.

'Ah, you are here! Good!' Ingrams moved forward, greeting each of the arrivals by name, then looked round to where the two archæologists stood. 'Well, gentlemen, I think we can now proceed at once.'

As the men moved to their positions beside the coffin, Harrison glanced about. The Dean's desire for secrecy had obviously been strictly observed as, apart from himself, the few that were there all attended in an official or semi-official capacity. Prebendary Richards, as Chapter Secretary, presumably was present to represent the cathedral administration. Standing next to him was the surprisingly jovial figure of the city pathologist. In tweed jacket and yellow waistcoat, pink-faced, with tight-curled hair and flamboyant side-burns, Dr Brooke looked a more suitable figure for the racecourse than for the macabre yet solemn occasion which he now attended. The only others not directly concerned with the actual operation were the Archdeacon and Simcocks. These two stood together immediately in front of the casket, the former—ice-pale, gaunt, tall, a beech in winter—stood head bowed, while his unlikely companion, already mopping his face from the heat of the lamps, stared in round-eyed wonder at every movement of the archæologists and their helpers.

Under Dr Kemp's direction, Dill and Pennyfeather applied their chisels to the base of the lid. Next moment the crypt rang to the crack of their hammers. Inch by inch, the two men began slowly moving apart, working their way round the oblong shape as they drove through the seal between the lid and the massive repository below.

As the hammers thudded in bursts, Harrison watched impassively.

After the devastating revelation in the dying woman's room and the subsequent collapse of all his theories about the murder, he'd felt nothing but a numbed confusion. After parting from Ingrams, he'd turned to the organization of the present event without any sense of anticipation or excitement at all, finding in it merely temporary relief from the confusion into which his mind had been thrown.

The glare of the arc lights, the incessant tap of the hammers, together with his weariness, brought on an almost trance-like state. As if in a dream, he observed all before him: the concentration on the men's faces; the gleam of the hammer-heads; the frozen expression of the other watchers; the dull greyness of the coffin itself.

Sudden silence jerked him back to reality: the hammers had stopped; Dill and Pennyfeather were straightening, grinning at each other across the loosened lid. A few hurried words, then the crowbars were inserted. A questioning glance from Kemp to the Dean and the pressure was applied. Dill and Pennyfeather leaning down on their bars, Keates lending his weight. A tearing cracking echoed through the low-roofed chamber.

The sound stopped abruptly; the men stepped back. After so many hundreds of years, so many lifetimes, the massive lid was free.

Now the seal had broken, it was as if some force or spirit within the coffin had been released. Harrison's endlessly revolving thoughts disappeared; his concentration and interest were now on the coffin, and almost involuntarily he took a step forward. Others did the same. Only Crocker didn't move. Instead, crossing himself, he began soundlessly moving his lips.

Keates, Pennyfeather and Dill, aided by Dr Kettle, each took a corner of the lid. Kemp, standing at the foot, glanced again at the Dean. Ingrams nodded briefly.

'Right, together then!'

At Kemp's voice, the lid was slowly raised; an inch of light gleamed below, then, struggling under its weight, the four moved it clear, finally laying it on the floor, its crudely-cut motif seeming more pronounced than ever in the glare of the lights.

Dr Brooke now took over. Stepping forward, he moved round the back of the coffin and peered into the opened recess. There was absolute silence. For moments, nothing moved in the entire crypt apart from the Archdeacon's lips quivering in prayer.

Dr Brooke remained staring down into the coffin, frowning as he did so. He at last looked up and stared round, wondering perplexity in his face. He then gazed down again into the coffin, his head shaking slightly as if either not understanding or believing what he saw.

In that frozen interval, Harrison's mind leapt to the scene of Thomas Cromwell's commissioners arriving at Durham Cathedral to ransack St Cuthbert's shrine—the flickering torch-light in the nave, the masons' hammers, a commissioner climbing up to peer into the opened tomb—then the startled voice ringing out as he saw, in horror and disbelief, not the dry bones and dust he'd expected, but the as-if-sleeping, utterly undecomposed body of the seven-hundred-years-dead saint.

Brooke leant further forward and began reaching in with both hands. There was a slight intake of breath from the Dean. From the corner of his eye, Harrison saw Simcocks's hand reach out to steady the now visibly trembling Archdeacon.

Slowly the pathologist straightened, lifting something out. Harrison felt the back of his neck tingle.

Brooke's hands emerged, then, like a priest with the chalice, he raised whatever it was up past his face into the blazing light. With a faint cry, Crocker fell upon his knees. The other onlookers, however, stood transfixed, gazing up as if mesmerized by the monstrosity held before them between the pathologist's hands.

It was a skull—huge, with massive jaw, hideous teeth, the forehead low and long—the whole thing shaped like the head of some grotesquely caricatured neolithic man.

'Heaven preserve us!' muttered Ingrams, face aghast.

'Merciful God! What is it, man?' cried out Prebendary Richards, one hand raised as if attempting to ward off a blow.

Incongruously, Dr Brooke suddenly laughed. In that brief moment Harrison, still reeling from the horror, wondered whether it was he or the pathologist going mad. Dr Brooke, however, laughed again, and the mirth was clear in his healthy, florid face. 'Pig!' he cried, holding the object towards them. 'See? The skull of your common-or-garden sixteenth-century hog!'

Brooke turned suddenly from officiating priest to party conjuror: his arms dived again into the coffin and rose again, a large bone in either hand. 'Tibia,' he announced triumphantly, holding out a blackened hunk of bone towards the onlookers. 'Probably ox,' he said turning the thing in the light. He looked to the other hand. 'Fibula.' Peering at it closely, he nodded. 'Horse,' he pronounced, grinning, 'Yes, definitely horse!'

Crocker had risen from the floor. He stood now in ghastly stillness, staring dumbstruck at the whiskered pathologist. For the others, however, the spell was broken. Harrison, with Kettle on one side and Ingrams on the other, moved forward to peer down at the bones at the bottom of the coffin.

Leaning in, Brooke raked through the debris with both hands. 'Sheep,' he said, lifting a bone and dropping it. He picked up another. 'Deer, perhaps.' He smiled round. 'All animal anyway. Kitchen refuse, I'd guess.'

'Sir, are you all right?'

Simcocks's voice was urgent. Harrison turned to see the Verger supporting the slumped body of the Archdeacon. Next moment, Ingrams and Richards were bending to assist. Between their hands, Harrison saw the Archdeacon's face, pale as a death-mask, mouth lolling.

'Help him home if you would, Mr Simcocks,' instructed Ingrams as Crocker's eyes opened and blinked uncomprehendingly at the circle of faces looking down. As Crocker was borne away, Ingrams turned to the two archaeologists. 'How is this possible?' he asked, waving down at the brittle, time-blackened bones.

Kemp shrugged: 'Very simple, Dean—a bluff, a decoy if you like.' He gave a short laugh. 'An almost literal attempt to throw dust into somebody's eyes!'

'I don't understand.' The Dean frowned. 'What do you mean? Dust into whose eyes?'

'King Henry's commissioners presumably,' answered Kemp. 'When they were reported on their way, the monks must have quickly secreted Becket's body, then shovelled a pile of dry bones into an old coffin, thrown in the first skull they could get, scratched a crude crozier on the lid and then buried it here in the desperate hope that if the puritans started digging around they'd find it and think they'd found Becket's bones.'

Dazed, Ingrams shook his head. 'But why animal bones? Surely that wouldn't have tricked them for a moment!'

Kemp smiled. 'I'm not so sure, Dean. We all tend to see what we expect.'

'*Surget Veritas!*'

All turned as Harrison spoke the words. He had stepped back and was staring at the emblazoned coat-of-arms and the motto on the weathered stone. From his look of horror and anger he might have been confronting some hideous demon who squatted gibbering and grinning at him, invisible to the rest.

'Richard, are you all right?'

For a second, Harrison's eyes met the Dean's, then he turned away. 'I'm sorry,' he said, 'but I must get home at once.' Before Ingrams could get out a word, he'd turned and hurried out.

With an impatient sigh, Winnie pressed the button on the television control. The screen faded and the room went silent.

Pushing herself to the window, she peered between the curtains into the dark. Nothing moved. Letting go the curtain, she turned back into the room and sat drumming her fingers on the rests of her chair.

Like her husband, she'd slept badly the night before. The speculation on Canon Cratchley's unaccountable visit to the Russian Archimandrite's residence in West London, then Richard's excited yet frustrated realization of Dorothy Crocker's role in those long-ago secret meetings and journeys had stirred and unsettled her, infecting her with the same tormenting sense of wrestling with ghosts and shadows that her husband had felt since the very start of the investigation. In the morning she'd woken irritable and nervy. The mood had persisted all day, and now with evening come and Richard away, she felt more feverishly restless than ever.

Suddenly she made up her mind. With a last furtive glance into the yard, she wheeled to the bureau and drew down the lid. From one of the small drawers, she withdrew a matchbox, ashtray and cigarette packet. Extracting a cigarette, she lit and inhaled deeply, relishing at once its soothing effect.

Like the majority of her contemporaries, she'd smoked regularly before her marriage, but the habit had jarred on her husband's fastidious nature; somehow, and she never quite understood why, he'd seen her smoking as an affront, almost as if it was some unworded criticism of their marriage. With some effort, therefore, she'd broken the addiction. In Cyprus, intermittently and furtively, she'd begun again. Not wanting to hurt or annoy him, she had never said a word; nevertheless, since then she had always kept a hidden supply of cigarettes close at hand.

Now, leaning back in the wheelchair, she savoured the temporary relief, smiling at herself as she did so: beside the pleasantly lulling effect of the nicotine there was also a slight but delicious whiff of rebellion about this girlishly clandestine act. She inhaled again, but just then there came a click from the gate and the sound of feet on the path. She froze, hardly able to believe he was back so early, then was plunging and screwing the cigarette in the bowl and stuffing ashtray, packet and matches back into the drawer. She flapped at the smoke as the latch-key turned, then swung round flushed and smiling as Harrison appeared.

'Hello,' she said brightly. 'I wasn't expecting you back for ages.'

Not answering, his face flushed, he strode straight for the window. Instead, however, of throwing it open as she expected, he halted and, bowing forward, let his forehead rest against the glass. Puzzled, she began to speak, but before she could do so, he'd turned, eyes burning.

'Christ, Winnie, tell me—do you think me an absolutely bloody fool?' His face contorted. 'A damned idiot, is that all I am?'

Her heart fell: his reaction was even worse than she'd expected. 'Look, darling,' she began, 'it's just that sometimes when my nerves get bad...'

Confused, she broke off: he didn't appear to be listening. Instead, clearly highly agitated, his hands trembling, he was pouring himself a whisky. Doubting suddenly the source of this passionate rage, she asked, 'Richard, whatever's the matter? Didn't the men turn up? Didn't they manage to open the coffin?'

'Oh yes!' he exclaimed bitterly and gulped down the rest of the glass. 'They opened it all right!'

'Well then? Aren't you going to tell me? What was in it?'

'Everything! The whole dammed thing!'

'What do you mean? Becket's body? His regalia?'

Harrison laughed scornfully. 'Bones, woman! A few poor animal bones! In other words, damn all!'

'But isn't that good? Why are you so upset? Isn't that what you and Matthew really wanted—no fuss?'

Not answering, he began pacing the room. 'Christ, God!' he suddenly cried. 'What a damned idiot! What a blind damned fool I've always been!'

Behind the anger, behind the lamentations, Winnie sensed something new: a savage and growing exultation. 'Richard, what is it?' she begged. 'What have you found out?'

Suddenly he was on his knees in front of her, his face staring up, intense wild excitement in his eyes.

'I told you,' he said. 'Everything! The whole caboodle!'

'But there was no body in the coffin?'

'Oh yes,' he answered, not shifting his gaze, his voice suddenly quiet, 'there was a body there all right.' He smiled grimly. 'And it was the body of a cleric too.' He took her hands. 'In that empty coffin, Winnie, I saw our good friend, Georgi Seferiades.'

She stiffened.

'Winnie, you know how Seferiades was killed?'

She nodded, looking away. 'They shot him at the petrol station?'

'Yes, but do you know how it was done? How his destruction was arranged? How the Brigadier and I set him up?'

Pale now, she waited.

'It was easy—we played on people's mistrust, on their propensity to see the worst.' He shrugged. 'On their paranoia, if you like.' He paused; then, as if willing himself on, continued. 'We used friendship to destroy him: all those visits you and I made to his house compromised him, created the first doubts in the minds of his followers. You can imagine it, a Greek-Cypriot nationalist with English friends visiting him at night and one of them an army officer working for British Military Intelligence! After that, it was easy: a whisper here and there, a forged letter or two. It was all that was needed, enough to make a couple of his own hotheads take their Sten guns and do the job we wanted.'

Winnie shook her head: 'Darling, what's the point of all this now? It was a long time ago.'

'The point?' The fury was back in his face. He got to his feet. 'Because it's returned. What the Brigadier and I did to Seferiades' followers has been tried on me.' He stood, clasping and unclasping his hands. 'Christ, hell, does the fellow really think I'm such a fool? After all I've known and done, did he really think I could be misled so easily? That I've no more judgement or perception than a couple of illiterate gunmen?'

'I still don't understand. Who are you talking about? Who has misled you?'

'Brigadier Greville—who else!'

Speechless, she stared at him.

'Yes, Winnie, the damned Brigadier—he's worked on me, used me, set me on.' Pulling up a chair, he faced her. 'Just now in the crypt I heard the archæologists telling Ingrams how the monks must have tried to trick Thomas Cromwell's commissioners. At that moment, I suddenly saw the whole case against Campion was as empty as that coffin—nothing in any of it, nothing but dust in the wind!'

Winnie shook her head. 'I don't understand. You're not saying poor Canon Cratchley isn't dead?'

'Oh, he's dead all right—dead and in his grave, but as for the rest, that's all been in my head—a germ given me, yes, but grown in my own thoughts.'

'But the rifled papers, the missing documents?'

'Greville's work, damn him.'

'But why? For what?'

Harrison laughed. 'Oh, that's easy—to destroy a controversial bishop who looks increasingly likely to become the next Archbishop of Canterbury. You can hear it, can't you? Campion just makes one attack too many on Government policy, then someone, a senior Civil Servant, a Minister perhaps, just like King Henry II, says "Who shall rid us of this turbulent priest?"—and some other voice, Greville's presumably, answers, "That fool Richard Harrison—who bloody else?"'

Reaching out, Winnie touched his shoulders.

'Richard, are you sure of this? It isn't all just something in your mind?'

For the first time since returning, Harrison laughed heartily.

'More of my paranoia, you mean?' He shook his head, his expression growing grave. 'Not this time, Winnie. I'm sure I now have the truth—the truth Dorothy Crocker gave me today.'

'What about the manuscript stolen from Sarah's flat?'

Harrison gave a bitter snort. 'Yes, the one stolen on the very day that I told Greville I was going to visit her to get it!'

'So you think he arranged the theft—and before that, rifled the Harvey-Watson papers?'

'It's obvious!'

'Is it?' Winnie looked doubtful.

'Yes—he had the manuscript stolen so I would think there was something evil hidden there. He did the same to the Harvey-Watson papers, but left me a few tantalizing glimpses of Russian names, of visits and meetings for me to think the worst.' Harrison smiled sadly. 'You see, Winnie, Greville knows me, in some ways better than you. He could trust my paranoia, could be certain I'd catch at threads to spin dark worlds out of, and finally write it all in that damned report he needs to discredit Campion with.'

A shadow crossed Winnie's face. 'But if what you think is right, that means Greville arranged Cratchley's death—that he actually had him murdered.'

'I don't know.' Harrison shook his head. 'My God, I just don't know, but I cannot believe it. Perhaps I don't want to: murdering a harmless old man just to set me adrift on my madness!'

Getting up, Harrison went to the window and stared out. At last Winnie broke the silence.

'If this is all true, how can you prove it?'

'God knows!' Harrison continued to stare out, then, suddenly turning, he strode to the bookshelves to stare for a moment through the glass. He spun round, face exultant. 'What is it now—January? Come on, Winnie, you're the literary expert, when is Robbie Burns's birthday?'

Winnie burst out laughing. 'What's that got to do with anything?'

'Come on! Just tell me! Isn't it Burns Night soon?'

She wrinkled her brow. 'I think it's on the twenty-fifth, but why...'

'That's next week! Just six days!' There was triumphant glee in his voice. 'Marvellous! We can do it before the Brigadier's deadline. What's the line—*"The best laid schemes o' mice and men gang aft a-gley?"*'

'Richard, will you please explain—'

'Oh yes,' he continued, 'and when we're finding just how our emigrant Scots celebrate their national poet, we'll also find out why Cratchley visited the Archimandrite of the Russian Orthodox Church in England.' He rubbed his hands. 'Yes, we'll make a little pilgrimage and find out exactly what, if anything, was Harvey-Watson's Soviet connection.'

Exuberant, he continued to pace the room. 'Right,' he burst out all at once, 'I'm going to fetch the *A to Z*. We can start planning our little day out.'

He'd hardly got through the door, however, when he stopped and looked back, smiling broadly.

'Oh yes, and before I forget: speaking of best laid schemes, perhaps it's time, my dear, you found somewhere else beside the bureau to hide those wretched cigarettes!'

CHAPTER THIRTEEN

In the days immediately following the opening of the coffin, the meteorological charts of Western Europe became positively labyrinthine with isobars twisting, snaking and looping as one depression after another swept in from the Atlantic. Storms raged across Ireland; there was extensive flooding in France; heavy snow fell from the Ardennes to the Appennines; even as far south as Rome the weather was felt, with the city gutters gurgling, spluttering and overrunning under an almost tropical downpour.

In a grey gloom, behind window-panes running with water, Dorothy Crocker died; with the rain drumming on her coffin, the wind clutching at her bearers, she was borne to St Mildred's graveyard, and there, behind the remains of the city wall, was lowered into the sodden dark earth, watched by a bedraggled circle of mourners, among which her brother stood white-faced, sheltered by the Dean's umbrella.

Peace returned to the cathedral. No more graffiti appeared; there were no further sightings of that frantic, dangerous spirit that had haunted the precincts. Despite the best efforts of the police, he or she seemed to have vanished as completely as the flowers before the Becket memorial and the queues to the crypt. Lloyd-Thomas returned to Bread Yard, and his face, as gloomily forbidding as ever, once more surveyed the choristers morning and evening in the great oval mirror over the organ-loft.

223

Though outwardly the even tenor of their lives resumed, Harrison and Winnie were on edge. For Harrison especially, the days before the planned journey to London were a torment. Although his belief in the Brigadier's deceit persisted, it increasingly fluctuated, rising and waning erratically like some wandering, orbitless moon. One moment he'd feel savage rage at the deception practised upon him; the next, he'd be wondering if his perception of the emptiness of the case against Campion was not a sickness itself, that his sense of being manipulated was not just another, more dangerous, form of paranoia. One thing above all, however, held him constant in his determination not to release his report until he'd at least met the mysterious Russian Cratchley had visited, and that was the already fading memory of the face lying now beneath half an inch of oak and six rain-sodden feet of earth in St Mildred's churchyard.

It was still raining on the morning of the twenty-fifth when the orange Volvo left the precincts. Once on the dual carriageway, Winnie and Harrison found themselves driving through an almost continuous cloud of spray. Little was said, and as he peered through the flicking wipers at the vehicles racing past, Harrison's mind returned to the telephone call he'd made to Acton the week before; he remembered the almost English voice that had answered and the polite, mild surprise that had met his request for a meeting. His despondency grew. What, he wondered, could possibly be learnt of conspiracy, secret meetings and clandestine journeys over coffee-cups in suburban west London? What were they doing, the pair of them, leaving Canterbury this wet winter morning? The sense of hopelessness grew. He saw himself driving on in his ageing car, still outside life, still the ineffectual dreamer grasping at shadows and attempting to shape absurd dreams.

In the mirror, the cathedral faded like a grey battleship into the haze. More than ever he wished the day over, that he was safely home, free at last to submit his report to Greville.

'Look, Richard! A rainbow!'

He glanced to where Winnie was pointing: over the fields a vast translucent arch stretched brilliantly coloured between the earth and the suddenly clearing skies. Feeling his heart rise, he increased the pressure on the accelerator.

'Morning coffee with an Archimandrite!' Winnie laughed. 'Well, darling, if nothing else, it will be different!'

'More coffee, Mrs Harrison?'

That it wasn't different was the trouble; whatever either he or Winnie had expected, it wasn't quite this, to be drinking coffee and nibbling rich tea biscuits in the sitting-room of a 1930's semi-detached house in such an ordinary, dull and respectable street. And the man sitting opposite them on the flower-covered armchair wasn't at all what they'd envisaged either. Archimandrite Nikolay—or Bishop Nicholas as he had introduced himself—was a large, broad-shouldered man, whose heavily grey-bearded face bore a surprising similarity to that of the late George the Fifth. Apart from the small double-barred cross hanging over his green cardigan and the jewelled ring on his hand, in tweed jacket and baggy cavalry twill trousers, with hand-knitted tie and heavy brogues, he could easily have passed for a convivial English country doctor or vet.

As Winnie's cup was refilled, Harrison looked forlornly at the desk with its spread papers and books. Noticing an open seed catalogue, his heart plunged still further. The whole journey to London, the struggle through the traffic, this meeting—it was all nothing but an embarrassing, futile waste. One thing, however, in that ordinary, so English room, had briefly fluttered his heart when he'd first entered. Now, drawn irresistibly, he turned to look once again at the two faces on the wall behind him. Jewelled bright against complete blackness, impassively serene, yet mysteriously living, Virgin and Child gazed back at him from beneath their golden haloes.

'You have an interest in icons, Colonel Harrison?' His host was smiling.

'Not really, I'm afraid.'

'A pity! That one's a beauty.'

For a few seconds the three gazed up at the icon in silent admiration.

'It was painted by Peter of Kiev in the eleventh century and once hung in the private chapel of Catherine the Great.' Archimandrite Nikolay paused momentarily as a siren wailed from an ambulance struggling through the traffic towards Shepherd's Bush. 'Your friend Canon Cratchley admired it greatly I remember. He displayed an extensive knowledge of the art.' He paused. 'But iconography was perhaps a particular interest of his?'

'I think he was interested in most things.' Winnie smiled. 'A bit of a magpie, perhaps.'

'Ah!' The Archimandrite sighed, and in the sound there was something that belonged somewhere far from the suburban streets outside, something as foreign and exotic as the cyrillic lettering on the book-spines on the desk or the haunting stillness of the pale faces gazing down from the wall. 'Yes,' he murmured, nodding, 'the canon was undoubtedly a true seeker—a very great loss I'm sure to his Church.'

Fifteen hundred feet above, an airliner passed overhead, banking on to its final approach for Heathrow. As the room quietened, the Archimandrite smiled at his two guests. 'Now, how can I help you? What was it you wanted to know?'

Harrison cleared his throat. 'Why Canon Cratchley came here. What his business was.'

A veil seemed to fall across the Russian's face; his expression grew as impenetrable almost as the two looking down from the wall. Harrison nevertheless pressed on. 'I take it his visit was something to do with his book? From the papers he was using, we know there was a Russian connection. We just don't quite understand what it was.'

Archimandrite Nikolay leaned back in his chair. 'Forgive me, Colonel, but is it necessary that you should know?'

'Yes.'

A few seconds passed before the Bishop spoke. 'You must understand that since nineteen-seventeen my country has passed, perhaps is still passing in spite of appearances, through an age almost as dark for Christianity as that experienced in this island after the Romans left or during the Danish invasions. The terrible forces of a militant atheism have been directed against not only the Orthodox, but all the churches of Russia. Ridicule, torture, spies, death—all have been used in an effort to tear out the heart and root of religion.'

'Yes,' began Harrison, 'but I don't see what possible—'

The Archimandrite held up his hand.

'As I say, Russian Christianity has been under siege since the Bolshevik Revolution. After the comparative easing of the war years, Stalin's grip tightened again. In the late 'forties and early 'fifties priests were arrested, seminaries closed and the tactics of terror re-employed. We in London, the Russian Church in exile, tried to help: we smuggled in bibles, news-letters and money, even priests.' He shrugged slightly and smiled. 'But we were poor and our resources small.'

'So you needed help,' interposed Winnie, her eyes lighting up. 'Of course!' She glanced round at her husband who sat, his brow puckered, his face still blank.

'Yes,' said their host, 'we needed help, and so looked to our sister Churches of the West.'

'Including the Anglican?'

Bishop Nicholas smiled. 'Your Church, Mrs Harrison, was very generous.'

'Look,' intervened Harrison, a trace of indignation in his

voice, 'am I getting this right? Are you saying Harvey-Watson was working against Stalin? Against the Soviet system?'

Again the Archimandrite smiled.

'He was working for God, Colonel, and for the Church Universal.'

For a moment Harrison stared at his host; then, pulling out his wallet and extracting a slip of paper, passed it over. 'These names I've listed, Bishop—the men that Harvey-Watson and his chaplain were meeting, do they mean anything at all to you?'

The Archimandrite glanced at the paper and nodded. 'Yes, they mean something,' he said, handing it back.

'Who were they?' Harrison hesitated. 'Are any still alive?'

A smile spread across the Bishop's face. 'One certainly is, Colonel—the third name.'

Harrison glanced at the paper. 'Uspensky!' He looked up. 'Who is he? Do you know where he is now? Can I speak to him?'

The smile broadened on the other's face. 'You are already speaking to him. He is here, Colonel; Uspensky is sitting in front of you now.' The Archimandrite laughed. 'Yes, my dear Colonel and Mrs Harrison, I am Nikolay Sergeyevich Uspensky, and yes, as a young monk, I did indeed have many dealings, both with dear Bishop William and our equally beloved brother and friend, Maurice Campion.'

Apparently motionless, the black blanket of water stole silently seawards as the river ebbed; a green navigation light shone in the darkness. Faintly, but growing in strength, came the deep, low throb of an engine. The petrol-barge slipped by, a low silhouette against the amber halo of light over the Isle of Dogs. The sound of its engine faded, and then came the wash, invisibly slapping along the wall towards Winnie and

Harrison. Passing under their feet, it set the floating pontoon of the rowing club bucking and rolling. A sucking and slurping came from beneath it and the securing chains groaned as they tightened.

The sound and the dark desolation released the ever-waiting horrors. From the deeps, the corpses again came bobbing—bodies fished from the slime of the irrigation ditch, bodies drifting through the blackness, bumping along under the hulls of moored lighters, caught and slashed in the churning propellers of tugs. With a shudder, Harrison thought of Cratchley—the old priest gazing upwards, the assassin creeping forward, needle raised. Had it been just for him the old man had been murdered? Had he been done to death there in the darkness merely to release the absurd, sick fantasies of his mind?

'Come on,' said Winnie, 'you're starting to shiver.'

'Right,' he murmured, relieved by the sound of her voice. He began wheeling her over the few yards of cobbles to the pillared porch of the waterside inn. Backing in, he dragged the chair through the double doors. Straightening, he looked round at the panelled walls, the odd assortment of pictures, high-ceilinged, spacious rooms stretching away, the bright glitter of glasses behind the bar, the great mirror over the fireplace. In a moment the appalling desolation he'd felt outside was gone. 'My God, Winnie,' he said, still looking about him, 'the old place has hardly changed.'

It was still early enough for there to be few customers, and they were able to occupy the small alcove immediately behind the doors that gave a direct view of the oak staircase leading to the dining-rooms above. Having helped Winnie on to the settle, he went to the bar.

'You remember it, don't you?' he said, returning with the drinks. 'We came here a lot when I was doing that explosives course at Woolwich.'

Winnie nodded, sipping her drink. Putting down her glass, she regarded him quizzically.

'Yes, I remember, but you haven't yet told me why we're here now.'

He smiled. 'I did—for Burns Night. Apparently the Trafalgar is the chosen venue for tonight's dinner of the South London Caledonian Society.'

For a moment she stared back blankly, then realization dawned. 'Of course! That evening at the Bugle-Horn! Greville's deputy, what's his name—Gillie? You think he'll be here?'

'I very much hope so.'

'How did you know?'

'About the dinner?' He laughed. 'Easy—it had to be somewhere. The Caledonian Society's in the phone directory. All I had to do was ring the Secretary.'

She smiled. 'You clever old thing!'

Harrison leaned back in the settle. 'You know, Winnie, it would be appropriate to finish the investigation here. Greenwich was the first town on the pilgrims' route to Canterbury. It was here somewhere by the river that Thomas Becket's saint, St Alphege, was murdered by the Danes.'

There was the sound of women's laughter outside. The doors swung open and a group entered—women in furs and evening dress, the men with lace ruffs at their necks and incongruous white socks below their coats. They stood a moment self-consciously in the bar, then moved to the staircase. From above came the first faint wail of bagpipes being warmed.

Harrison glanced at his watch. 'Quarter past! We must keep our eyes open now.'

Dinner guests began arriving in greater numbers. Around them the bar was filling fast. The buzz of conversation grew louder; more laughter. Harrison felt his tension increase. Every opening of the swing doors seemed to carry in more of the terrible desolation he'd felt outside. The serpent was back in his belly. As the minutes passed, it coiled tighter. For a moment he almost wished that Gillie wouldn't appear, that he wouldn't have to know who had ordered the killing—for whom exactly Cratchley had died.

As if sensing his thoughts, Winnie reached out and touched his hand.

It was just three minutes before the half-hour when he saw Gillie's tall figure pushing through the crush at the foot of the stairs.

'Right,' said Harrison, getting up, his face pale. 'I'll nab him before he gets upstairs.'

From the look of startled dismay in the face that looked down over the banisters, the interruption was obviously quite as unwelcome as it was unexpected.

'I must speak to you for a moment in private.' Gillie shook his head, amazement giving way to annoyance. 'Can't you see, man, I've got a dinner-party just beginning.'

'I'm sorry,' insisted Harrison, his hand still gripping the other's wrist through the bars, 'but I really must have a word.'

There was a squeal from the pipes above. Gillie looked towards the sound.

'The matter is important.'

Seeing the fixed determination in the other's face, Gillie gave up. He looked round to the woman in a silver lamé dress at his side. 'I won't be a moment.' Angrily he pushed down through the crush and followed Harrison over to the alcove.

'So what is this?' Pale and stern, he sat and faced the couple on the opposite settle.

Winnie smiled charmingly. 'My husband wants to know why you were in Canterbury before Christmas.'

Irritation seemed to sharpen Gillie's thin features. 'I told him at the time. I was attending the Society's breakaway weekend.'

'And that was all?'

Above, the pipes again wailed.

'I must go,' said Gillie, starting to get up.

'What happened to the investigation into Cratchley's death?'

Gillie stared at the other man. 'What do you mean?'

'The investigation! Where did it get to?'

'Get to? What are you talking about. There wasn't one-there was nothing.'

'What the hell do you mean?' Harrison's face reddened as his temper flared. 'For God's sake, you removed Cratchley's body, didn't you? There was that delay to the funeral.'

The same invisible veil that had fallen over the Russian's face that morning fell now over the Scot's. 'You know very well, Colonel, that this is all covered by the Official Secrets Act.'

'Confound the Act! I want to know who killed Cratchley.'

Again blank amazement filled Gillie's face. He glanced about, then, leaning forward, looked directly into his interrogator's face. 'Nobody killed Cratchley, Colonel,' he whispered, his grey eyes cold. 'The old man died of a heart attack.'

'Heart attack?' Harrison stared.

'Why the surprise? Wasn't that just what you yourself suggested? I remember you telling us that the man had a weak heart.'

'But then why...' Harrison's voice trailed away. Glancing quickly at Winnie, he leaned forward again. Customers crushed against the table. 'Are you certain of this? No ricin? No poison at all? You're saying there was no murder? Nothing?'

'Nothing—that's right. Just a heart attack.' Gillie began to get up, but, seeing the bewilderment in the two faces looking up at him, reluctantly lowered himself back on to the settle. 'I myself collected the pathologist's report,' he said in a whisper. 'There's no doubt. Canon Cratchley died of natural causes.'

Harrison's fist slammed on to the table between them.

'Damn that infernal man!' he cried, his face scarlet with fury.

Gillie frowned, but before he could say a word, Winnie was speaking. 'Thank you very much for telling us. Since your visit that afternoon with Brigadier Greville, the whole affair has been somewhat on our minds.' She smiled appealingly. 'We've brooded on it rather. You understand, Canon Cratchley was a very dear friend of us both.'

'Of course.' Gillie nodded, anger gone. He turned to Harrison. 'I'm sorry, Colonel. On behalf of the Department, I do apologize. Someone should have been in touch at the time and set your mind at rest.'

Apart from the man on the bench, both platforms of the station were deserted. A woman who looked hardly more than a schoolgirl paused from pushing a pram across the pedestrian bridge to stare uncuriously down at the solitary figure who sat, apparently absorbed in his newspaper. With a yell to the child dawdling behind, she continued on. Over the waves of monotonous rooftops a ship wailed from the invisible Thames.

At the sound, Harrison glanced at his watch. The stopping train from Canterbury had been late; he'd been relieved on disembarking to find the station empty. However, gradually over the thirty-five minutes or so as he'd waited, his initial relief had transformed, first to impatience, then to anxiety.

Narrowing his eyes, he stared up the double track running bar-straight until merging and finally vanishing at the base of the Colossus-like tower-block dominating the western horizon. Peering, he made out a dark shape, apparently motionless, but perceptibly growing in size as it rushed towards him. Sunlight flashed on a windscreen. There was the raucous blast of a horn. Folding his paper, he got to his feet as the train squealed to a standstill beside him.

Doors opened—suddenly there was the Brigadier, conspicuous in bowler and tweed coat. Seeing Harrison, he strode over.

'So why here, damn it?' He glowered round at the small grey houses hedging the station. 'What was the idea of insisting on this godforsaken place?'

Harrison shrugged. 'I thought it convenient. No man's land, if you like.'

'You can say that again! Suburban South-East bloody London!' His umbrella rang on the platform. 'God damned end of the world!'

The train began rumbling away. Suddenly the two men were facing each other on a once again deserted platform. Greville glanced at the briefcase in Harrison's hand. 'So—' he smiled grimly—'it's finished at last?'

A couple of youths began crossing the bridge above, one banging loudly on the steel parapet as he went.

'Let's find somewhere not quite so overlooked,' said Harrison.

Despite the density of the buildings, the street outside was curiously deserted. In silence the two men walked up the slope to the main road. Turning left at a graffiti-scrawled bridge, littered beneath with cardboard and broken bottles, they followed the increasingly modern buildings. Still they did not speak, the remembrance of their last parting moving, as it were, like some third figure between them, inhibiting speech. However, as the buildings on their right abruptly ended and there opened a vista of low wooded hills and grassland, the Brigadier looked round.

'You know this place?'

Harrison nodded. 'I came here once or twice when you sent me on that course at Woolwich.'

Turning off the pavement, he led the way up a track running beside the fence of municipal gardens and park. At a gate he paused, looking back across the vast housing estate with its series of interconnected tower-blocks sprawling out below them towards a distant line of trees fringing the river. 'Back then, all that was open marshland right down to the water. Look at it now!' He waved towards the estates. 'Imagine living there! It's not surprising there's all the violence and drugs! The wonder is that people retain the humanity they do.'

Before the Brigadier could answer, he'd walked on. Greville hurried to follow, but as he reached the top of the rise ahead, he stopped. Before them, hidden until now by the fold of the ground, spread a large ruin.

From first appearance it might have been Roman, so little of it remained—nothing much more than a pattern of roofless walls, most just a foot or so above the ground, the highest not much greater than the height of a man. Even the support pillars had gone, stolen and re-used presumably centuries back; now only their stone bases lay regularly spaced across the mown grass, and apart from the couple of Norman-arched doorways still standing, the whole place gave the impression of a fossilized imprint, a mere skeletal outline of the original ground-plan to what had obviously once been a large complex of buildings nestling at the foot of the wooded slopes beyond.

'What the hell is it?' murmured the Brigadier.

'Lesnes Abbey,' replied Harrison, walking on.

Frowning, Greville followed him through an archway into the walled rectangle of grass. Once inside, both halted, looking around. 'So what's the idea?' Greville eyed the other narrowly. 'Why here?'

Harrison shrugged. 'It seemed appropriate somehow. This abbey was built by Richard de Luci, one of Becket's murderers. He built this place as an act of penance. He came to die here as a monk himself.'

'All right, Dickie. Fascinating, I'm sure. Now let's get on with it.' Greville stepped forward. 'Let's have your report.'

Harrison extracted a thick envelope from his briefcase and held it out.

For a moment Greville didn't take it. Instead he gazed quizzically at the other's face, then, without a word, snatched and tore open the envelope, dragging out the thick, typed document inside. For a moment he bent over it, then straightened, his face crimson. 'What's this? *The Rationalization of Ecclesiastical Property in the Canterbury Diocese!* What damnfool joke are you playing? This is a matter of national security.'

'I promised you a report. I had this one going spare.'

Just for a moment, Harrison thought he was going to be struck. Glowering, Greville raised his stick. Its ferrule hovered, quivering high above him in the sunlight for a second, then, faltering, drooped and sank back to the ground.

❈ ❈ ❈

A flight of rooks rose simultaneously from a bunch of elms on the hillside. Flapping down across the wooded slopes, they wheeled, cawing loudly, over the ruined abbey and the two figures facing each other among its broken walls.

The harsh cries of the birds seemed to release a spring: suddenly all the anger Harrison had held back since Gillie's revelation was spilling out. 'Did you really think me such a blind, damned fool? Could you really believe you would use me so easily?'

His back against the wall, the Brigadier eyed him impassively.

'It's so damned obvious. Cratchley dies, you lie, lead me to think it was murder. Then you have his manuscript stolen and, finally, you tamper with his source material—Christ God!'

As if deliberately goading him, Greville remained silent, for all the world a disdainful parent observing the tantrums of a child.

'And I was just made for your use, wasn't I? Ex-Military Intelligence and actually working for the Church—and my guilt over Seferiades to be used as a lever to get me to destroy somebody else!' He broke off, choking on his fury. For a second or two he struggled for self-control, then forced himself on. 'Anyway, merely out of interest, what were you intending to do with my report— slip it under the eyes of some of the more gullible backbenchers and Cabinet members? Or would it have gone even higher?'

Half smiling, Greville shrugged, then turned and walked out through the arch, leaving Harrison to catch him up.

'Bastard creatures!'

The Brigadier had halted on the path, and as the other came to his side he pointed up with his umbrella to the line of rooks now sweeping back towards the elms. Together, the two men watched the birds until they'd vanished among the trees, then Harrison, calm again, looked round. 'Why all this effort to discredit Campion anyway? Whatever threat is he?'

'You know as well as I do!'

'Because he preaches trust and calls for disarmament? Because he dares to criticize the Government? Because he demands social justice? I may not agree with everything he says, but for God's sake, hasn't the chap the right to say it?'

The Brigadier spun round. 'Not from Lambeth Palace, he hasn't! Not as Archbishop of Canterbury! Let him make himself a martyr if he wants, but he's not going to threaten everything we've built in this country for generations—not if I can help it, that is!'

'You?' Incredulously Harrison studied the other's face. 'You mean this whole plot was your idea? Just your own? It didn't go higher?'

'Bugger off!'

Greville swung away, but Harrison had already seen and understood—the bewildered fear of a man facing retirement, seeing the world and his power being torn away. Greville was an ageing man, seeing Europe and Britain changing, the great enemy becoming the possible friend—everything he'd dedicated himself to, measured and valued himself by, already crumbling into the past, leaving him valueless, an empty relic, a hollow nothing, a collection of brittle bones and sagging flesh to face death, the work of a lifetime mocked by every lessening of the tension between East and West.

'Campion will help rot from the inside—further muddy our view.' Greville had turned and was again looking up to where a faint cawing came from the ragged bundles of nests high in the elms. 'Between him and those oily-mouthed bastards in Moscow, we're being softened up for the chopping-block.'

'Nonsense,' said Harrison quietly. 'The Soviet Empire's like this damned place, it's in ruins. Anyway, we can't go on fighting this century's wars for ever.' He paused. 'Sometime we've got to let the past go.'

Greville gave no answer. In a silence broken only by the faint sounds of the rooks and the occasional heavy vehicle passing on the road below, they walked on through the gardens.

'Well,' said the Brigadier at last, 'I take it I'm not going to get my report?'

Harrison shook his head.

Stopping, Greville prodded the soft earth of a flowerbed with his umbrella. 'Those bloody clerics have all ganged up, Dickie. They're virtually all behind Campion, soft little liberals to the most hard-line of the conservatives. With old Haverwell pulled out, the PM has no option: the Church will have to be given what it wants.'

'It looks like it,' answered Harrison. 'I was just reading the article in *The Times* when I was waiting.'

'Think about it, Dickie, I beg you; think while there's still time.' The Brigadier was looking at him intently. 'I wouldn't like to think of anything more being laid on that tender conscience of yours.'

Harrison laughed self-consciously. 'I'll be all right. Anyway, over these last few weeks, I've come to think Maurice Campion may be what this country needs—someone to balance our present materialism and greed. I didn't realize until yesterday they'd even closed the Seaman's Hospital in Greenwich. Great charitable foundations chucked away like so much rubbish! We're adrift. We need someone to anchor us back to the best of our history.' He shrugged, pausing. 'Anyway, it doesn't matter what I think. Thank God, I'm out of it now at last!'

Brigadier Greville smiled; momentarily there came to his eyes a look of affection, an almost feminine tenderness, which startled and shocked Harrison. And there was something else in the look—another emotion that for the moment he couldn't name. Before he could speak, Greville had turned and was striding away between the bare flowerbeds back in the direction they'd come.

Harrison watched him go for a moment, then walked back to the ruins. Entering a gap between the few-inches-high wall surrounding what had been the monastery church, he crossed the mown grass to where the stone of the high altar still lay. Gazing down, he felt the warmth of the sun on his face. He looked up. 'Thank God,' he murmured aloud, 'it's finished at last!'

Even as he spoke, he remembered that final lingering look in Greville's eyes. The joy drained from him: in the heart of that surprising affection there had been an almost infinite pity. Suddenly apprehensive, he turned to look back across the gardens, but the Brigadier had already disappeared.

CHAPTER FOURTEEN

The scaffolding removed, Christ Church gatehouse stood resplendent in all its original Tudor glory. The stonework and the heavily carved door-panelling had been cleaned and fully restored, and now the gorgeous ranks of repainted saints, angels and shield-motifs gleamed in the summer sunlight.

Harrison gazed up from a crowded Buttermarket with a profound mixture of satisfaction and relief. Four months had passed since he'd parted from the Brigadier, four months in which he'd returned happily to the comparatively mundane cares of diocesan work, finding in that and his marriage a happiness and content he'd never known before. However, while he'd followed the regular routine of his life, out in the great world beyond the expected decision on the Primacy was finally made: from Windsor Castle, on St Valentine's Day, Maurice Patrick Campion, Bishop of Derby, was proclaimed chosen successor to the See of Canterbury and future Archbishop.

The appointment was received with remarkable enthusiasm in a country for the most part only nominally Christian. A surprising range of public figures, covering among them almost the entire spectrum of British politics, welcomed the news. For many, Christians and non-Christians alike, Bishop Campion represented hope—in him, it was thought, lay a strength and simplicity of faith which, seasoned by the accumulated wisdom and traditions of an ancient Church, would provide a moral and spiritual direction to a nation poised somewhat uncertain and fearful before a new millennium.

Campion was not without his critics, however. Even within the Church opinions were divided. From all ranks of the clergy, there were numbers who feared that the future Archbishop's unyielding and unbending leadership could well lead to an irrevocable split between Church and State. Others saw him as an impediment to theological debate and development. For the most part, however, the Church greeted his appointment with undisguised joy. A new vitality grew, congregational numbers increased and there was a general quickening of the pulse. Even Harrison, locked away in his office with the material concerns of ecclesiastical walls, roofs and guttering, became conscious of the reviving breeze beginning to blow through the institution which employed him—though not a wind strong enough, he thought, smiling wryly to himself as he looked up at the gatehouse, to stir the obstinate, sluggish spirit of Keates.

Ever since the date of Campion's enthronement had been announced, Harrison's struggles with the cathedral Clerk-of-Works had been like that of Abraham and the angel. To get the building and grounds ready on time to welcome the guests, royal, civic and ecclesiastic, he and the Dean had alternatively to plead, badger and threaten. Now, just in time, the work was at last done; the ancient cathedral, mother church of the Anglican Communion, was ready, dressed in all her finery, to greet and proclaim before the world the next day, the 104th Primate of all England.

Re-entering the precincts, he headed back to his office. Closed now to the public, the grounds were almost silent as the last preparations were made. Television pantechnicons were parked under the west front, white satellite dishes sprouting like upturned mushrooms on the lawns beside them. The sight of them reminded him of the short-lived burst of interest that had followed the discovery of the casket which now lay, already growing dusty, in the vaults of the city museum. His thoughts moved to Crocker. The Archdeacon was rarely seen now: the double blow, the death of his beloved sister and the overthrow of his hopes regarding the coffin, had left him a solitary figure, moving grey and silent, untouched and untouchable by a hurrying, changing world.

Dr Crocker was still in Harrison's mind as he mounted the stairs to his office. His thoughts, however, were cut short by his secretary as he entered. 'Oh, thank goodness you're back, Colonel! The Dean's waiting in your office.' Glancing towards the closed inner door, Mary lowered her voice. 'I don't know what's the matter, but he looks upset.' Harrison's heart fell: had that blasted Keates missed something after all?

❈ ❈ ❈

Ingrams swung round from the window as he entered. 'Ah, here you are!' His face was grave. 'I'm sorry to intrude like this, but there's something you should see. I'm afraid to say that something rather alarming has emerged—or rather, re-emerged.'

'Re-emerged?'

'Apparently so.' Ingrams went to the door. 'Richard, I want you to come with me at once and see what I've discovered.'

Together, the two men left the office. With the Dean leading, they headed towards the north-east corner of the cathedral, and then on to the Oaks. Following the path round the oval of grass, they halted at the gate to what had been Cratchley's garden. Through a tangle of vegetation, the empty cottage, still awaiting renovation, appeared to have snuggled down out of the sunlight, half invisible behind the foliage.

The Dean turned to his companion. 'I borrowed the keys from the Archdeacon's office. Tomorrow's ceremony has been rather on my mind. I was looking for some peace. Instead, I'm more on edge than ever.'

'What is it you've found?'

'Come and see for yourself.'

Harrison followed Ingrams up the narrow path. With the scent of lilac about him and the even hum of the foraging bees, he waited as the other unlocked the now dusty front door.

It opened, rasping slightly on unused hinges.

There was a shocking nakedness to the hallway. Now that the hallstand, watercolours and the mounds of books and magazines had disappeared, the narrow vestibule, with its stained bare boards and empty rusting hooks, had a look of almost sordid desolation. Strangely enough, cleared and unfurnished, the house appeared meaner and smaller than it ever had when packed to bursting with the accumulated paraphernalia of the dead man's life.

Harrison followed into the sitting-room, but as he stepped inside, he stopped: on the wall above the mantelpiece where the mirror had stood, was scrawled the message:

οτι ημεραι εχδιχησεωϐ ανται εισι

The incomprehensible words were smeared large and vivid red on the white expanse of plaster which the mirror had protected from the sunlight. Appalled, Harrison looked round at Ingrams. 'What is it, for heaven's sake? What does it say?'

Softly the Dean recited the words aloud; against the sounds of the summer garden outside, the long-dead language echoed through the empty house as through the dry hollowness of a tomb. He paused, looking at the other steadily. *'For these are the days of vengeance.'*

An ice-cold hand seemed to finger the back of Harrison's neck.

'It's the beginning of a verse from St Luke,' continued the

other. 'Fully, the sentence reads: *For these are the days of vengeance to fulfil all that has been written.*'

After so many peaceful months, it was if a tiger had leapt from a garden. Visions of the earlier graffiti rushed to Harrison's brain; all at once, he was again seeing the figure dashing from him from under the organ-loft, hearing Lloyd-Thomas's terrified scream through the darkness. He glanced round listening, half expecting, half dreading to hear the sound of a footstep or the rustle of clothing. There was nothing apart from the birdsong and the hum of bees among the lilac. A disturbed bluebottle rose and hummed across the room to bump and whirr against the window. He turned back to the Dean.

'Could this have been here since the winter?'

Ingrams shook his head. 'Sarah would have said something when she cleared the house. Anyway, until then the mirror would have covered that whole section of wall.'

Going over, Harrison touched the lettering lightly and glanced at his fingertip: there was now a faint red smear on it. 'You're right,' he said. 'This has been done in the last day or two.'

The bluebottle whirred and bumped against each of the panes in turn, its drone growing more frantic by the second.

'What I don't understand,' said Harrison after a moment, 'is why now? Back in the winter, with all the excitement over that blasted coffin, there was some explanation, but...'

'That's it, Richard!' The Dean looked excited. 'My dear fellow, you've got it! It's the Becket factor again. Of course! That's what's caused this.'

'Becket factor?' Harrison stared. A terrible thought came. 'Keates hasn't dug up something new, has he?'

With a slight smile, the Dean shook his head. 'You haven't heard? I thought everyone knew. Immediately after the enthronement itself, the Archbishop intends to go down to the martyrdom pavings accompanied by two of the cathedral clergy.'

'In the middle of the service!'

'It's his own idea. His wish is to dedicate his Primacy to the memory of St Thomas Becket.'

Harrison stared at the garish scrawl on the wall. 'And you think this woman, whoever she is, has heard and is now...' He broke off.

'It fits,' said the Dean thoughtfully. 'The first attack, the one on Cratchley, came the evening after the Pope and the Archbishop prayed together before the martyrdom stones; the attack on Lloyd-Thomas was on the night of the commemoration service. In other words, at a time when Thomas Becket was more than usually in our thoughts.' He pointed at the wall. 'Now this appears just before another public act of veneration to the martyr's memory.'

'What will you do?'

Ingrams shrugged. 'Inform the authorities. I was given a number to ring if anything unusual was spotted in the grounds. With Royalty here tomorrow and Government ministers, they're terrified of bombs. You may think me silly, but I feel I have no choice but to tell them of this: unlikely as I trust it is, we must at least be prepared for another attack.'

'But why Greek?'

'Why not?' Ingrams looked round from re-locking the door in mild surprise. 'My dear fellow, it is, after all, the language of the New Testament.'

'Oh, quite,' murmured Harrison, disconcerted, 'but all the same, is it likely: a mad woman knowing Ancient Greek?'

The Dean laughed.

'Really, Richard, you do display a charmingly old-fashioned belief in the merits of a classical education!' He shook his head. 'Sadly, a knowledge of dead languages is no proof, I'm afraid, against insanity.' He smiled. 'If anything, rather the opposite, I fear—I remember a don at All Souls' positively insisting that his Hebrew translations were guided by the nightly visitations of the Archangel Gabriel!'

Harrison laughed politely. 'Do you think Campion could be persuaded to cancel this dedication thing?'

Ingrams chuckled. 'You clearly don't know our new Archbishop, Richard.'

'I imagine, Dean,' said Harrison as they began to walk back towards the cathedral, 'you'll be one of the two clergy attending him?'

'Yes.'

'And the other?'

'Ah!' Ingrams smiled. 'That I think was a very happy choice: our Archdeacon will be the third of our little party. I'm sure you agree that there is no one more suitable than poor Stephen to pray beside the Archbishop and myself on the martyrdom stones. You know, Richard,' he said, glancing round, 'when I asked him to accompany us, I saw a joy in that unhappy man's eyes I wouldn't have believed possible.' He laughed shortly. 'I could have been offering the poor fellow the very keys of Paradise!'

Harrison was surprised how free the Dean seemed now of the gnawing anxiety possessing him earlier: to so social, so clubbable a person as Ingrams, to share a problem was almost to solve it. Having shown the ominous message and having discussed its meaning and decided his course of action, his mind was again free in a manner astonishing and almost inexplicable to one of Harrison's brooding, solitary nature.

'Anyway,' continued Ingrams, 'you mustn't let this little matter concern you. I shall inform the authorities at once. The important thing for you is to relax after your labours. Do you still intend watching the service on television at home with Winifred?'

There was no answer. He turned to find his companion had halted and was staring up at the Bell Harry Tower above them.

'Richard, what is it?' he asked, walking back.

'Those people up there.'

Ingrams followed the other's gaze. Two figures were looking down at them over the tower parapets. 'Security.' He laughed. 'They're quite taking us over. Mind you, after what we've seen, I'm rather pleased they're going to so much trouble.'

Where Ingrams had seen two figures, Harrison had seen three. That invisible third was there for him alone. Stirred from his memory by the shock of the words in the cottage, he saw as vividly as the first time, the dark figure, insect-small, black against grey, grotesquely waving over the parapet. The scrawled quotation had shaken him, certainly, but he'd not found it frightening. What did it represent, after all, but the cry of an anguished soul, howling pathetically in its confused and tormented isolation? Now, however, looking at that which was not there—that invisible third—he tasted fear, a fear all the stronger for that it was completely irrational, based on nothing more than a memory of a figure waving as if in frantic warning or in mockery at his puny efforts to understand and avoid whatever fate was moving towards him.

He returned to his office determined to bury his absurd and illogical sense of dread under a bout of concentrated work. He was unable to settle, however. Restlessly he paced about, the spasmodic bursts of the typewriter next door further jarring his nerves. At last, making his excuses to Mary, he left.

Stepping into the sunlight of Green Court, he found that the quiet backwater had been selected as the base of the security operation next day. Since lunch-time, two marquees had been erected on the central lawn. Beside them stood a mobile police communications centre, its whip-like aerial protruding high above its perspex dome. The scene was reminiscent of a divisional field headquarters: the faint sounds of radios being netted, plain-clothes and uniformed figures moving purposefully between tents and control-centre, white tapes being laid over the grass for the vehicles carrying in reinforcements. All was order and efficiency, and, observing the scene, his half-acknowledged sense of impending catastrophe appeared simply ludicrous, a mere neurotic fancy grown of the same dark sickness infecting the mind of whoever it was that had scrawled the secret warning or threat.

Just then, the stocky figure of Inspector Dowley emerged from the nearer marquee. Both men paused and faced each other across the few yards of grass.

Dowley's sudden appearance gave Harrison a jolt: he remembered the chaos of his office back in the winter—the strewn papers, the upturned furniture, the whole order of things torn apart. His misgivings returned. Almost perversely, the Inspector's appearance of tough dependability made him doubt suddenly the organization he represented: the whole paraphernalia of vehicles, radios and computers seemed momentarily nothing more than frail tissue serving only to disguise the fallible, weak nature of its inventors. In the same place, among the same walls as the monks had walked, there came a terrifying vision of the vulnerability of the individual, the sheer inadequacy and limitation of human mind and perception set against vast destructive forces, moving unseen, without and within.

He took a step towards Dowley, then stopped. The moment had passed; once more the formidable certainties of the police operation stood before him, mocking his fears. With a slight nod, he turned away, telling himself that Ingrams must have already passed on what was written in the cottage to forces altogether more formidable than that of a mere local CID officer. Nevertheless, as he continued towards Bread Yard, he had a vague sense of an opportunity missed.

In the early hours he awoke to find the bedroom bright with moonlight. He lay, eyes open, gazing up, listening to Winnie's regular breathing. When he'd hurried from the office, his intention had been to share with her that intangible sense of dread he'd felt seeing the figures on the tower, but having glimpsed the extent of the security operation, he'd said nothing. As planned, they'd gone to the theatre that evening and then on to dinner.

Whatever lingering echoes of his forebodings survived the play and the meal were finally dispelled when walking back through Bread Yard after garaging the car. A light had been on downstairs in Canon Rope's cottage; the curtains were open, and as he passed, he'd casually glanced in.

The elderly man was reading, peering through a magnifying-glass at the open volume on his lap. A partly-consumed meal—some sort of cold pie—lay congealed on a plate beside him; over the fireplace hung a large framed photograph, browned and fading with age, of what he took to be a Chinese pagoda with snow-covered mountains beyond.

Rope's face was in profile, and Harrison saw, as on silent film, the extraordinary animation of the reader's features. From the working of the mouth and the expression, it seemed as if whatever was in the book was being simultaneously ravished and devoured. Harrison was fascinated and repelled: it was almost a parody of himself sitting alone those months before, bent over the Harvey-Watson papers. A wave of something like nausea—nausea and pity together—swept over him: the solitary, manic excitement of the figure in the booklined, unpeopled room visually represented the abstracted, isolated, self-absorbed and self-regarding part of himself that he feared, that self-created, deluding prison-house of his mind, the dark, solitary cell where the fantasies flourished and the paranoias grew.

Turning from the window, he'd finally dismissed his fears: his world was the rational; it lay in material reality, in his work and in his relationship with Winnie. As for any danger or threat, that could be safely left to the Dean, the police and all those responsible for the massive security operation.

With the moon full on his face, he lay in bed listening to his wife's peaceful breathing, more than ever glad he'd mentioned nothing to her of Ingrams's bizarre discovery. With relish, he thought of all the completed work on the cathedral and the Christ Church gatehouse, visualizing the cleaned and restored stonework ghostly-white in the moonlight. Again, his thoughts returned to the cottage and the scrawled quotation, now presumably, like all the rest, illuminated by the moon.

For these are the days of vengeance. He smiled to himself. In the soothing moonlight, the phrase seemed more pathetic than ever. Closing his eyes, he snuggled down against his wife, leaving the acres of stone and all the vast preparations—the white tapes, the crowd-barriers, the now dew-damp marquees, the cables and satellite dishes—all to await in silence the coming day.

'You're up early!'

Winnie smiled up at her husband who stood beside the bed, holding out a cup of tea. Blinking the sleep from her eyes, she pulled herself up against the pillows.

'It's absolutely lovely outside.' Harrison opened the curtains. The cathedral towers gleamed almost white against absolute blue.

Winnie sipped her tea. 'You know, darling,' she said, 'I'd be perfectly all right here on my own if you want to take part in the service.'

'Nonsense!' He smiled. 'You know how I hate crowds.'

The two of them were enjoying a leisurely breakfast when a helicopter flew low overhead, vibrating the windows as it passed. There was the sound of coaches pulling into Green Court. Conscious of the huge security operation already in progress, Harrison relaxed: his responsibilities were over; the day belonged to Campion and the Church.

Over the washing-up, Winnie and he saw increasing signs of the bustle outside: two policemen entered the courtyard, looked around and went; through the archway, they glimpsed a crocodile of choirboys passing round the quadrangle; Lloyd-Thomas departed, music case under his arm, his expression as doleful and gloomy as the weather was bright. In complete contrast, Canon Rope's countenance was as gleefully animated as ever as he passed by arm-in-arm with Prebendary Richards. Spotting the couple at the window, he waved. Just then the helicopter again swept low over the courtyard. Looking up, Rope gestured towards it and yelled something to his companion above the roaring clatter of the machine.

'Come on,' said Harrison as the two disappeared, 'let's get this finished or we'll miss the beginning of the show.'

With the sitting-room curtains closed, the television was switched on. The programme had begun. The scene before them was of the crowds gathered in the Buttermarket, the camera looking up the curving sweep of the road leading into the Christ

Church gatehouse where a solid mass of spectators pressed against the crush barriers on either side.

A commentator was speaking:

> In the last half-hour, the crowds here in the Buttermarket have seen the cars of numerous dignitaries pass through this magnificent entrance into the precincts. Among them, they've seen the Home Secretary, the Lord Chancellor, the retiring Archbishop and his wife, various ambassadors, including Cardinal Cellini, the Papal Nuncio.

The shot widened, taking in the entire gatehouse.

> As we await the arrival of the royal cars, for a few moments we can enjoy the sight of this lovely Tudor gatehouse. The work on its restoration has only just been completed; now it stands as colourful and impressive as when it was first completed in 1541—an appropriate emblem perhaps of the new Archbishop's term of office which many believe promises to bring about the long-awaited revitalization of the Anglican Church.

The camera angle opened still further, until on the screen, the entire gatehouse stood framed against the cathedral towers and the cloudless sky.

Winnie smiled round. 'He's quite right, dear. It looks lovely. You and Mr Keates have really achieved a miracle.'

Before Harrison could reply, from both the television and through the open window came the pealing of the Bell Harry Tower. The commentator's voice suddenly grew excited as the camera closed on a black limousine moving between the crowds.

> And now the first of the royal cars is in sight. There it is! The feathered crest of the Prince of Wales above the windscreen! And there, within, we can see both...

The sound of bells swelled up, as the city churches, like so many lesser vessels, joined in their flagship's greeting. Faint, almost plaintive, behind the tremendous sound came the cheering of the crowd.

The Prince's car turns through the arch. It disappears. And yes, here is the Queen's car now, just coming into sight!

Winnie shook her head. 'I don't know,' she said, 'it seems perverse sitting watching in here when it's all happening just a few hundred yards away.' She looked anxiously round. 'Richard, you could still go. You've got that pass Matthew gave you.'

Harrison shook his head. 'I'll see much more on the television than stuck at the back of the nave.'

On the screen the two royal cars drew up before the west front where Ingrams and Prebendary Richards waited to greet them.

The Dean bowing now as the doors are opened. He welcomes his visitors. A proud day for him. Now they all turn to enter through the western porch.

The scene changed to the interior of the cathedral; as it did so, the commentator's voice became hushed.

The Prince and Princess of Wales, followed by the Queen and Prince Philip, being led to their stalls by the imposing figure of Mr Simcocks, the Head Verger.

The confidence of the murmuring organ, the solemnity of the scene and the commentator's reverential tone had a peculiarly lulling effect. Outside, the bells had gone quiet. Harrison leaned back, enjoying the sight of Simcocks bowing himself back from the royal party.

The first stroke of ten rang across the precincts. As it did so, almost simultaneously, the organ music ceased; a hush fell over the vast congregation; a few moments of absolute stillness, and then the great west doors opened. With the organ roaring, the procession of choristers entered.

Slowly and solemnly they advanced, led by a silver cross, singing the psalm *Venite Exultemus Domino*. Behind the choir came the cathedral clergy, the furs and colours of their academic hoods vivid against the white of their surplices. Steadily they moved, passing in twos across the screen. Momentarily there was Crocker, moving in slow step beside the Precentor, his cadaverous face, haggard and drawn, staring up like some spectral sleepwalker at the cross rising as it mounted the steps towards the pulpitum-screen. Then came the Dean, beaming round at the congregation either side of him as Simcocks led him behind his curiously ill-assorted and mismatched little flock.

Again the organ roared as the procession of bishops began. Resplendent in copes and mitres of cloth-of-gold, each with his silver crozier, they advanced, appearing, as the camera looked down from high above, like so many gorgeous, self-propelled chess pieces sweeping across the diagonally-laid paving of the central aisle. And then suddenly there was Campion, alone at the back. Stepping out of the sunlight through the great west doors, he paused, looking up the length of the nave before him, a fierce, stern intensity to his face, the haft of his tall crozier, thick as a quarter-staff, gripped in his hand.

'Good grief,' murmured Harrison, 'talk about an eagle among doves.'

The cameras turned back to the choir, now singing the *Benedicite* as they filed into their stalls.

'There's Simon!' exclaimed Winnie. 'Doesn't he look sweet?'

Harrison laughed. 'Hardly, my dear. A whitened sepulchre, I'm afraid, just like the rest.'

'Oh no, they all look so sweet!' she protested. 'Look at them! It isn't just the boys, it's the men too. Positively angelic! What is it about a cassock that gives them that strangely androgynous look?'

'Androgynous?'

'Yes, dear, like angels, neither male or female.'

Harrison frowned; suddenly, in that hot, curtained room, he was again seeing the figure flitting before him into the shadows of the nave and the figure waving from the tower. 'My God, Winnie!' Excited, he jumped to his feet. 'That's it, androgynous—sexless—it was exactly that!'

'Whatever's the matter?'

'The figure I saw in the cathedral, it wasn't a woman, damn it! My God, no wonder they couldn't find her! It was a man I saw, a man in a cassock!' He stared at her. 'Christ, I can see it now: it was a man, I'm absolutely sure! And that person who first stabbed Cratchley, what was all that about Nell Cook and a seventeenth-century dress? It was the length and the shape of a cassock that the old fellow saw!'

> Now the Archbishop of York, with the Bishop of London beside him, moves towards the throne, the great stone chair of Purbeck marble—the Sedes Marmorea—in which, from time immemorial, archbishops have been enthroned.

'Darling—' Winnie stretched out her hand—'does it matter at this moment? Can't we just sit and enjoy the service?'

'With a psychopath loose in the cathedral! It could be any of them, clergy or choir!'

'Calm down, my dear. Nothing is going to happen in the middle of—'

'Greek!' he burst out, cutting her off. 'Ancient Greek, Winnie!' There was frenzy in his eyes. 'Who reads that these days but priests? And who but a priest can move about a deserted cathedral without it being remarked on?'

'What are you talking about?'

Harrison waved again at the screen, where the clergy in their serried ranks had sat to listen to the first of the epistles. 'It could be any of them! Any of those could have stabbed Lloyd-Thomas, and before that, Cratchley.'

'...that after my departing shall grievous wolves enter in among you, not sparing the flock. Also of your own selves shall men arise...'

'It could be any one of them,' he repeated, horror growing in his voice, 'and with this Becket thing again...' His voice faded away: before him, caught by the prowling lens, was the Archdeacon's face, haggard, emaciated, unearthly pale. Staring as if mesmerized at the screen, he breathed the word out, 'Crocker?' He swung round. 'Of course! Who else? Who but he would go about writing on walls in Ancient Greek? Who was the person so worked up by the coffin? God, the man was always...' His voice died.

'Always what?'

'Mad! He asked me to rationalize diocesan expenditure, then refused to have anything changed! Unused churches kept open just because they're old! And now, in a few minutes, Campion is going to pray at the martyrdom stones, and Ingrams, the fool, has chosen a maniac to go with him!'

'Darling, where are you going?'

'To warn Ingrams—I can't just sit here! God knows what might happen!'

'But Richard...' It was too late. She heard the front door slam. From the television came the hushed tone of the commentary:

We see Bishop Campion moving now, led by two of his brother bishops, to take his oath to protect the Church and its people—the same oath taken on the same spot as Thomas Becket took in 1162.

The day was heating like a furnace under the blaze of the sun. As Harrison ran, perspiration sprang from his face. Through the salt of his sweat and the blinding glare of the light, walls and towers, marquees and empty police coaches, shimmered and blended into an indistinct blur of shape and size.

Crocker!

The image of the tormented face staring over the coffin stood before him, precise and distinct; he ran, breath rasping in his lungs, heading across Green Court for the cathedral itself.

Crocker!

The rattle of iron through the crypt, white knuckles on the bars of the gate: a Bedlam inmate tearing at his cage. Again came the picture of the Archdeacon's agonized face above the coffin.

He ran faster. Then came a loud shout from behind. Stopping, he turned. A figure, black against the white canvas of the marquee, waved and began to move towards him. Uncertain, Harrison waited, breath coming in gulps, his mouth parched from the running. In the distance came the throbbing return of the helicopter. Then from the corner of his eye, he caught the sudden flash from the top of the Bell Harry; looking up, he saw the vague shapes of the watchers behind the parapet. Then another dazzling flash as the binoculars caught the sun—and suddenly he saw that ominous solitary figure waving its warning—an image more vivid, more palpable, than anything he could make out through his sweat and the blinding light.

A second shout from behind, closer now, but Harrison was again running towards Dark Entry. From dazzling sunlight he passed into shadow abruptly. Momentarily blind, his feet thundering between the walls, he raced down the deserted passage, seeing Ingrams, Crocker and Campion descending the martyrdom transept, then kneeling and suddenly the cage bursting open, the madman leaping, hand upraised.

The days of Vengeance!

As his dread rose, one part of his mind rebelled. It was absurd. Impossible. Wasn't Crocker high church? Hadn't he, above all, always venerated the martyr? Had the changes in the Church deranged him? The move towards women's ordination? Or was it grief over Dorothy? Was it disappointment? Did Crocker hate Becket because he hadn't intervened to save his sister? As the questions reeled sickeningly round, he thought he heard other feet than his own echoing through the passageway.

Stumbling up the steps of the north-east transept, he reached the iron-studded door. Grabbing the handle, he turned and pushed. It was useless. The solid unyielding mass was locked against him. Desperately he rattled the handle and beat with his fist.

'Colonel Harrison!'

Inspector Dowley was behind him, moving up the steps, face wary, eyes fixed on his.

'I've got to get in,' gasped Harrison, slamming his elbow back against the door. Turning, he put his ear to the wood; through the solid oak, he heard the faint murmur of the organ within like the hum of a giant hive.

Dowley took another step up. 'What do you want in the cathedral so urgently, Colonel?'

'That warning in the cottage!' panted Harrison.

'Warning?' If anything, Dowley's suspicion had deepened.

'You don't know?' Harrison stared down into the broad face

below his, then glanced over the policeman's shoulder down the passage behind. 'Good God, where are your men, Inspector? How the hell could I have got this far without anyone stopping me?' The sound of the distant helicopter seemed suddenly the forlorn, pathetic drone of the frantic bluebottle trapped in the cottage. 'Where are all the men coached in this morning?'

Dowley hesitated. 'We're only responsible for the crowd-control in the city and the security of the outer precincts.'

'And here? Around the building and inside—who's responsible?'

A sardonic smile touched the heavy face looking up the steps. 'Your people, Colonel.'

'Mine?'

'London is coordinating the security operation. Your people in Whitehall have overall responsibility for the cathedral and its immediate environs.'

'And they haven't passed on to you what was found in the cottage yesterday? What are they playing at?' He looked again down the empty passage behind, then towards Great Cloister.

'My people, you say?'

Suddenly, he was four months back, standing outside the ruins of Lesnes Abbey with the Brigadier's face before him; again he heard Greville's voice speaking against the cawing of the rooks. 'I wouldn't want anything more to lie on that tender conscience of yours, Dickie.' He remembered the pity in the other's eyes, and then with ice-cold rock certainty he understood. Numbly, he faced the policeman. 'Inspector, I have good reason to think that there may be an attack on the Archbishop. One of the two priests who will escort him to the martyrdom transept immediately after the enthronement is, I believe, mentally deranged and is the same person who ransacked my office before Christmas and stabbed Mr Lloyd-Thomas.' He paused. 'I also have good reason to think that the Archbishop is being deliberately left unguarded.'

The formality and calm precision with which he spoke had their effect. On Dowley's face incredulity gave way to alarm. 'You're sure of this, sir?'

'I think there's a strong possibility. Good God, look around you, man, there's just the two of us here.'

The Inspector glanced at the locked door. 'How long before the Archbishop enters the transept?'

Harrison glanced at his watch. 'A few minutes at the most.'

Dowley pushed past. Kneeling at the door, he drew out a ring of thin spikes, bent at the top, which Harrison recognized at once as a set of lock-picks. Steadying himself against the arch of the door, he watched the deft, expert turns of the Inspector's wrist, seeing the Brigadier's pitying smile and fighting against a sickening sense of coming defeat.

Through the cavernous cool depths a chorister's voice soared in the distance, unearthly pure. Harrison, with the Inspector behind him, hurried forward on tiptoe, seeing between the pillars and the lattice-work ahead the glow of candles on the high altar and the light streaming down in rainbow shafts from the stained-glass windows of the choir. The child's voice echoed in the vaulting above.

At the presbytery entrance he stopped and leaned round the pillared arch, Dowley panting at his ear; before him swam a pageant of colour—black, red and white of cassock and surplice; gold and green of vestment; scarlet and blue of uniform and gown. For a few seconds he searched hopelessly among the multitudinous blur of faces, then shrank back. 'I can't see the Archbishop!' He turned to gaze for a moment at the empty, high-backed throne standing below the high altar, bathed now in the same crimson-red glow as when he'd seen it that afternoon with Rope. *Throne of blood!* The absurd phrase rushed back; suddenly, he could almost hear the Canon's high-pitched laugh and the eager, nervous rubbing of the old man's hands.

The memory jerked him from his reverie. He swung round.

'They've already gone to the martyrdom transept—come on!'

Half-running, the two headed down the shadowed passage of the north aisle, tombs and monuments on the one side, light from the choir streaming through the grilles and barred arches on the other. Figures stood ahead in the gloom: a small circle of gowned men clustered beneath the first of the massive support arches of the Bell Harry. Hope rising, Harrison increased his speed, but as he neared, the faces turned towards him. They were just those of the Head Verger and his ushers.

The circle broke before him. Simcocks was now in his path, arms spread wide, the loose cloth of his gown like cormorants' wings.

'Colonel Harrison, sir!' The Verger gaped in astonishment.

'Where's the Archbishop, man? Dr Crocker and the Archbishop, where are they?'

'Down below.' Simcocks pointed back across the marble landing to the steps leading down to the transept. 'They've both gone down with the Dean.'

'Out of my way!' Harrison pushed past.

'But, sir, they're at prayer!'

The cry was behind, ahead the stairs. As he reached the top step, a thunderous roar rolled through the cathedral as the organ began the anthem. He raced down the first flight, the Inspector behind. He turned for the second, began to descend, then stopped. Aghast, he leaned over the balustrade, staring down to where in the dimness the three bodies, bright in their vestments, lay prone, face downwards, arms outstretched.

'No!'

Even as the cry burst from him, he felt Dowley's checking hand; then he was seeing the three heads rising almost in unison to stare up at him in bewilderment.

Ingrams, the nearest to him, began to get up: Crocker, furthest away, blinked through his spectacles. The figure in the centre, however, remained motionless, arms still outstretched in the form of a cross, continuing to observe Harrison as steadily as when he had gazed from the chancel at him half a year before.

Dowley's grip tightened; he felt himself being drawn back. He resisted, gripping at the stone balustrade.

This was the time, he was certain, this the place to which all things had been rushing since that dark winter afternoon when he'd first looked down from the choirstall into those eyes now again looking up into his.

He glanced towards Crocker: the Archdeacon was standing now, gaunt, ashen-grey, and taller by far than the cassocked shape he remembered darting away from him into the nave. He'd been wrong: Crocker was tragic, not mad. Then from whom was the blow to come? Greville was at the heart of it, he was certain. There was still something in the whole tapestry of events he'd missed—one stitch—that tiny something that didn't fit.

Archbishop Campion was rising now. Harrison's mind again returned to that winter afternoon: the tall figure in the dark overcoat buttoned to the neck to hide the clerical collar and purple stock—then the other figure, also holding his coat-collar closed, hurrying after him calling his name; the lights of Green Court through the drizzle; that strange giggling laughter ringing through Bread Yard.

'Think of it, Colonel, a bee in December!'—that was it: the phrase that had delivered him into Greville's grasp—the trigger of the whole filthy conspiracy. But there had been no poison, and therefore no bee or sting! Momentarily he saw the grinning face, the gleaming teeth and the keys of Cratchley's cottage dangling over the table like ripe fruit.

'Rope!'

Simultaneously came his realization and cry: in the same instant there was a brilliant flash of light and a huge crash as the calefactorium door flew open—and Rope was before him, a black shape silhouetted against the blinding light from the cloisters behind—there as if conjured by the call of his name.

'Canon Rope!' Through the frozen moment came the Dean's startled voice. Rope was before them all, eyes burning, mouth working, a trickle of saliva crawling towards the chin. Suddenly the chamber went bright as he sprang forward with hideous, manic agility. Sunlight caught the blade of the outstretched knife.

As under a sea, it seemed to happen. Against the distant rumble of the organ, Campion turning as if in slow motion to face the fury rushing upon him, the knife-point plunging at the centre of the crossed white cordons on his gorgeous cope; the Dean reaching out ineffectually—then the Archdeacon throwing himself sideways, falling between the lunging blade and the golden vestment—a low thud, a scrape of steel on bone, a gasped cry, and then the furious force of the blow throwing Crocker back against the Archbishop's chest.

Harrison stood paralysed as Dowley thrust past; men entered the open door. Rope was thrown against the wall, pinned there for a moment, then vanishing behind a wedge of shoulders: a wild shriek, fingers tearing the air, and for the last time, the madman's face, the demented eyes, appeared over the heads as he was hustled out. Then suddenly stillness, the only sound, the repeated wailing cry fading away outside.

Still gripping the balustrade, Harrison turned from the empty doorway to the tableau below: Campion kneeling, Crocker in his arms, Ingrams beside him, their hands exploring the front of the surplice across which the red stain was spreading over the white. Then Simcocks was there, kneeling on the other side, taking the Archdeacon's hand in his.

Ingrams's voice was anguished. 'Stephen, my dear chap! My dear fellow!'

Crocker appeared to smile; his face, supported by Campion,

was looking directly at Harrison. His free hand half raised, then fell; his head slipped deeper into his Archbishop's arms.

Blood on gold; blood crawling over the worn pavings, seeping through the runnels and gouges of the ancient pavings.

Above, the organ had stopped. In the silence, Harrison continued to stare numbly down.

Campion's lips were moving as he bent forward, nestling the man in his arms. '...*our dear brother into the hands of a faithful Creator and most merciful Saviour...*' Crocker's eyes closed; his head lolled back into the cradling arms. Simcocks was sobbing, shoulders heaving, pressing the limp hand between his.

And still the quiet voice of the Archbishop:

'*And may thy portion this day be peace, and thy dwelling the Heavenly Jerusalem.*'

EPILOGUE

'It was good of you both to stay for the dedication.'

Harrison and Winnie turned to find Dean Ingrams had entered through the calefactorium door. From the sunlit passage outside came the drowsy hum and twitter of high summer, the sounds amplified by the high ceiling and stone walls and floor. In silence the three of them turned and stood gazing up at the grey, rectangular slab of Portland granite on the wall beyond the roped-off divide. After a moment or two, the Dean sighed heavily. 'Poor dear Stephen! How delighted he would have been to know he'd have a memorial here.' Ingrams looked tired; to Harrison and Winnie, he seemed much older of late: his hair was much greyer, his face more lined.

'Richard,' said Winnie quietly, 'I think we should be getting back to finish the packing.'

Harrison wheeled her out into Great Cloister, exchanging as he did so the blessed cool of the transept for the sultry heat of the August afternoon. Ingrams followed. Together the three of them began following the roofed walkway round the cloister.

Pausing, the Dean pulled his pipe from his cassock pocket. He filled and lit it, gazing out as he did so between the piers of the latticed arches to where a pair of swallows were diving and darting low across the horizontal tombslabs on the grass.

He took his pipe from his mouth. 'It's the deanery cricket match on Saturday. We'll miss Stephen's bowling. He could be depended on to send down one or two of the most extraordinary googlies.' There was infinite regret in his voice. He took another puff on his pipe. 'God knows, our late Archdeacon could be a difficult man at times, but I never knew anyone play a straighter bat.'

'Quite,' murmured Harrison, staring out across the lawn.

'Matthew,' said Winnie, turning to the Dean, 'you really mustn't blame yourself, you know.'

'But I do, Winifred! I do!' The Dean stared across the enclosed lawn. He shook his head. 'I always shall.'

'Why? You couldn't possibly have known what would happen.'

'I should have guessed.' Ingrams tapped his pipe sharply on the stonework. 'I knew poor Rope was ill, and I knew his terrible history, of course.'

'I had some idea he'd been in China,' said Harrison, 'but until the inquest I'd no idea he'd been a prisoner of the Japanese.'

'Four years.' Relighting his pipe, Ingrams spoke through a haze of smoke. 'His wife died of dysentery in the camps; he himself was beaten and starved almost to death. Apparently, from that and scurvy, he came out in nineteen forty-five like a wizened old man. Not a tooth left in his head, and the poor fellow wasn't quite thirty!'

Harrison winced inwardly, remembering the fascinated repugnance with which he'd watched the old man's obsessive gulping and gnawing, his revulsion at the sight of those over-white dentures, too large for the shrunken face.

'And it didn't end there,' continued the Dean. 'The poor fellow insisted on staying in China. He was in Nanking when the communists took the city. He saw his entire flock slaughtered, and came home to a mental hospital. When he came out, letting him have a place to live in the precincts seemed the least the Church could do. The trouble was, of course, over the years, his bouts of mania got steadily worse.'

'Even so, nobody could have guessed just how dangerous his obsessions were!'

'Yes, but I could see he was getting worse.' Ingrams shook his head unhappily. 'I just didn't know what to do. Before, there had always been Cratchley to keep an eye on him and calm him down.' He sucked thoughtfully at his pipe. 'Extraordinary man!'

'Cratchley?'

The Dean nodded. 'You know, he once even managed to cure a dog of mine that had gone off its head.'

'Yes,' said Harrison quietly, 'I remember someone telling me.'

'How was Canon Rope when you went to visit him?' asked Winnie.

Ingrams shrugged. 'Calmer, but still mad as a hatter—absolutely refused to see the Archbishop, still insists he's the anti-Christ and an agent of Moscow. I fear it means Broadmoor now for the rest of his life.'

'What I don't understand,' said Winnie, 'is why the terrible reaction to Thomas Becket. What was so intolerable about such a distant historical figure?'

'A mystery, my dear Winifred! A mystery. On a simple level, it may have been a typical low-church reaction to idols of any sort—an irrational fear perhaps of Catholicism, of foreign and alien domination. At a deeper level, I don't know. Did the thoughts of a Christian martyr conjure again the fate of his congregation in China and the fate of his wife? Was Becket the past he could not let rest in the infinite mercy of God?'

The three of them walked on, passing through Dark Entry and out into the brightness of Green Court. At the deanery, Ingrams held out his hand. 'I am going to miss you both.' He looked suddenly anxious. 'Tuscany—you will be careful, won't you? It's a long drive.'

'Oh, we'll take it in easy stages,' answered Harrison, glancing at Winnie.

Ingrams smiled at them both benevolently. 'God bless you,' he said, 'and bring you both safely back to Canterbury.'

A breeze, cool and refreshing, blew over the Appennine hills, swaying the topmost branches of the pines on the wooded slopes and stirring veils of dust from the roads. The leaves rustled on the vine-clad pergola, setting their shadows dancing across the white marble table at which Winnie sat writing her cards.

She looked up and, brushing a fly from her cup, sipped her coffee. As she did so, she heard her name called and, turning, saw her husband making towards her among the tables of the hotel balcony grinning broadly, holding out a folded newspaper as he came.

'Well?' said Winnie, smiling up at his sun-bronzed face, 'what's pleased you so much?'

'In our absence,' he said, unfolding the paper and putting it before her, 'our new Archbishop appears to be managing to lay about him with his usual effect!'

Before her was the headline:

CAMPION LASHES GOVERNMENT OVER PRICE-TAGGED REFUGEE STATUS: CONFERENCE UPROAR AT PRIMATE'S SCORN.

Harrison took the seat opposite as she began reading through the article aloud.

'Cabinet of new-model samaritans who would cross the road only to check on the victim's credit-rating!'

She broke off, clicking her tongue in mock disapproval. 'Oh dear,' she said, smiling mischievously, 'it does rather look as if the ravaging beast is again on the loose!'

Harrison turned away, the shape of Canon Rope momentarily rising before him, framed in the calefactorium doorway; once more it blocked out the sun, sending now its vast shadow spreading over the summer hills and the wide valley beneath. Leaning towards him, Winnie touched his arm. 'Darling, what do you think?' She held out the card she'd finished writing. 'I chose it for Sarah. Do you think it will do?'

Taking it, he looked down: before him was the head of Michelangelo's *David*, the same face that together he and Winnie had gazed at only the previous morning on their visit to the Accademia. As he gazed at the serene marble face of the youth the demon face faded into the sunlight.

'Well?' prompted Winnie anxiously. 'Do you think Sarah will like it?'

He smiled. 'Of course she will. It's very nice.'

The waiter brought more coffee. In silence they drank, then Winnie returned to her cards. Harrison, taking up his paper, attempted to read. The breeze returned, fluttering and tugging at the pages; the postcards began slithering across the marble table-top as if drawn by invisible hands. Again, as the leaves quivered on the pergola framework, the shadows danced and ran over their faces in a dappled pattern of dark and light, then down the wind came the tinkle of the chapel bell from Fiesole.

The bell ceased its ringing. In the silence, Winnie heard Harrison's sudden intake of breath. Opening her eyes, she saw him staring down at the paper.

'What now?' she sat up.

He thrust the open sheets towards her. 'That!' He pointed to a short paragraph at the bottom of the third page, captioned: Commuter Trampled in Crush.

Recently retired senior civil servant, Brigadier J. M. Greville MC. KCB (69), died yesterday of a heart attack after falling during the evening rush-hour at Cannon Street Station.

According to station master, A. N. Anpu, there were larger than usual crowds on the platforms due to a local industrial dispute involving signalling staff...

'What a way to go!' exclaimed Harrison, 'Poor devil!' Winnie looked at him coldly. 'Are you forgetting, due to him, one man is dead and another will be in an asylum for the rest of his life?' She paused. 'Well? Isn't it true?'

Harrison looked away. 'I suppose he saw a duty,' he murmured.

'Duty!' She scoffed. 'What, doing murder by proxy? Trying to silence someone because you don't happen to like their opinions?' Her tone was withering, and as she saw the effect of her words, her hoarded resentment against Greville swelled and quickened. 'I don't understand. How you can grieve for a man who continuously misled you, who treated you with contempt?' She paused, leaning forward, staring into his face. 'What is it in you that can respect, even admire, a soulless killer cunning and cold enough to work on other people's irrational fears, inciting them to do his filthy work for him? When you failed him, who did he use, this hero of yours? An emotional cripple like Canon Rope! Worked on the poor man, played on his past, incensing him with his talk about communism, idolatry or whatever until—' She broke off. 'Richard, he was disgusting—evil, can't you see?'

'No!' Lumbering to his feet, Harrison waved towards the hills. 'Damn it, he was fighting here, risking his life for our liberties when we were both still at school.'

'Listen to you! Even now, you're still fixated! In God's name, what was this hold he had on you?'

Harrison looked down into the valley, seeing again the coffin as it had lain in the crypt, its ambiguous emblem, the crude question-mark, gouged in the weathered lid. Turning, he smiled sadly, shaking his head. 'In the end, each of us is a mysterious closed casket, locked even to ourselves. Even the most logical of us, the most balanced, is a maze of contradictions beyond analysis. We're all, every one, a mystery within a mystery; a whirling mass of atoms and energy without any consistency or certainty whatever.'

Reaching for his hand, Winnie drew him down. 'We have loved and can love.' She smiled tenderly. 'That is our consistency and our hope.'

'Perhaps.'

'Oh yes, my dear,' she said. 'All of us, Stephen, Dorothy, you and I, even poor Canon Rope are bound together in that.'

Together they sat looking down to where, dim through a haze of heat and light, the towers and terracotta roofs of Florence lay woven through by the greenish-glint of the Arno. There they remained, hands touching, under the shade of the vine, feeling the cool of the breeze on their faces and hearing, above and around them, the continuing sigh of the leaves.